Country Roads

Country Roads Series: Book One

Grea Warner

The characters and events in this book are fictitious. Any similarity to real persons, living or dead, places, or events is coincidental and not intended by the author.

If you purchase this book without a cover you should be aware that this book may have been stolen property and reported as "unsold and destroyed" to the publisher. In such case the author has not received any payment for this "stripped book."

Country Roads
Copyright © 2018 Grea Warner
All rights reserved.

ISBN: (ebook): 978-1-945910-52-4
(print) 978-1-945910-72-2

Inkspell Publishing
5764 Woodbine Ave.
Pinckney, MI 48169

Edited By Vicky Burkholder
Cover art By Najla Qamber

This book, or parts thereof, may not be reproduced in any form without permission. The copying, scanning, uploading, and distribution of this book via the internet or via any other means without the permission of the publisher is illegal and punishable by law. Please purchase only authorized electronic or print editions, and do not participate in or encourage piracy of copyrighted materials. Your support of the author's rights is appreciated.

OTHER BOOKS BY GREA WARNER

All My Memories in Can't Buy Me Love Boxset

Almost Heaven (coming soon!)

GREA WARNER

DEDICATION

This book is dedicated with much love and respect to my parents who played country tunes in the car when I was growing up. Little did they know what they had started…

And, to my brother who had the seat right next to me and still loves music as much as I do.

CHAPTER ONE

    Back where I grew up, the roads went from cement to gravel to dirt and back again with no rhyme or reason. They twisted and turned. They intersected weedy railroad tracks and climbed hills with no guardrail to guide. These roads were surrounded by pine covered woods filled with Mother Nature's creatures who, only part of the time, knew their forest-like boundaries. People gave directions not by street names but by landmarks like a country inn or a local market. It was on these roads that I found my freedom…that I learned to escape. I could go miles without seeing a soul and get lost in the simplicity of nothingness.

    It's funny how similar the city is. The subway's darkness burrows underground and leads you directly into a hub encompassed by the pure chaos of millions. Everyone walks fast among the buzzing noise and brilliant lights, not daring to make eye contact. Again, I have nowhere particular to go. There are masses around me, but I am still alone. I feel that sense of solitary freedom, and that is all that is important.

    The truth is, it doesn't matter what your surroundings—be it the big city, suburbia, or a quaint country town—your heart and your memory follow you wherever you go. There is no escaping what lies deep down in your innermost self. And while there are things that you might want to forget, there are also those precious few keystones that you wish you could not just conjure up but bring back to life with a click of your heels. That only happens in fairy tales, though. And, every once in a while, when the cities and the towns become that cliché small world rolled into one, it happens in schools too.

***

"My uncle can sing!" first grader Wyatt blurted out in the computer club I was in charge of toward the end of each school day.

"Oh, okay. Well, that's a good idea. But maybe instead of your uncle, we can have a talent show and some kids can sing." I didn't want to totally douse his idea. "Your uncle can come and watch us perform, Wyatt. In fact, I'm sure he would like that better than singing himself."

The brown-haired child's offer had been in response to a sad topic we had been asked to talk about with the club classes. One of the students had been diagnosed with cardiomyopathy. The principal and school counselor wanted to develop a plan for helping the family. Because of the numerous hospital visits, they were trying to find ways to raise money to assist with some of the costs. And they also wanted the students to be aware, empathize, and help if they could with fundraising ideas. There were reasonable suggestions like selling popcorn or cookies, having a car wash, and making artwork to sell. But having a family member sing was surely not one of them.

"But he's good, Miss Faulkner."

"I'm sure he is, Wyatt. I wrote it down." I added his idea to the paper but had no real intention of having it actually make the official list I would give to Principal Lennock. Uncle "Joe Shmoe" could thank me later for the save, I smirked internally.

***

When Xenia Lennock walked into the computer lab the next day during second grade's club period, I assumed she was just doing a quick walk-through. I was pleased how the students were on task, writing their names in the computer paint program and having fun learning. I enjoyed working with the kids, and that forty minutes with a different grade level each day was my only real chance. The rest of my job, as technology coordinator for a private elementary school in upstate New York, was administrative, dealing with everything from webpage design and upkeep to technical assistance.

Xenia motioned me over with a wave of her hand. "Would you be able to meet with a parent? It's Mrs. Jamison. I told her you had some free time after club." She nodded her head in a way that I knew her words were more of a directive than an actual question.

"Wyatt's mom?" I was glad to place the last name with the student as it was still so early in the school year.

"Wyatt. Yes. It's his mother." She looked around the lab as the kids yelled out "done," "look at mine," and "cool."

"If you get done, we can print them out," I told the class. "Just give me a minute." Then, turning to Xenia, "Sure, I can meet with her." Although I wanted to say that I had a million things to do—make copies, write notes, shut down the computers, check my e-mail, etc. But you don't say that to a principal, especially one with a parent request. "Do you know what it's about?"

I couldn't imagine. Parent conferences with me were not a frequent occurrence and, if they did happen, the parent usually had something they thought they needed to gripe about. Wyatt was a good kid. He was new to the school but adjusting well. I had briefly met both his parents during his new school orientation tour. They seemed easy going and interested in their child without being overbearing.

"I don't know. Something about what you talked about in club."

The parts of a computer? Taking care of a keyboard? My goodness what did we talk about that warranted a parent visit? We were only nearing the end of the second week of school. I hoped this Wyatt wasn't a student who told false tales at home just to get attention.

"She seemed very nice. I don't think it's anything to worry about." Just as she finished reassuring me, an announcement came over the general loud speaker requesting that Mrs. Lennock report to the office—another crisis for Xenia to divert for sure.

***

Curiosity mixed with caution as I entered the school counselor's office for the mysterious meeting. Inside, I found a toddler with crayons and a piece of paper sitting at the solitary table in the colorful, comfy room. Next to her sat a woman around my age.

"Hi. Wyatt's mom, right?" I stuck out my hand to shake hers.

"Miss Faulkner, so nice to see you again."

A smile. Okay. That's good.

"Nola Jamison," she confirmed. "Wyatt really seems to like you. He says how funny you are."

"Thanks. I try. It keeps them going." Sitting across from her, I acknowledged the smaller being in the room. "And this is?"

"Kelsea, say 'hi'," Mrs. Jamison prompted her mini-me.

Beautiful with bouncy blonde curls, Kelsea looked up wide-eyed and inched a little closer to Mrs. Jamison. "Hi."

"Sorry, she's a little shy with new people."

"That's okay. I understand. I'm like that too. Kelsea,

how old are you?" When she held up two fingers, I continued, "Two years old! Wow! You're a big girl. In just a few years you'll be going to school too. Wyatt showed me a picture of the two of you at the beach." I remembered, happy to make a personal connection. "Did you have fun?"

A smile crossed her face. "I made a castle."

"He seems like a good big brother," I told Wyatt's mom. What else could I say? Why were we here?

"Sometimes." She laughed. "But when he's not, he's not. Overall, he's really good with her, though."

"I understand. I have an older brother too," I volunteered. "Some things never change."

"Or with younger brothers for that matter." She slightly shook her head. "Listen, speaking of, I don't want to take up your time. Wyatt mentioned that he volunteered my brother to sing…something about a sick child."

So that's what this was about? What? Was she upset? We wouldn't make anyone sing.

"Oh, right. Yeah, one of the students is pretty sick. It's his heart. We're looking to do a fundraiser. Yvonne, our counselor, asked that we talk with the kids." Just as I finished, Yvonne entered her office. I was glad to have a comrade in the room especially because she was more knowledgeable on the subject. "Here she is. Yvonne, do you know Wyatt's mom, Mrs. Jamison?"

"No. Nice to meet you." Yvonne mimicked my earlier handshake and sat down to join us. "I heard what you were talking about as I was coming in."

Mrs. Jamison continued, "Wyatt loves his uncle. We all do. And he's great with the kids. But we try not to draw attention because we want them to lead a normal life. Wyatt doesn't understand. He's a talker." She smiled. "In case you haven't noticed."

Now I was curious. Maybe this uncle wasn't some schmuck I was gracefully trying to save from a bad karaoke experience. He might actually be "someone." But, really, how famous could he be?

"Who's your brother?" I went ahead and asked.

"Finn."

Even though she said it distinctly, I needed the clarification or just simply to slow down the moment so I could process. "Finn?" His name stuck in my mouth and came out a sputtered whisper.

Much louder, Yvonne's voice echoed mine. "Finn Murphy?"

"Uh-huh. That's my baby brother. Oh, I thought you knew. I thought Wyatt said."

"No! Wow! He's one of my favorite singers." Yvonne acted absolutely star-struck without even seeing the actual star.

"Finn?" I managed to spit out again.

"Yeah. Do you listen to country music? I know it's not everyone's cup of tea." Mrs. Jamison turned to me. "He's—"

"I know who he is." Why couldn't I speak above a whisper? And why did his name affect me like that?

Yvonne turned to me. "Lara, you listen to country?"

"I do, but, um…I actually know Finn."

Mrs. Jamison's eyes ever-so-slightly pierced the distance between us. "You do?"

"He and I went to college together. We had mutual friends. We hung out some."

"Miss Faulkner," Mrs. Jamison examined me closer. "Your first name is Lara?"

"Yeah."

"Oh, I just never put it together. I mean, what a small world," Wyatt's mother said. "You're that Lara?"

That Lara? "Uh, well, I don't know. I guess. Did Finn mention—"

"You knew Finn Murphy in college?" Yvonne pushed my arm. Could this woman gain some composure and act just a tad bit professional? Gosh, she was nearly twice my age.

"Yeah. We were friends."

"You're Lara. I remember him talking about you and calling you one time when I was with him."

"Maybe."

"Lara, uh, sorry, Miss Faulkner, God, he was so in love with you," Nola divulged.

Feeling a rush of heat fill my cheeks, I said, "Oh, please, I think you can call me Lara. And, no. No, I don't think so. He wasn't."

Finn's sister! Huh, how about that? Finn and I had been friends and that was all. There might have been a fleeting moment when I thought he was thinking otherwise, or later when I thought I was thinking otherwise. But we were never on the same page besides a friendship, which ended up drifting apart, like so many do, when the real world began.

"Anyway…," Mrs. Jamison hesitated, clearly feeling a little awkward after her reveal about her brother's feelings.

Attempting to fill the silence, I asked, "How is he?"

"He's good." She smiled while scanning me over, I swear, in a whole new way. "He just finished his tour. He's been in the city this week." She spoke of nearby Manhattan. "He's meeting with execs for the new single and for the CMA announcements. He got three nods this year." She beamed like a proud sister should. "Did you happen to catch it?"

"No—work." I gave the excuse but omitted the fact that I read about the nominations online.

"Right. Well, I texted him last night about Wyatt's little offer. He called back this morning and said he would like to help. He would just need some more details. And that was before he knew…well, before we knew about you. For sure he'll do something."

"Lara," Yvonne said. "I still can't believe this—you and Finn Murphy."

She needed to stop. I could just picture her running around the building singing "Lara and Finn sitting in a tree." And nothing was further from the truth.

Not a usual blusher, I felt another one creep onto my cheeks. After shooting a glare at Yvonne, I focused on Wyatt's mother. "That's great. What does he have in mind?"

"Maybe quietly come into town, do a last-minute concert where all the proceeds go to the family—that sort of thing. Is that what you have in mind?"

"Well, quite frankly, I had none of this in mind." I semi-laughed, still stunned by the fact that Finn's sister was sitting across from me.

"Yeah, I guess not."

"Mommy, I wanta go," Kelsea whined.

"You're being very patient. Just a couple more minutes," Nola pacified.

"Is she allowed a piece of candy?" Yvonne whispered to Mrs. Jamison in case she wasn't.

"Sure."

Nola unwrapped the candy before handing it to Kelsea and then, like any good mother, prompted her daughter, "What do you say Kelsea?"

"Thank you." She shyly smiled up at us.

"Did you know Miss Faulkner knows Uncle Finn?"

I couldn't help but smile at Kelsea whose eyes got real big. "Let's organize something right away," I said regrouping. "I'll check with Mrs. Lennock, but I think any time that works for Finn, we can make work here too. I'll call you." I paused momentarily lost in thought…lost in the past. "It'll be great to see him. It's been a long time."

***

After the phone's third ring, I was preparing myself for the message I was going to leave on voice mail. It was the day after I had met with Yvonne and Finn's sister. Xenia and some of the administrators had given me a few dates to suggest to Finn via the Jamisons. So there I was, after official dismissal time, with the school phone up to my ear. But instead of a recorded voice, a live person answered the Jamison phone.

"Hi, uh, Mr. Jamison?" I said.

"No. He's not here. Do you want to leave a message?"

Too old to be Wyatt, I concluded. "Who's this?" But I already knew.

"Hi, Lara. It's Finn."

I was so glad we weren't on any type of video chat as I suddenly felt like I didn't know how to act or what to say. I stood up from the rolling chair and started to pace for as long as the business phone cord would allow me. "Sorry, I guess it was just the male voice."

"Yeah, I don't sound like him at all." Finn laughed the laugh I remembered. "How are you?"

"I'm good." And immediately I wanted to pull out the thesaurus and edit my boring answer. Instead, I forged on to a topic that took the spotlight off me. "Congratulations on, well, everything."

"Thanks."

"So, I was calling to talk with your sister—"

"Oh, I guess I could get her."

"No. No. Don't bother her. I can just talk to you. Do you have a few minutes to discuss the whole concert thing?"

"Concert thing?" he repeated as if not comprehending.

"Yeah. Your sister said she talked with you about doing a benefit concert for a student who's sick."

"Nola, did you promise that I would do something for the school?" I heard him holler away from the phone.

God, I would feel like such a fool if she hadn't actually asked him. "Uh, hey," I tried to get his attention back from across the line. "I can call back another time."

"No. You don't need to do that. We're good. I was just teasing. When am I going to come to this school of yours?"

Relieved, I sat back down, but this time it was on the

floor—a chair with wheels still seemed a little unsteady in my state. "As soon as you can. And I see you haven't changed."

"You thought I would?"

"It's been a while." I grabbed a piece of printer paper and a pen and started doodling circles and such.

"It has. So what's up with you besides the job? Not married yet?"

"Ha! No."

"Would have lost that bet. Totally saw you married by now. Y'know, a photo with matching shirts, three kids."

"Hardly," I spit out more than laughed and then felt a need to explain/fib. "I've dated but nobody worth the long haul."

"Yeah?" he prompted for more—of course.

"One of my co-workers is attempting to set me up. We'll see." Not wanting to think any more about that, I changed the subject. "But enough about me. Happy pre-birthday."

"Huh? Yeah. I can't believe you remembered that."

In a world of electronic calendars and reminders, how could I not? "Well, it's not a day anyone forgets, do they?" I thought with melancholy of Finn's September 11 birthday.

"No. The sad stories get so depressing every year. That's why we're celebrating today."

"Something special?"

"Just pizza with Wyatt and Kels. I have an early flight back to Nashville tomorrow. But let's see what we can do about getting me to come back to New York to help this kid."

Finn and I chatted for a few minutes longer. We were able to schedule the benefit concert for exactly two weeks out. Finn would do the concert completely complimentary with all proceeds going to the family. But he did want to keep it an intimate school function. In other words, he wasn't going to bring his band. It was just going to be him and his guitar. And he didn't want a three-ring media circus. This was about the student, not him.

Talking with Finn was so natural. It was as if it had been seven days and not seven years that had passed. I was ready to tell him that when we were interrupted.

"Mom said not to bother you, that you're talking with Miss Faulkner." It was Wyatt's voice.

"Then why are you bothering me, Earp?" Finn jokingly replied to his nephew.

"What is Miss Faulkner telling you?"

"What do you think she's telling me, huh? Are you getting bad reports in school?" Finn teased.

"No." I heard Finn laugh before Wyatt continued. "Can I talk with Miss Faulkner?"

"No, Wy."

"Why not?" Finn's nephew asked.

"Because I'm talking with her."

"Uncle Finn, please," his excited voice pleaded.

"Do you mind?" Finn's question was now directed to me.

"No, that's okay. Go ahead."

"Hi, Miss Faulkner!" Wyatt sounded even more excited than his usual enthusiastic self.

"Hi, Wyatt," I answered.

"Hi, Miss Faulkner," he repeated.

"You're having a birthday party?" I asked.

"Yeah, for my uncle. I told you he would sing."

I couldn't mistake Nola's voice directed at her son, "Wyatt Jamison! I told you to let Uncle Finn talk."

"Miss Faulkner, I have to go. See you tomorrow!"

"Tomorrow's the weekend, Wyatt," I corrected.

"Oh, okay." And before I could tell him to put Finn back on, the line went dead.

I hung up the phone and contemplated about whether to call back. There really wasn't a reason to. Finn and I had solidified as much of the concert arrangements as we could at that point. Yet I didn't have a chance to say goodbye just like I hadn't in the past.

CHAPTER TWO

I tried to put Finn out of my mind as I shut down the computer, but it was nearly impossible. It had been seven years since I had seen him and just a little less since we had last spoken. And while I couldn't help being reminded of him on occasion due to hit songs on the radio and television appearances, I wasn't truly transported back until I had heard his voice on the phone. And then he was all I could think about. Like a fog had cascaded over the room, I wasn't hearing or seeing anything—just the memory of one of the last times Finn and I had seen one another…

It had been well past one in the morning. I had been lying on the newer sofa in the upstairs lounge of my co-ed dorm nestled in the West Virginia countryside. I heard the front door suddenly fling open and, quickly afterward, witnessed two, obviously drunk, college boys bounding up the stairs. They were mumbling something and were clearly amused with themselves.

I couldn't resist laughing at the two whose arms were wrapped around each other for support. "Hello, boys."

With hair in a windswept brown mess, Finn managed to slowly string two words together. "Lara…hello."

"What are you two doing?" I shook my head, stifling my own laughter. It was fun to see them so happy and carefree, especially after a week of final exams. But it didn't surprise me. Finn, drinking or not, was almost always a happy person, and that's what mattered.

"Decan here is being all poli-sci guy. We were tossing the pigskin around ala Kennedy. He's trying to drum up business."

"You were playing football now?" I referred to the late hour.

"Yep," Finn answered with a near chuckle.

"Here, Lara." Decan, a senior in the house and one of Finn's best friends, handed me a bona fide candidate's button with his name on it. "Vote Mickelson for Mayor."

"That really is so cool, Decan," I spoke of the fact that Decan was actively running for mayor in his hometown. "I can't believe you're actually doing this."

"Uh, Lara, thank you for my vote." He clung onto Finn while adjusting his Harry S. Truman style glasses. "Um, your, uh—"

I heard Finn teasing Decan about mixing up his words as I went to close the doors that led to the bedrooms. In their intoxicated state, the two were getting a little on the loud side, and I didn't want them to wake up any of our housemates. "I don't live in your town or state for that matter." I informed Decan of my voting status as I made my way back onto the sofa. "Besides, I'm not registered."

"Oh, boy." Finn dipped his head backward and exhaled an undeniably loud groan.

"What!?" Decan bellowed as Finn rolled his eyes at me. "You're not registered to vote?"

"No," I said matter-of-factly, knowing now the reason for Finn's reaction.

"How can you not be registered?" Decan pulled away from Finn. "That is your duty. Your duty as an American citizen. Your right."

"I just never did. I had a lot going on when it was time to vote and I was eighteen. And now I'm here, away from home—"

"You need to register to vote, Lara. You can get an absentee ballot," Decan countered. "There's no excuse. It's—"

"Hey, Susan B., settle down. Give the girl a break." Finn placed his hand on Decan's shoulder.

"Pretty good, there, Finnster. Susan B. Anthony did advocate voter's rights…women's rights. All the more reason—"

"I do listen sometimes in class, Numb Nuts."

"Don't be a hater, man. I gotta bounce, anyway. Going to call the old lady." He smiled, referencing his girlfriend.

"Good night, Decan," I said as he sauntered toward his room.

Finn fell more than sat next to me on the sofa. "Why did you have to provoke him?"

"It's like one in the morning. I wasn't thinking."

"Drink?" He extended his hand, red Solo cup intact, toward me.

"Neh."

"Neh?" he slurred.

"Not thirsty. Besides, I don't really like beer. Why drink it if you don't like it? I could never understand that."

"You don't drink too much do you, Lar?"

Somehow, I felt like I had to defend that. "I drink."

He mumbled something about an occasional beer not counting and then said, "I'd like to see you drunk. I mean really drunk. I'll have to take you to a bar some time and line up shots."

"It wouldn't affect me. It's all mind over matter." I tapped my head to exaggerate the point.

"Not a chance. I'd pay to see you drunk. Not buzzed—drunk."

"Well, it's not going to happen tonight."

"Yeah, probably not. More for me, I guess." And he took a big gulp from his cup. "What are you doing out here, anyway?"

"Checking out the scenery, counting the drunk graduates to be, thinking how much it sucks that it's not me." I had my penance to pay with another half year of schooling left in my collegiate career—all because of destructive past decisions and consequently transferring schools.

"Offer stands. We can get you drunk."

"Not the drinking—the graduating." I laughed and changed the subject. "I got bit by something." I showed him my ballooning thumb.

"Youch. What the hell did that?"

Withdrawing my hand, I said, "I don't know. I guess spider? It actually woke me up. I was sound asleep and felt the pinch. I'm just keeping an eye on it—making sure it doesn't get any worse. I'm not really anxious to get back into my room."

"I don't blame you. That's nasty."

"Thanks a lot."

He placed the cup on the end table. "Want me to keep you company for a little while?"

"Sure." It would be nice to have someone to talk to and not let my mind wander to the dark things I often resorted to thinking about in the middle of the night. And Finn was the perfect person. Because of our mutual friends, Sam and Olivia, we had become friends, and he was one of the few people I could count on.

"Okay," Finn agreed. "Gotta share the blankie then."

I adjusted the blanket covering my legs so that it would envelope both of us. "You didn't play tonight?" I spoke of his college band.

"Nope. We're done until after graduation." He stretched his long legs out onto the coffee table. As my legs mimicked his, he spoke again, "We're going to do a gig in Pittsburgh, though—early summer. Got it lined up.

On the South Side. Is that anywhere near where you live? Maybe you could come—bring some friends."

"It's about an hour away. We'll see."

"That would be cool."

"You're still going to LA, though, right?" I leaned my head against his shoulder, feeling a little sleepy.

"Yeah." He paused for the final swig of beer. "At the end of summer." Referring to his internship at a major record label, he continued, "I still can't believe it. That place is iconic."

"The best. They had to have really liked the samples you submitted, especially with how steep the competition must have been."

"Well, it is unpaid grunt work."

"But, God, there are hundreds of people who would die for the opportunity. It's your talent."

"And luck."

"How about perseverance?" I offered at his modesty. "It's going to open doors. I know it will."

"And, if not, I'll still have that good ole college degree that the folks wanted. I'll have something to fall back on and not just, 'Do you want fries with that.'" He smiled, but I saw a flash of doubt.

"Finn, if anyone can do it, you can. You'll be a big star."

"God, I—" Finn started and then suddenly went mute for the slightest of moments. Then, just as quickly, he touched the side of my face with his index finger and pulled away so I was forced to sit up and look at him. "Lara, if I wasn't seeing Audrey," he spoke of the redhead he saw every other weekend since she went to school a few hours away in his hometown of Louisville. "would you go out with me?" He looked me straight in the eyes and suddenly seemed seriously sober.

"Finn…" my voice wavered. *Where was this coming from?*

His lips, still wet from the beer, met mine tentatively. "We would be good together."

"You're drunk. You don't know what you're saying. And, you *are* seeing Audrey. You two will move to the West Coast, and you'll forget all about me."

"I doubt that." He leaned his forehead against mine and looked into my eyes. After a pause, where I didn't know if I was breathing or not, he released our heads and patted me on the leg. "Night night, sleep tight, don't let the bed bugs bite." He smiled a drunk smile, got up, waltzed down the stairs, and went out the front door, leaving me as still as a statue.

"God, Lara, I have been trying to see you all day!" Vanessa, the school's reading specialist, bustled into the room, forcing me back to present day. Her long, dark, wavy hair was bouncing right along with her arms.

"Huh?" I tried to refocus my thoughts on someone besides Finn and our phone conversation just moments before.

"Earth to Lara!" My friend and co-worker waved her hand in front of my face.

"Sorry." I attempted again. "Yeah, I was in meetings in administration."

"I heard. What's this about Finn Murphy?"

My eyes rolled slightly back. So much for dislodging myself out of the past. Here we go. "Who told you?"

"Yvonne."

"Of course." Another eye-roll on my part.

"Did you two date?"

"No! No. God, she wasn't listening." I shook my head that time.

It couldn't be further from the truth. It had been one kiss—one kiss that I had chalked up to a drunken impulse—certainly not a true, profound declaration of any kind. But then, that subsequent night years before, when I had heard his voice in the common area outside my dorm bedroom, I had frozen. I hadn't known how to react or what to say. What was he doing in the house? Was he visiting Decan? Or maybe someone else? Maybe, I thought, he wouldn't even stop in.

My door had been half way open, and I had been lying on my bed, back to the door, watching the season finale of a television show that hadn't even made it to the next season. I sensed his body in the room and I heard him say my name, but I hadn't dared move besides the slight breathing action that I thought mimicked sleep. I knew if he had gotten any closer or touched me, I would probably have been made. But he hadn't. I guess he must have taken me for my "non" word, and I felt more than heard when he exited my room.

I had waited a long while to give up the guise of sleep and then slowly got up, closed my door completely, sat back on the bed, and looked out the window. The way the housing had been laid out, I could see the window of Finn's frat house bedroom. His room appeared dark. I wondered where he had gone. To the bar to hang out with friends? Or someplace quiet to call Audrey? I wondered why I cared so much where he had gone. And I wondered why, if I cared so much, I hadn't just spoken with him in the first place. And then I damned him for saying what he had on that sofa. Nothing would have ever even entered my mind. But that's all it had taken—a question and a drunken kiss, and it had been embedded in my brain. But then graduation, departures just days after that, and years in between had helped resolve any of those mixed feelings.

"Yvonne said his sister said he was soooo in love with you," Vanessa once again brought me back to present day.

"Finn thought everyone was in love with me," I explained. "Like right after I graduated, I was teaching a Computers 101 class at a senior citizen home. He thought all the old guys would have crushes on me." When Vanessa leaned up against my desk in an obvious stance that said she was there to stay and question me some more, I realized something. "He mentioned Wyatt during that phone call all those years ago. He was crying in the background. He was just a baby. He told me he was a keeper." I remembered thinking how important that was. It had also been the very last conversation Finn and I had had besides a few meaningless texts shortly after. Had I realized then that it would have been the last time, I would have paid more attention. But you never really know when the end is the end.

"Finn lived here?"

"No. He was visiting his family in Louisville for the holidays. He was still living in California with Audrey."

"Audrey?"

"Fiancée."

Why did acid run a race up and down my esophagus just like it had the first time I heard they were engaged? It had been at the after-graduation concert near Pittsburgh. Blindsided by Audrey and the beaming ring on her left hand, most of that evening had been a blur. I remembered congratulating Audrey and making small talk about the ring but not wanting to know the details of the proposal. I remembered Finn coming up to me, still sweaty, and giving me a hug and then kissing Audrey. I remembered thinking I wanted to forget.

"But I thought he liked—"

"Vanessa!"

"All right. What happened with this Audrey girl?"

I looked at the phone. I knew it was hung up, but yet, I felt like somehow Finn was still listening. I didn't like to gossip, but Vanessa was my best friend, and it was nice to talk with someone about what happened back then. "When he moved to Nashville that next summer, Audrey was supposed to follow him shortly after, but she didn't. She stayed in California."

"Why?"

"The classy 'she was sleeping with her boss' and never let Finn know." Vanessa's mouth dropped open and her eyes enlarged as I continued. "I only know that because my friend's husband was friends with Finn. I never heard from Finn after he moved to Nashville. I guess he took the break-up pretty hard."

"You never talked again?"

"No. I moved here. I didn't have his new contact info. He lost touch with everyone. I mean, I knew a little about his music from the radio, television, whatever. His career really took off right away. But then…then there was the whole thing with…the drugs."

That time in Finn's life was, unfortunately, documented in the media too. Wild, reckless, partying behavior and pictures with long, leggy blondes were followed by a stint in rehab. It stunned me when I read about it. It certainly wasn't the Finn I had known. But if anyone knew how addictions could overpower lives, I did.

"But he's not like that now, right? I saw when he won a couple of those awards, and he's always nominated. I mean, he seems like a good guy on interviews."

"He always was. Just one of those natural, down-to-earth, fun type of guys."

"A good guy. Doesn't seem like my type," she sassed.

"You like every type of guy," I practically screeched.

"So, so true."

"Anyway, when I talked with him on the phone, it didn't seem like he's changed at all." When she tilted her head and eye-balled me, I answered the non-verbal question, "Just now."

"Way to bury the lead, Faulkner!" she cried out.

I lightly chuckled at her exasperation. "We were just talking about him coming here to sing."

"So he *is* doing that?"

"He is," I confirmed.

"So cool. I'm paying for the good seats. Maybe I'll even be in the mosh pit."

I laughed. The details of the concert hadn't even started to be ironed out. But there definitely was not going to be a mosh pit, and I was pretty sure it was going to be a one-price event.

She glanced at the clock on the wall. "Sheez, I gotta run. I need to get ready. Date number three tonight, my friend. This might be turning into something serious."

I shook my head. Vanessa didn't seem to do serious with men or anything in her life. But she had fun and that I envied.

"When am I going to get you to come out with us—do that double date?" She persisted in trying to set me up.

"Some things just aren't meant to be. It was written in the stars long ago," I concluded while remembering a night, long before even meeting Finn, that had cemented my thoughts on the matter. It was the part of my life that I kept running from—first to college and then to New York. It was the part that made me the person I was—reserved, alone, but safe.

***

And those characteristics ideally matched my chosen profession. I loved the solitude that, for the most part, my job entailed. Researching, adding data, fixing issues, creating documents, and so on, gave me the freedom of working alone yet still having the opportunity to interact.

Now with two major events happening within a day of one another—Open House and then Finn's concert—I was in full work mode. The stuff I had to get done for the open house had become pretty routine over the past few years. So that wasn't so bad. But I was also in charge of getting the word out for the fundraiser too. While Xenia became the contact with Finn via Nola, I was busy creating flyers to send home and posting information on our private social media group pages so that our school families could be informed of the special event.

So, of course, that involved research. I wanted to attach Finn's bio information, video links, song lists, etc. to our resources. And, admittedly, doing all this, drew me into all things Finn Murphy. I found myself not only looking online and listening a little more to country on the radio, but also going back and digging up old photos, yearbooks, and other memorabilia from our collegiate days. It had been such a good time in my life after such a turbulent nineteen years before, I couldn't help but smile at each object.

There was definitely a buzz around the building during those days leading up to Finn's appearance, not only because it was such a huge deal to have a big celebrity in our teeny, tiny community, but also because of the generosity and meaning of his presence which, thankfully, no one forgot. They were all getting ready to meet a superstar. But for me? I couldn't wait to see my good friend again.

CHAPTER THREE

Just hours before the evening open house, I was on a time crunch. Creating my own one-person assembly line, I began stuffing folders with a number of papers describing the school's technology use. In an attempt to make the task not so monotonous, I started to sway more than walk down the line. I knew I was doing the swaying part, I just didn't realize it was accompanied by my singing until I heard light laughter. Swirling around to face the computer lab door, I immediately ceased both of my actions.

"I hope that's a Finn Murphy song."

It would have been embarrassing enough to be caught by one of my co-workers, but, no, it was the artist himself. Geesh! No one had told me he was coming. If I had known, I would have fixed my hair into something more than a simple headband, put on more make-up, worn a more flattering top…you know, like getting ready for a class reunion. But nope. No. Of course not.

Instead, I put on my false bravado and quickly sang a couple more words to his latest tune. "It sure is," I concluded with.

Finn's eyes possibly smiled brighter than his mouth as he remained leaning in the doorway. He was skinnier yet more muscular and fit than I remembered him. He seemed older but not necessarily in a bad way. His hair was shorter, yet relaxed. Wearing jeans and a form-fitting white T-shirt, he appeared different than any of the album covers or videos. He didn't look like a music great. He looked natural. He looked like someone's uncle. He looked like Finn.

He hugged me before I had a chance to debate on whether to stick my hand out or to embrace him. "You look good," he half whispered, half said in my ear.

I broke our lock but, still standing right next to him, said, "I didn't know you were going to be here today. I—"

"You look good," he repeated slower, and I wondered if he wanted to make sure I had heard him or if it was just to reiterate the fact in his own mind.

"Thanks." I suddenly felt good.

And then the moment was gone. Before anything else could be said, a stampede of first graders entered the room. Both of our eyes swung to the students as they hurried to their assigned seats.

Paige, though, who had the job that week of classroom greeter, timidly went up to Finn and held out her hand. "Welcome to our class," she said.

As Finn started to shake her hand, amused, Wyatt yelled out, "Uncle Finn!"

"Thanks. What nice"—Finn was forced to pause for a second as Wyatt energetically adhered himself to Finn's side— "manners," he finished while looking from Paige to me.

"We try." I was impressed myself if I had to admit it.

"Hey, Buddy." Finn ruffled Wyatt's hair. "Shouldn't you be doing what the other kids are doing?"

Ignoring the question, obviously excited, Wyatt turned to me. "Miss Faulkner, this is my Uncle Finn."

"I see that." I smiled.

"C'mon, Uncle Finn. Come sit with me." He took Finn's hand and practically dragged him toward his computer spot in the back of the room.

I knew that if the class had any more free time, the crowd would become restless and not as manageable. So, I clapped my hands three times and in a sing-song voice said, "Everybody listen."

The students echoed me and put their fingers up to their lips for the quiet sign. Even Finn, from the back of the room, although mockingly, put his finger up to his lips and smiled. I tried not to laugh.

"Boys and girls, get on my website. We're going to play Bingo."

Chairs squeaked with movement and voices squeaked with glee. Word Bingo was already a class favorite. Little did the students know that they were learning while having fun. As hands started manipulating the computers and the Bingo screens started to appear, I wove my way to the back of the room and to Finn and Wyatt.

"Do I need to do anything for you for the concert tomorrow or are you just here to play Bingo?" I asked.

"Nola's downstairs talking with someone about tomorrow. I stopped in to see you, but I'd love to play Bingo if I can."

"Yeah, Uncle Finn, play with us," Wyatt cried out.

"Fine, but I'm putting you to work," I half-joked.

"Okay," he smiled. "I'm yours. What do you want me to do?"

I reciprocated the grin, still a little shell-shocked that Finn was actually there, and let him sit at my computer to manipulate the interactive whiteboard. "You're the word caller. Read one word at a time…slowly," I cautioned. "They'll cross them out. Five in a row and they'll yell out 'Dude!'"

"They'll yell out what?"

"You heard me. 'Bingo' is so last century." I laughed.

"Lara, you always did make me wonder."

"Start calling out the words or they'll eat you up." I shook my head and turned to the class. "Everybody have

Free Bingo Space marked off? Remember that is the one with all capital letters. Five in a row and you win. Wyatt's uncle is going to call out the words." And then to Finn, "They're all yours."

While Finn called out the words, I walked around the classroom and helped the struggling readers sound out the word on their Bingo page and click the mouse to cover the space. Finn did a nice job. Although, on occasion, I had to remind him to slow down because words like "the" and "is" and "on" and "an" weren't automatic yet to a six-year old.

We were on the third round when I heard a slight knock on my open door. I looked up to discover Finn's sister standing there. I motioned for her to come in as she smiled and shook her head at the sight of Finn playing Bingo. I met Nola at Wyatt's computer as Finn called out the word "did."

"I was wondering if I could take, well, both of my boys." She tilted her head amusingly toward Finn. "I'm staying to help for Open House, and I wanted to make sure that Wyatt knew not to go on the bus."

"Dude!" one of the students yelled out.

I went to check their board. "Yep, it's a good Dude. Everybody, close out Bingo and line up. It's time to go back to homeroom."

As the disappointed students scurried on their mission, Nola laughed at Finn who was now at her side. "Having a good time?"

Joining them, I said to Finn, "You get a gold star for today."

"Cute," Finn replied.

Nola looked back and forth between us and then said to her brother, "I've got to help set up the cafeteria and then the PTO has me getting pizza for the teachers for dinner before tonight."

"I'll stay for pizza. Maybe I can meet some of the staff before I perform tomorrow."

"They don't have much time to get ready for tonight. I'm sure they're going to be eating and running, right Miss Faulkner?" She turned to me. It was true, but she could tell I wasn't going to get in the middle of it. "Besides, Munch, don't you have your date?"

Finn's mood seemed to slightly change. "I don't know what your matchmaker mother-in-law expects. This is not a date. It's dinner."

"What? I don't think Iva would think that," she challenged. "You've gone out with her enough times to constitute—"

"I can count the number of times on one hand," he immediately countered.

"But that's because you're not in the same city. I'm sure you somehow keep in touch in between."

I was beginning to feel awkward. You could totally tell these two were siblings with the no-holds barred banter between them. I was glad the students were swarming into line near us.

"Yeah, but you know we're both busy. I think I hear more from your mother-in-law asking what the status is than the actual status." Finn turned to me. "I'm going to have to go, but I want to catch up. Do you want to meet up after the show tomorrow? Maybe get a drink?"

"Sure," I heard myself instantly reply. "But Finn, I'll be at Wyatt's birthday party the next day. I thought I'd see you then."

I usually turned down invitations to those things, but Nola only invited me once she found out Finn and I went to college together. She was actually having Wyatt's party a couple weeks early because Finn was going to be in town for the benefit. It was just the family celebration at the Jamison house—not the one where they were taking a bunch of kids to an indoor playground.

"Oh, right. Well, that doesn't count. You deserve a drink after dealing with this all week." He smiled, looking around the room.

"That sounds great if you want to."

"Yeah, I'll take you. I'd love to." He gave me a half-hug as I was being tapped on and waved to as the class started out the door.

"Okay, Munch," I teased wondering why his sister had called him that.

"Nola!" he half-heartedly bellowed, but she was already out the door. "The name kinda stuck. Growing up, she always blamed me for eating all the after-school snacks before she could get home," he rationalized his nickname to me.

"Bye, Wyatt." I directed my attention to the person I should be focused on. "See you tonight. Take care of your uncle. Make sure he can sing tomorrow."

"He can sing, Miss Faulkner." Wyatt looked at me like I had said the most ridiculous thing in the world and took Finn's hand as they left.

***

The school auditorium was packed, which of course, had to do with Finn's fame but also with the caring, small town New York community. I managed to find a seat—not that many of us were sitting the whole time Finn was on stage—around the fourth row but all the way to the extreme left. It was, actually, pretty ideal for the silent observer in me. I could watch and appreciate his talent and personality without being within direct eyeshot of the performer.

It took a while for the crowd to dissipate because so many wanted to say something to the country music star. But, finally, I made my way over and took my turn. Finn was standing next to a woman with an average build and blonde hair that flowed in soft waves past her shoulders.

When he smiled on my approach, I acknowledged his performance. "That was great. And I see you got to speak with Harlan's parents. I'm sure they really appreciated it."

"Yeah," Finn answered. "I can't imagine what they're going through. I hope that little kiddo gets whatever help he needs."

"This definitely helped," I offered and then, not wanting to feel sad after such an energizing show, I changed the subject by reaching out my hand to the blonde stranger in front of me. "I'm—"

"Sorry, Lar, this is Iva," Finn apologized giving the name I had assumed. He turned to Iva. "Lara is who I was talking about. She's my friend from college. She is amazing at her job."

"God, no, I'm not." My eyes dipped on the accolade. I absolutely dread and am kind of notorious for not wanting any attention drawn toward me.

And, of course, he didn't let up. "You should see the webpage she's in charge of. Not just her page but the entire school's site," he said making me wonder when *he* had seen all of it. "And you should see her interact with the kids. My nephew just loves her."

"I like my job. It's as simple as that." I tried to put an end to the Lara spotlight.

"If only we all could love what we do," Iva offered. "I work for the government. Enough said."

"Hey, there're advantages and disadvantages to most jobs," Finn tried. "At least you have stability. Mine can be taken away in a heartbeat."

"Not likely," Vanessa interrupted. "Hi, I'm Vanessa. That was an awesome show." She grabbed Finn's hand for a shake.

"Thanks." He loosened his hand from hers.

"The guy I'm dating, he's into rap, but I'm a country girl all the way." She turned to me willing with a flash of wide eyes not to call her out on the mini-lie. Vanessa's music taste was very eclectic. To say she was a country girl was a bit of a stretch. "Hey, Lar," she forged right on so that I didn't. "Why don't you take Robb's friend to the birthday thing tomorrow? It would be a perfect time to set you two up."

"Uh—" I started.

But I was quickly interrupted by Finn. "Oh, no!"

"No?" I asked curious at his immediate reaction. "Why?"

"You don't want a whole crowd watching you on a first date," was his response.

"Hmmm, maybe," I admitted but actually felt the exact opposite. "But, the thing is, I don't know the guy. So, maybe more people around would be better—more people to add to the conversation." If I was going to go on this date, I wanted to feel comfortable.

"I totally know where you are coming from," Iva chimed in. "Maybe you, this guy, Finn, and I can meet up afterward. That way, it won't be a whole crowd, but you won't be alone either."

"No," Finn replied before I could decide.

"Why not?" It was Iva's turn.

"I have to take off the next morning. I've got to get stuff done and can't go out after."

"Oh." Iva's shoulders dipped, and her voice lost some of its bounce. "All right. Well, I tried." She briefly looked at me and then turned again to Finn. "I gotta get to that bachelorette party. Walk me out?"

"Sure." He offered his arm to Iva and turned to me. "You'll be here when I come back?"

"Yeah," I acknowledged.

"Good." He smiled before walking in stride with Iva.

After watching them leave, I turned to Vanessa and told her I didn't think it was really appropriate to bring a guest to Wyatt's birthday party. Vanessa pouted, frustrated to be put off again. I told her to let the school year get settled and I would go out with Robb's friend. Who knew—maybe he was the love of my life? Or not.

When Finn returned, everyone had cleared out except for the janitorial staff. I asked him how things were going with Iva. It was two nights in a row after all.

"I don't know. She's…." His voice trailed off.

"She seemed happy, like you guys were good."

"Yeah," he agreed. "We were listening to her tunes last night. Pretty decent list."

"What? All Finn Murphys?" I joked.

"No. There was some country but not all. That's cool. We have similar tastes."

"Well, that's good."

"But she not into my obsession with HGTV. So, I don't know…." His voice lightened and trailed, but I couldn't tell if he was joking or not.

"Are you serious?"

"Yeah. Don't you watch those *House Hunters*?"

"No."

"C'mon, are you ready? Where are we going?" He changed the subject and put on the light gray hoodie he had been holding.

"Coffee?"

"I thought you would need something stronger."

"Probably, but there's a cute coffee shop just a few blocks down. We can walk."

When he gripped my hand in his, it took me by surprise. I wasn't expecting it, and it felt a little foreign to me. But before my brain or hand could react, he clasped tighter with a confident, kind squeeze, and it made me recall how secure I had felt with Finn as a friend all those years ago.

As we walked out the door and crossed the parking lot, Finn glanced around and pulled the hood part of the sweatshirt on top of his head. "So," he noted, "still not a drinker, huh?"

"I drink," I defended. "Coffee, water, iced tea…," I listed, knowing very well what he was referring to.

"I'm not making fun. I've just always been curious."

"I do drink a little, but… well, for one thing, you remember when my dad died?"

"Yeah," he replied with the consideration of being

solemn.

The ironic part was, I hardly considered my childhood or my dad something worthy of mourning. But Finn had been a comforting blanket when I had first found out my father had died. It had been the year before my graduation, and Finn had sat and talked with me until my brother, Lane, only a year older than me, had come to pick me up.

"Do you remember how he died?"

"ATV accident," he stated and added a personal addendum, "Haven't wanted to even look at one since."

My hand squirmed a little in his. That initial awkwardness was back. But it wasn't necessarily because of Finn. It was just that everything always felt a little closed in when I thought of my past.

So, as we walked down the adjoining street, I let go of his hand and elaborated on the part of my father's death that Finn hadn't been aware of. "Nothing is wrong with ATVs. They're safe when you wear a helmet and you aren't so intoxicated that you can't say your own name. And Finn, that's how he was all his life—as far back as I can remember. He lived life more drunk than sober and the sad part was, after a while, he became, actually, more tolerable when he was drinking. It was his self-medication—his regulator. Unless, of course, he took it to an extreme which, unfortunately, he did on more than one occasion. But we learned the patterns of that too, and quickly acquired the art of avoidance and pacification. Sometimes, though, neither of those solutions would work. When my father got really drunk, I mean nasty drunk, he needed a punching bag. And for years, that was Lane and me—never our mother. He got to her emotionally, which, as far as I'm concerned, was far worse. Now, it was never terrible, terrible. My father was discreet, and my brother and I knew we deserved the lashings we got. We had the misfortune of getting in his way—sometimes just because we had been born."

I looked at Finn. He was intently listening to me, but I

could see how his eyes had changed—the sympathy…the sadness. I didn't want that. It wasn't why I was telling him.

"Write this down." I tried to lighten the mood and did a friendly swipe at his arm. "It would make a great song."

"Lara—" Even in just the two syllables that it took to say my name, I could hear the pity.

"Oh, Finn, please. I'm just trying to tell you why I personally don't care for alcohol a whole lot. If you know how to control yourself, have fun, be responsible, and not hurt anyone, then fine. I don't have a problem with someone drinking. It's just when it has the power to turn you into a mean son-of-a-bitch that I have an issue. And as far as him hitting us—when my brother got old enough, he fought back and that not only protected him but me too. It was good as long as Lane was around."

"But Lane wasn't always around." He got it.

"No." I paused in a reflection that seemed to mimic the dark, still, quiet night surrounding us. "After a sports injury, Lane lost his scholarship and gave up the idea of college. It was so terrible. And he certainly wasn't going to stay in our town. His destination then was purely 'out of this hell hole.'"

"Where's he at now?"

"North Carolina." I smiled thinking of Lane. "We don't see each other often but we're still pretty close. He works at a hotel and he's married."

As we turned onto the street that housed Java Mug, we saw a woman sitting on a bench, playing a guitar, and singing a folksy song. She was rather good. I started to sway my hips as we neared her.

Finn laughed and dug into his pocket to add a bill to the guitar player's case. "This is new."

"What?" I asked.

"You."

"What's that mean?" We started walking again.

"Not bad. Just…." His eyes scanned mine as if they would give him the correct words to say. "You're the same but more alive or something."

"I guess I'll take that as a compliment," I offered, glad we were off the topic of my dad and his damning issues.

"For sure. This is the second time already that I've seen you dancing. And, if I recall, you were not a fan."

I smiled thinking, as surely Finn was, of me asking Audrey to cut in on Finn and me when we were doing the groomsman/bridesmaid dance at Sam and Olivia's wedding right after college. "Hmmm. Still not. You caught me swaying. Dancing? Nope. Not a chance."

"Might have to find a way to change that."

"Ha! No." I stopped in front of the entrance to Java Mug. "Here. We're here."

Finn held the door open for me. After stepping inside, he asked, "Do you know what you want?"

"I'll get it."

"Grab a seat," he directed and, before I could protest, "What do you want?"

"A large, hot Nutty Honey—no whip."

"That's quite a memorable name."

I laughed at his reaction. "You asked."

As I sat down on a red cushioned chair against the wall, I heard the owner/barista, Dinah, say to Finn, "Is this for Lara?"

"It is." Finn, sounding a bit bewildered, nodded his head in my direction.

"Oh, hey, Lara!" Dinah called across the café.

"Hi, Dinah." I waved in response. To keep my hands and mind occupied, I started flipping through a local magazine lying on the table as Dinah completed our order.

Finn handed me my coffee, placed two fruit muffins on the table, and sat down on the chair next to me. "Dinah said you would probably want one of these too."

"Yeah, most of the time I get a cookie or some sort of muffin. But that's my favorite." I said, taking a sip of the hot, delectable beverage.

"How did she know as soon as I mentioned that coffee

that it was for you?"

"You're not the only celebrity around here, you know!" I joked, knowing that I was not only a regular at Java Mug, but Dinah and I had become friends. "What did you get?" I asked as Finn took a sip of his coffee.

"I usually just like it straight black, but I couldn't resist the Caramel Irishman."

"And?"

"Scrumptious, especially with the whip action." He lifted his eyebrows.

A sudden cheer from fellow coffee patrons caused Finn and I to look up. On the muted television screen, an NHL game was being broadcast and it had the attention of almost everyone in the shop. Finn removed his hood as the replay showed the Islanders scoring to take the lead against the Penguins.

"They call that a goal?" I half grumbled half shouted. "That was goalie interference."

Finn's eyes widened as his shoulders shook briefly. "You're a hockey fan?"

"Not really. That was the sport Lane played. So I know it pretty well." And then I repeated, "And that was goalie interference."

"You just say that because you're from Pittsburgh and a Pens fan."

"And the Islander uniforms are ugly," I teased.

"Oh, geez." He playfully nudged me.

"Let's bet."

"Okay." Amused, Finn nodded. "What's the wager?"

"Whoever loses buys a chocolate treat for the walk back."

"You're on, girl. Besides, I already got the first round, so it's only fair that you get the second." He smiled in a joking way and took a bite of his muffin.

"We'll see." I was up for a lighthearted challenge.

"So, Lar, I have to ask—what happened to Blondie?" He touched the ends of my now darker strawberry blonde hair.

"Went natural after graduation." No more dying it platinum.

"I like it and like that it's long again. I don't know what you were thinking when you chopped off all your hair right before Sam and Olivia's wedding."

I had been thinking I was all alone at that wedding. Olivia had Sam, Finn had Audrey, and I had no one. I was hurting and wanted to cut something. My hair was the safest, most liberating thing at the time.

I didn't say all of that, though. Instead, I turned the tables on him. "You're one to speak. What's with the eyes?"

"Touché."

"Seriously, Finn, colored contacts?" I said referencing his miraculously green eyes that had always been gray.

"That's what the label likes. Something about making them pop and playing up the whole Irish thing," he answered almost apologetically. "You really don't like them?"

"Eh, it's just…it's not you. It's not my you."

"Your you, huh?" A puzzled but happy smile crossed his face.

My standing up so abruptly caused Finn's body to jerk a little. "I'm going to use the restroom." I copped out of trying to explain my idiotic comment. And since I couldn't exactly pretend to be asleep this time, the old "powder my nose routine" would have to suffice. "Do you need anything while I'm up?" A slight memory lapse, perhaps?

"Uh, no, Lara." He gallantly half stood as I made my way back toward the restroom and away from the conversation.

I looked in the simple bathroom mirror and shut my eyes, condemning myself. Why had I worded it that way? Of course I was excited to see Finn again. When we spoke on the phone and I saw him in the school, I remembered my old friend and mentally noted the years that had passed and how we had changed. But, now, in that coffee shop, I was noticing our not-skip-a-beat friendship and how much had *not* changed. And I wondered if part of that were those feelings that blurred the line oh so many years ago.

CHAPTER FOUR

"You should have just stayed hidden in the bathroom."

What? My eyes widened at Finn as he said those words and I inched my way back to my chair. Was he totally calling me on my bluff? He wouldn't do that, would he?

"Look at the television. The Islanders just scored."

"Oh." Oh. "Dang it," I added.

"You want me to take my contacts out?"

"No, of course not." Geez, let it go.

"I remember you didn't exactly like my choice of eyewear the first time we met, either."

"What? What are you talking about? You didn't have contacts then."

"Glasses."

"Oh." I did remember that little tidbit. "Oh, right."

"You were mean."

"I…I was not."

I remembered how nervous I had been. I never liked meeting new people. But, regardless, there I had been, smooshing my what suddenly felt like thunderous thighs into the back seat of Sam's car right next to a co-ed I had never met. His bandmate, Bryan, was on his other side.

After the opening introductions, Bryan put on a pair of mock, studious-looking glasses. "So, what do you think?" He tilted his head a couple ways. "We're thinking one of us should add glasses to break up the look. We picked these up at a thrift shop." He then handed them to Finn who tried them on and looked at me only inches away.

Feeling uncomfortable making conversation with these two new boys, I resorted to my sarcastic, sassy façade to get me through. "Well, you," I nodded to Bryan. "they look good on. You," I directed my glance as much as I could to Finn. "not so much."

"Ha!" Bryan laughed at Finn.

"You might do better putting on a cowboy hat too, instead of a ball cap. You look like a cancer patient instead of a country singer." I felt awkward sitting so close to an unfamiliar guy. So, that weird, straight-laced humor really came out in full force.

"Bro, you look fine in the baseball hat," Sam offered from the driver's seat.

"Really?"

"Now, who are you going to trust?" I continued talking. "Someone who is your friend and is obligated to tell you that you look good, or someone who you don't know and has no reason to lie to you?"

"You don't think that was mean?" Finn brought his coffee mug down and interrupted my re-telling of the collegiate story.

"No. I didn't mean it that way. I didn't know you. I told you—" I stopped and decided to turn the story onto him. "I noticed right away how you and Olivia switched seats on the way back."

"Really?"

"Yeah, you probably don't remember, though. You were pretty drunk—rum from what I recall."

"I remember not wanting to sit on the middle back hump again, especially with Sam blasting the air conditioner right in my face."

"Yeah, you did keep boohooing about needing more layers."

"I didn't boohoo."

"Then you said, 'Well, I guess I won't see you again.' and I said, 'Oh, sure, when these two get married,' because Olivia was already planning it years out despite not actually being engaged, and she had already asked me to be a part of the wedding."

"What a fiasco." Finn referred to Olivia and Sam's eventual divorce. "You still in touch with them?"

"I get Christmas cards from Olivia. Sam—no. I guess sides had to be drawn. You?"

"Sam showed up once at one of my gigs, but it's been years."

"By the way, how did you think you weren't going to see me again? It wasn't exactly a huge campus."

Finn looked slightly awkward and then admitted, "I just meant, you know, not go out, like on a date."

"Really? I wasn't thinking that at all."

"No kidding. You didn't give me the time of day."

I hadn't thought of that day in almost that many years and now, reliving it with Finn, I saw it in a whole new light. "Do you think they were trying to set us up?" It had never dawned on me.

"It wouldn't have been the first of Liv's friends, and Sam always had crazy ideas."

"I was just so excited that a big project I was working on was done, and I was ready to let loose. I wasn't thinking about anything else."

Finn literally spit out part of his latte. "That was letting loose?"

"Yeah." I said handing him a napkin. "If I recall, I was even a little bit buzzed from that beer all of you coaxed me into drinking."

"Lara, I thought you were so stuck up at first."

"Really?" I was genuinely shocked. I would never, ever consider myself stuck-up. "I was just shy." Before he could reply or I could continue, the Islanders scored again. "Shit!"

Finn smirked and said, "That's not shy and definitely not school talk."

"I don't see chalkboards and playgrounds around, do you?" I exaggerated a comical turn around. "As long as I'm not at work, I should be able to curse and drink like the rest of society. Just don't tag me in a post online."

"You have a personal page online?" He sounded shocked. "And you drink?"

"Well, no, and, I told you, a little."

"Uh-huh." He said in knowing way. "Anyway, it didn't matter, did it?"

"What?"

"Thanks to Sam's lousy car again, I got to know the real—not stuck-up—you."

"A lousy car it was, but that had nothing to do with it. It was that damn deer that ran out in front of it."

A few months or so after the concert episode, Sam, Olivia, and I were in a car accident. We were all taken to the hospital via ambulance. Sam, who was unconscious momentarily, suffered a concussion and had a broken arm. Olivia broke her foot and had a punctured lung. They both had to stay at the hospital. Since my only injury had been two bruised knees—the result of slamming into the back of the driver's seat—I was free to go. I was consoling Olivia and agreeing to take care of her cats at her off-campus apartment when Finn had walked in. Because the accident happened so close to campus, news hadn't taken long to get around. Finn offered to give me a ride back, helped me check on the cats, and bought me pizza when he heard my stomach growling and realized I hadn't eaten all day. We became friends, going in groups to movies or sporting events. But there had not been one ounce or inkling of anything else until that night before graduation on that sofa. And then that turned into nothing too.

"I loved that Jeep of yours," I brought my thoughts back to current day while referencing the red Wrangler Finn had in college. "It was sharp and felt so free. I always wanted one like that."

"Yeah, that was the car, huh?"

"Guess you don't still have it, then."

"Nope," He glanced at the television with a smile. The final score proved Finn the winner. "Looks like you owe me, Roxanne." He grinned like the Cheshire cat, and I knew it was not only because of his victory but because of the name he used for me.

"Stop that." I bellowed but, nonetheless, laughed. "My red lava lamp was not an advertisement for prostitution."

"Roxanne, Roxanne…." He started singing part of the red-light Police song that had prompted the ridiculous, nothing-could-be-further-from-the-truth nickname he had appointed to me in college.

"I'll get that chocolate treat." I stood, shaking my head.

"Lar, you don't have to. I'll get it."

"No. A bet's a bet. Throw the trash away. I'll get it." I walked to the counter and asked Dinah for two chocolate-covered pretzel rods. When I tried to pay her for them, she told me they were on the house. "Why?" No matter how good of a friend I was, Dinah never offered even a buy-so-many-get-one-free card because she was young and still trying to make her business a success.

"Your friend there put a really nice tip in the jar earlier."

"Still, Dinah, I want to pay you."

"It's two pretzels."

"Are you sure?"

"Yeah. Next time, though, I want an autograph," she whispered smiling at me.

"You do know." And I thought others were starting to suspect too now that the hockey game was over and their attention wasn't diverted. It was then that I realized why Finn had worn the hoodie despite the warmer weather—it was a disguise of sorts.

"I figured it out because I heard about the benefit thing. But a customer is a customer. I want the scoop next time you're in, though."

"No scoop, just old friends," I said as Finn appeared beside me. I turned and handed him a pretzel rod. "Here you go."

He stuck it in his mouth and mumbled "bye" and "great place" to Dinah as we walked out the door. We strolled in silence most of the way back to the parking lot. After giving me a hug, Finn made sure I got into my used compact car and told me he would see me the next day for Wyatt's birthday party.

***

I hadn't seen Finn in seven years and now it was three times in three days. How strange life can be. How quickly things can change and, yet, how things can still remain the same.

The weather didn't know if it wanted to cooperate or not, going from overcast to bright sunshine to drizzle. We were outside on the patio. We were inside the Jamison house. We were playing cornhole and having a BBQ. We were watching football on TV and having cake and ice cream in the living room. But, most importantly, Wyatt was having a good time parading around like he was king of the universe. Kelsea would follow him around like a lost puppy, and most of the time, Wyatt would tolerate her since she was the only one remotely his age. But he also liked telling her the things she couldn't do because she wasn't three years old yet.

Mr. Jamison's mother and aunt flew in for the concert and the first part of the birthday party but left before dusk to catch their flight back home to Boston. Nola and Finn's parents flew in early that morning and Mrs. Murphy's brother, Eoin, who was a restaurant owner in Manhattan, also came in. I could see where Finn got his personality and charm by the way the entire clan welcomed me in such a warm and hospitable manner.

Of course, since they were all familiar with each other and not me, I was the one who got bombarded with the questions. I told them how I ended up working at Wyatt's school and how, yes, I was still single. Then Finn, Eoin—a divorcee with three teen to twenty-something year old kids—and I told our nightmare dating stories. That was when I found out why Iva was noticeably absent from the festivities. As maid-of-honor for her sister's wedding, which was only one week away, she had venue plans with the bride.

"You know my mom's going to ask," Will, a.k.a. Mr. Jamison, prompted Finn about Iva.

"She already did before she left. I don't know, man. She's a nice girl. But is she the one?" Finn replied.

"One? Nephew, I thought you would have at least three. I would," Eoin offered.

"And not know any of their names—a girl for every city." Finn went along with it. "Call one while dropping the other one off. Get a number and throw it in the trash."

"What do you think of that, Lara?" Mrs. Murphy asked.

"I think that is horrible for all womankind. You wouldn't do that." I looked at Finn, remembering the boy I knew. But then I recalled the time when his career had just been taking off and he had gotten all wrapped up in the rock star lifestyle.

"Hmmm," he teased. "No. Besides, Uncle Eoin would need a little blue pill to keep up that pace."

"I hear watermelon rinds have a similar effect," I offered.

All eyes swirled to me as Finn and his dad said simultaneously, "Really?"

"Yeah, I heard it on the radio," I said more softly while

thinking, *what did I just say in front of virtual strangers and someone's parents?*

Mr. Murphy raised his eyebrows at his wife, making me think how different my parents' relationship had been compared to theirs. "We have watermelon?"

"Ew, Lara, see, there's something I just didn't need to hear." Finn laughed as Wyatt, Nola, and Kelsea entered the patio, dragging me and Mrs. Murphy inside to play the new interactive video game Wyatt had gotten for his birthday.

After a few rounds, Nola decided to get Kelsea and Wyatt into their pajamas early so they would be ready when it was bedtime. And Mrs. Murphy wanted to put away some of the food in the kitchen so it wouldn't spoil. I offered to help her, but she insisted that I was a guest.

So I retreated back to the patio where all the men—minus Will who was dealing with his Wall Street job—were still gathered. In typical Lara fashion, I found a need to say something since the atmosphere had suddenly grown awkwardly quiet with all eyes on me. "What were you boys doing while I was gone?"

"We were talking about you," Mr. Murphy answered solidly.

"What? What a lousy cook I am?" I referred to the baguette chips and pizza dip I had brought that was more than a bit on the watery side.

"No," Finn's dad replied but didn't offer anything else, making the room grow even more eerily quiet.

Because I couldn't handle the silence, I was the first to speak, "Wyatt gave me a real workout on that game. I'm going to have to get in better shape." Silence. "Or, get a beer."

Finn reached into the cooler near his feet, pulled out a bottle, opened it, and handed it to me as I sat down next to him. I was surprised he didn't make a crack about me drinking. I was surprised I was drinking. I couldn't remember the last time I had a beer. It still was not, by any means, my drink of choice. But the awkwardness made me suddenly desire one.

That's when Mrs. Murphy entered and sat down. Finn changed seats, sitting, instead, next to his mother. They started a conversation about his music and how he was thinking of trying some new sounds on his next album. I asked if he would give us an example. Finn hummed a few bars which sounded bluesy. It was a nice contrast to his usual country rock. We all tossed around other performers who had similar sounds. Finn's Uncle Eoin didn't know one from the other, and Finn's dad was wondering which ones were straight. The mood, thankfully, was changing to a more relaxed one again.

A little later, after using the restroom, I opened the front door to take a moment to myself and soak in the now dark evening. It was peaceful and what I needed in order to reflect on all that had happened in the past couple of days. I was leaning against the doorframe when Finn joined me.

"Whatcha doing?" he asked softly as if trying to read my thoughts.

I turned in his direction. "I was just admiring how crystal clear the sky is tonight. You can see every star."

"Hmmm." He leaned outside and briefly looked with me before straightening back up. "I feel like there's something in my eye. I've got to go wash it out. It's like I have my contacts in, and I don't."

"I noticed." Gray.

But before he could exit, Finn's cell phone rang from inside his pocket. He pulled it out, looked at the caller ID, and answered with a generic "Hello." I looked at him and offered to leave so that he could have some privacy.

"No, no that's okay." He pulled the phone slightly away so that I knew he was directing his comment to me. "It'll just be a minute." And then, once again, he talked into the phone, "No, I was talking with Lara." He listened to the other end. "Yep, we're still here." Another pause to listen. "No. You knew that." He listened again. "Hey Iva,

Wyatt really liked your gift."

Regardless of Finn's silent protest, I went back into the house. He, in turn, walked farther outside, shutting the door behind him. Listening to someone else's phone conversation always seemed awkward, especially when it was someone's... whatever Finn and Iva were calling their relationship. I made my way back to the living room. Nola had just made it back downstairs with both wound-up kids. I started saying my goodbyes, thank yous, and nice to meet yous. They took turns giving me hugs like they had known me forever. Some families are like that. Mine surely wasn't.

The only two I had not said goodbye to were Will and Finn—who was now off his phone. They were outside on the driveway near the cars. I made my way toward them.

"Lara, you're not going, are you?" Will directed his eyes toward my purse and jingling keys.

"I am. Thanks for having me." I made a point of looking at both men.

After the smallest of silences, Finn asked, "You going to give me a hug goodbye?"

"Thanks for helping out with the concert." I initiated that hug.

"For sure." He broke our embrace, and I noticed Will silently walking back inside the house.

"Why are you leaving?" Finn seemed genuinely disappointed before he started razzing me. "You going on that date? Hunka, hunka burning love?"

"No," I said and momentarily covered my face in embarrassment. "He's probably like four or five inches shorter than me or 650 pounds or has complete attitude. The men people set me up with…." I shook my head with exaggeration.

"What's up, Lara? You had guys want you in college and, yet, I never really saw you with anyone. There was that one kid…." His voice drifted as he suddenly turned serious.

"Yeah, Oystein," I said referring to the foreign exchange student I hung out with for a little while mid-way through college. "He was a good guy. I liked him. I just…." Was scared. Wasn't ready. Instead, I said a variation of the truth, "I mean, he was a whole year older than us and was heading back to Norway. It was never gonna work out."

There was a moment of silence between us before Finn spoke. "Lara?" He paused but didn't lose eye contact with me. "Are you…? I mean, not that there's anything wrong…." It was one of the only times I had ever witnessed Finn stumble on his words.

But I knew what he meant. And I often wondered if other people thought that of me too. He was the only one that had ever—sort of—asked, though.

"Not that there's anything wrong with that?" I finished for him and then answered immediately. "No, Finn, I am not gay. Not at all."

Even though I'm sure he was trying to disguise it, I couldn't help but notice the slight relaxation in his shoulders and lightest of exhales from his nose. "Sorry. Maybe I shouldn't have asked. I work with gay people, have friends who are gay. I really don't have a problem with it. It's just…you…. It would break so many guys' hearts."

I shook my head at his vision of me being a heartbreaker and his absurd theory that all these guys liked me. That also wasn't true. But he had always attested to that. And even though it wasn't the case, it made me feel a little bit empowered.

Reconnecting with Finn over the past couple of days was, in a way, therapeutic. Partly because it was so natural. Partly because he brought back memories of a time that had been the best in my life—not that I had a lot to choose from. Talking with him made me also realize how far I had come since. Not only starting fresh at the college where we had met but also since graduation. I was a whole different person and, maybe, someone who should truly let go of her past.

While I pondered those thoughts, I walked slowly toward the low concrete block wall that bordered one side of the driveway. Finn followed, but silently, as if he knew I needed that moment for decision. Just as I hoisted myself up onto the wall, his phone rang. After glancing at the screen, he put his index finger up as the universal symbol for me to wait and strolled off to answer the phone.

I did wait, and I did think. My stomach started to slightly churn. I had never told anyone—not anyone in ten years—the truth. And now, I wanted to because it was Finn and how natural our friendship was to me. He had already heard about my destructive dad and certainly hadn't judged. And really, my story wasn't all that different than that of many girls. It was just that after it had happened, I had successfully tucked it away under lock and key and tried to re-invent myself. The stomach rumblings and slight cloudiness in my head signified the definite nerves and uncertainty of telling someone. But they were mixed in with possibility—the possibility of being just a little free.

His return was within only a couple minutes. "Sorry 'bout that." He used his defined arms to help position himself on the ledge next to me.

"Who was it? One of the girls from every city?" I used my go-to sarcasm.

He ignored it. "It was my dad. He said he forgot to tell you thanks for the watermelon trick."

I couldn't help but give a short snort. And then, "The stars really are spectacular." It was a natural stall, but I didn't really need it. I was ready. "If you really want to know why I'm the way I am, I'll tell you, Finn. But it's not a pretty story, and if you don't want to hear it, that's okay. It's just seeing you again, I don't know, I realize how much I've changed and have gotten past it, and maybe I shouldn't be so ashamed. Maybe it will help to tell someone."

He spoke with conviction. "I'm here. You tell me what you want."

I looked into his eyes, those honest gray eyes, for a long moment, just to reassure myself that this was the thing to do. A wash of calmness spread through my body. I felt at peace with my decision.

CHAPTER FIVE

I took a deep breath. This…this was it. "My senior year of high school—I felt so lost…so abandoned. Lane was gone. So, I got to be…because I had to be…braver. But at the same time, I became more reckless. I, unfortunately, followed in my dad's footsteps and started drinking. Not a lot, but recreationally when I never had before. I also started dating a boy named Miller. He was rough around the edges, I guess, but he had the sweetest heart. We were together for most of our senior year and into that summer. I was accepted into Pitt and was really looking forward to finally escaping the hell hole too."

The slight strain in Finn's face mimicked the seriousness of the conversation, and I considered just stopping there. But I knew it would be a cop-out. I took a deep breath, really and truly wanting to cleanse my mind. I had put so much of the past in a reserved, closed, mental vault that I thought I was good. But I wasn't. I needed that release. I needed to tell someone. And with my friendship with Finn seemingly picking up so naturally, I was willing to venture down that bumpy road with him. The smallest of buzzes I had from the beer, admittedly, helped too.

"It was early August. I was at Miller's house. His

parents were out of town, and he and his fraternal twin brother, Macon, were having a little, you know, gathering." I smirked—everyone knew what a teenage gathering while parents were away entailed. "There weren't so many of us that the neighbors would be alerted but enough so that it was interesting. Miller, who was already a few beers in, and I were out on the back porch talking and, you know, kissing. But neither of us were really into it. So, I told him to have fun, but it was time for me to go home. I would call him in the morning."

"Okay." From the sound of Finn's content voice, I could tell he liked that as an end to my tale, but, unfortunately, it wasn't anywhere near.

"When I got home, my dad was off his rocker drunk. It had been a while since I had seen him like that. I should have just gone up to my bedroom, curled up, and gone to sleep. But I was the fearless Lara now, especially having had a beer at Miller's. So, I confronted him. My mother tried to intervene, but it did no good. He hit me and he hit me hard. It was a smack that literally sent me sailing across the room. I was stunned and scared. So, I did the only thing I knew to do. I hurried back to my safety net—the one I shouldn't have left in the first place."

"Good. I mean," Finn clarified. "good for you for getting out. I can't imagine…your dad," his voice nearly growled.

"When I arrived back at Miller's house, it was Macon who answered the door. He was well beyond the buzzed stage and almost stumbling drunk. He told me everyone was back in the woods and that he was just coming in for a refill of the punch creation they had made. When I took a cup and drank it in one swallow, he told me to take it easy but, nonetheless, poured me a second. I didn't care. I knew I wasn't going anywhere else that night. I was staying."

I saw Finn shake his head like he knew where the story was going. He couldn't possibly. I know I would have preferred whatever version he was concocting in his mind.

"So, we made our way back to the waterfall in the woods where I saw the small group gathered. They were sitting in a haphazard half-circle laughing in the way that only drunks do. And then, I couldn't believe my eyes. Miller, who hadn't noticed us approach, had a short, pudgy, curly blonde in his lap." I closed my eyes momentarily at the memory—the real turning point. "It took him a moment to notice me and then it was shock—pure shock. I tried a glare, but I was losing my bravado. All I wanted was for him to tell me he was sorry, or that it was a mistake, or I wasn't seeing things right, or that she was their long-lost sister. But he didn't say any of those things. Between the shock of Miller's actions and the alcohol kicking in big time, I wasn't sure what was happening. But I did know I didn't want to be there. So, I ran off."

"I'm sorry, Lara."

"Finn, that…that's not it." I let out a gust of air. My shoulders were tight and my stomach was in knots, but I was on a roll, and I needed to get it out. All of it. "Just…just try not to judge, okay?"

"What? No."

I sighed, doubting the truth of his statement but dove back into the tale with a now-or-never attitude. "Somewhere down the path, I lost my footing and fell. I scraped my knee and got a tiny gash near my eye. I started to cry, which was not like me at all. I had learned quite successfully how to hold back my feelings, especially when it came to being hurt. But the combination of physical and emotional wounds caught up to me. I didn't realize Macon was behind me until he crouched down and handed me his drink. Foolishly, I finished that one too. Macon held me at arm's length, looking me up and down as if it were a debate. And then, when his inner judge, I guess, ruled a verdict, he put his mouth up to mine. I should have been surprised, but I wasn't even thinking. Or, if I was, it was to return the favor and make Miller jealous. Macon's kiss was the next thing I drank in." I took a deep breath but couldn't look at Finn. And I rambled the next part off like I was a train that had lost its brakes and was accelerating down a hill. "Before I knew it, we were off the path, behind a tree, and my clothes seemed to be missing. The punch was like nothing I had ever had. It made things flash like a psych ward in my brain and literally in front of my eyes. At the same time, I felt absolutely numb. I heard hooting and hollering from two of Macon's buddies and saw that they were there—I mean right there—next to us, watching. I felt Macon in me before everything went black."

"Shit." Finn's jaw was clenched as he tried to stifle his own curse.

I looked away again and continued, "When I woke up the next morning, I was on the sofa in Miller and Macon's house. I was dressed only in my T-shirt, which luckily was on the longer side. I flashbacked to the night before and subconsciously curled into a ball. I wanted to vomit. My stomach felt like I was deep sea fishing on a raft built for two in the middle of a hurricane. I couldn't believe what I had done. I had no feelings for Macon. Miller came in from his room and I could see the spite…the hatred in his entire being. If I hadn't been sure what he knew, I knew then. He told me the girl was only hitting on him and he got rid of her and went to look for me. And then, he couldn't say anything more. He just left. I went to the bathroom to hopefully vomit or, at the very least, pee. But when I looked in the mirror, it was horrible. My hair was a tangled mess, there was dried up blood near my eye from the cut, there was a bruise on my cheek from where my father had smacked me, and my knee was raw from where I had fallen." I glanced over at Finn. I couldn't believe I was going to tell him this part, but when he placed his hand on top of mine in a comforting way, I did. It was not only our friendship that I was relying on—it was the maturity of the years that had passed. "But…the pain, it wasn't just external." I paused slightly again. "Of all the times Miller and I had sex, it never felt like that. Not even the first time. I had no idea what happened. It made me sick. So, I promptly did what I set out to do. I threw up."

I slowly lifted my head to glance at Finn. I hadn't dared look up while telling that last part. I was not only afraid of his reaction, but it took every ounce for me to actually speak the words. His eyes searched mine like he was trying to find a way to help or even take it all back.

"That tiny scar near your eye." He chose one of the easier injuries to talk about. "You have to really look to notice it."

"It's faded a lot. You can only see it sometimes, ironically, when I smile," I offered. "You know, it's weird to say all this out loud. It's almost like it happened to another person."

"You know what happened, though, don't you?" he asked gently.

"I'm not sure that I knew immediately, but yes. I know that it went beyond…beyond what was right."

"The other two…the ones who were, God, watching, do you think they actually—"

I couldn't let him go on for my sake and for his. "I don't know, Finn. I just don't know."

"That makes me sick. That Macon creep never should have done that to you."

"Finn, I did kiss him. I do remember that. I was drinking. I own that. I do. I wasn't completely innocent."

"But in the state you were in, he—"

"We were all kids."

"You…no one deserves—"

"I—"

He didn't let me finish. "No. No one." With a soft swipe of his hand, he removed a tear from my cheek that I hadn't realized was falling.

"I'm sorry. I didn't think this would still affect me so much."

"God, why wouldn't it?" he said. "Lara, I'm so glad you

felt like you could tell me."

It was my turn to search his eyes. I got up and paced, doing a couple messy figure eights before stopping directly in front of him. "Finn, there's one more thing. It's kind of a biggie." I had come this far. I might as well tell him all of it. "You want me to stop, I totally understand."

Finn put out his hand to help me back up to the concrete wall. "If you want to tell me, I want to listen. But I'm sorry that you have more to tell."

"By the time I was six days late, I pretty much knew. I didn't have it confirmed, though, until weeks later. I was eighteen years old, it was the third day of classes at Pitt, I was finally out of my home, and I was pregnant."

Out of the corner of my eye, I saw Finn bring both of his hands up to cover his eyes, nose, and mouth. He left out an exhale, as if he knew it was coming but was shocked just the same, and dropped his fingers to his chin. He slowly nodded his head, let his one hand drop to my side, and waited for me to clasp it. When I did, he laced his fingers through mine and said, "Go on, Lara."

"I was scared to death. This was something so far removed from my life plan, I couldn't even imagine what it meant. I didn't know what to do or where to go or who to talk to. I sat on it a couple of days, which just made matters fester in my head. I couldn't concentrate at Pitt or even begin to think of making friends in my new environment. What would be the point, anyway? My life was in shambles."

Finn remained solid. He remained steady. He hadn't wavered in how he was looking at me or the interest in what I was saying. Part of that amazed me, part of it didn't surprise me at all. After all, that was the reason I had thrown my trust into telling him my story when "trust" might as well have been a four-letter word in my mind.

"God, what a way to bring down a seven-year-old's birthday party, huh?" I jested.

He didn't want my sarcasm, though. "Lara, what

happened? What happened with the baby?"

He didn't ask it as if he had an inquiring mind. He asked it in such a soft, calm way, that I could swear he was prompting me so I could do what I was really setting out to do that night—release myself from the past. Or, maybe, that's just the way I wanted to hear it.

"I called Miller."

"Not…not Macon?"

"No. I hadn't spoken with either of them since that night of the party. But I had been in a relationship with Miller. I was hoping we could at least talk. And he had as much of a chance as being the father. But, as you can imagine, the conversation…well, it…it wasn't pretty."

Oh, God, it was starting to sink in that I was telling someone all this, and it was Finn. Voicing it made it seem somehow even worse. And I thought it was horrendous in the first place. It was like I reciting a storyline from *Days of Our Lives* and not something that could have actually happened. Yet it did. To me.

"Yeah." He sighed. "So, what happened? Did you have the baby or…?" I could only imagine the questions forming in his brain.

"I did. I gave it up for adoption. It was the only choice I felt like I could make. The baby…he was born on May first. May Day. Kind of ironic, huh?" I did a half-hearted smile.

"A boy."

"Yeah."

"Neither Miller or Macon wanted any parts of any of it. They didn't even want to know whose it was."

"But did you? Did you find out?"

"Yeah. After the baby was born. I just…I don't know…I kinda felt like I needed to know with everything that went down tha—" I stopped as a piercing flashback of that night struck me like a sword in the side.

"That's okay." Finn cringed watching me do the same. Then, ever so carefully, he said, "I know it's not any of my business, but who was the…?" He trailed off his question.

And I gave him a light-hearted out. "The results are in. You are not the father." I jokingly mimicked. "Maury would have paid big time to have me on his show."

"Lara, how can you joke about—"

"Macon," I blurted out emotionless.

"Hmmm. I'm sorry."

"Yeah." I reflected for a millisecond. "But in a way, it made it easier. I had had feelings for Miller. Macon and I were a mistake." I patted his hand. "Well, there you go. Explains a lot, doesn't it?" I resorted once again to my cynical side. "It's probably why you thought I was stuck up. I really wasn't. I was just a stupid girl who gave a baby up and didn't want anyone to know. I wanted to start fresh with platinum hair and a new college." I acknowledged the West Virginia school where I would eventually meet Finn. "I just had a hard time forgetting and letting go."

"God, Lara, I can't believe all that you…geez. I mean, how did you keep that all inside? No. No one would have ever guessed. No one would have ever known. And you're not stupid. You're pretty damn amazing."

"I *was* stupid. But, in the end, I did the right thing. I know I did. I think about that baby a lot, even though I never saw or knew anything about him since that day."

"What about the brothers?"

"Them either. Both moved out of town. I know it's all for the best." I paused. "In a way, I think getting pregnant might have actually saved me."

His eyebrows furrowed. "What do you mean?"

"I was so out of control that last year of high school—reckless…not caring. Being pregnant made me think of someone else. It made me realize how bad things had become—like how much I was drinking and the wrong choices I was making. It made me more aware of things too, maybe a little too much. I know I don't trust people like I should. I have to really get to know you to let you in."

Finn put his hand back on top of mine. "I'm glad you trusted me. I know that couldn't have been easy."

But that was exactly the thing. I did trust him. It was kind of weird after not speaking for so many years in any capacity. But, yet, it was so natural. He had truly been one of my core few friends in college. Someone who was so easy to just sit down and talk to and hang out with. I wouldn't have dared told my tale back then, though. It wasn't something the collegiate crowd would have accepted, plus I wasn't the more secure person I was today. Well, with everything except with feelings of the heart. I knew that. I knew that was my greatest trust issue. And I was pretty sure it could never be mended.

We sat there silently for a few minutes both staring at the endless sky. And then the vibrating of Finn's phone broke the serenity. It wasn't the first time during our conversation. And it had been preceded by many throughout the party too.

"Your pocket is buzzing again." I was glad to add a little levity after such a long, emotional conversation.

"It's just a text. People can't leave me alone," he complained and looked at the caller ID. Pressing a button, he ignored whoever was sending a message.

"I know you're busy. You have a flight out tomorrow. You should go spend time with your family." I hopped off the ledge.

"Lara—" he started as he jumped off too.

"Listen, Finn. Please." I looked at him now standing directly in front of me. "Do me a favor. Don't tell anyone what I told you tonight, okay? Please. Besides my mom, you're the first person I've told since back then, and I'm not even sure why." I was beginning to feel weird…awkward about it. Buyer's remorse and coming down from the high of telling the tale was starting to stab my mind. "And, seriously, don't write any of my drama into a song. The residuals wouldn't be worth my sanity." I resorted to my sarcastic side.

"Of course no—"

"The thing is, it's not really something that I think…. Just…please. I'm sorry, don't tell your sister or your family. I don't want them to think that I…." Was a slut, whore, throwaway mom…. Choose your derogatory noun.

"Lara, I'm not telling anyone, okay?" he said calmly. "But they wouldn't—*we* wouldn't—think any differently of you. But I understand." He purposefully made a point to pause with a stare and a confirming blink. "You have my word."

"Thanks for listening."

"That's what I'm here for."

I wanted to disagree. He was there for his nephew's birthday. He was there to help a sick child's parents. He wasn't there for me.

"I should go," I said, not only because I had monopolized his time, but I was feeling embarrassed by all that is Lara Faulkner.

"You sure? How far away do you live?"

"Not far at all—just the next town over."

"Are you all right to drive?"

"Yeah," I chuckled. "I only had one beer."

"I know. But emotionally, are you all right?"

Touched by his concern, I reassured him, "I'm fine." I started walking toward my car while pressing the unlock on the key fob.

As I opened the car door, Finn said, "Let me give you my phone number. Call or text me when you get in."

"Finn, I'm all right."

"I know you are. But you should have it, anyway. We don't have to go another—What? Seven years?—without chatting again, right?"

"No." I fished my phone out of my purse, started a new contact, and handed it to him. "Here, add it so I can be another person bothering you."

"You call me, Lara," he said seriously while entering his info. "And that deal we have about me not telling anyone?

Same thing applies here. I can't give my phone number out to just anyone. So, please don't—"

"Don't worry. I won't." I took my phone back.

He gave me a tight hug goodbye and tucked me into the driver's seat, shutting the door after I sat. "Be safe."

I took a last glance as I pulled away. Finn put his hand up to his ear and mouth to signal for me to call him. I laughed, although I knew he couldn't tell.

***

When I got back to my apartment, I double-checked the door to make sure it was locked, turned on my laptop, and changed into my pajamas for the night. I had been thinking of Finn the entire ride back. He still embodied so many of the genuine, fun, and compassionate qualities of that boy I had known back in college. But now they were also mixed with a maturity and confidence that made me appreciate him that much more. And even though I hoped I had gained some of that too, it was nice to feel like someone was looking out for me. Being alone and independent for so long, I wasn't used to that. It was a good feeling even if I knew it was a fleeting feeling. Finn would go back to his life, and I would go back to my demons.

I took out my phone, found his contact, and sent him a text. *I'm home. Safe and sound—Lara*

His response came within a minute. He texted a smiley face accompanied by, *Didn't want to have to hunt U down.*

I shook my head at his non-threat. *No need. U have my # now & U know where I work.*

My phone buzzed again with a new incoming text. *I've missed U.*

That made my heart skip for a second. I knew it shouldn't have, but it did. I had to stop for a moment and think before texting him back. What he had typed was so innocent. I had to realize that.

Because I didn't respond immediately back, Finn texted again. *What's up?*

Trying to be honest, I responded with, *Was thinking how nice it was for U to say that.*

His rapid response was, *I didn't just say it, y'know?*

What? What does that mean? I hate texting! Regardless, I sent one back. *No, got it. U should get back to your fam. & quit texting me.*

Call U once I'm back in TN?

Sure that would be great. I attached an out, though, so he wouldn't feel obligated and, admittedly, so I wouldn't have any expectations. *But I know U are busy. Have a safe flight.*

Talk w/ya soon, then. Night, Lara.

G'night back.

I waited for another text but, obviously, saying "Night" was the equivalent of "10-4 good buddy" on a CB radio. We were over and out. I just hoped it wasn't the case forever.

CHAPTER SIX

"Quit texting me…or calling. Get the hint, Lara. I don't want to talk to you—just like before…just like all those years ago." And the silence across the line told me he had hung up.

I had never, ever heard or seen Finn act that way. And I was flabbergasted, shocked, confused…sad. I thought we had resumed our friendship. I thought we had such a nice time catching up…that we would stay in touch. Hadn't he said so? I had trusted and revealed so much to him. And now? I was spinning.

And the worst part was, I was in public. So I couldn't let it show as I walked out the main doors of the local mall. As I placed my phone back in my purse, flashbulbs stunned my eyes with brightness. They were everywhere pointing right at me. The sounds I heard were more like chants. "Whore!" "Slut!" "Pathetic." And in the midst of me trying to get away, I heard a baby crying. Its wails were getting louder and more urgent by the second.

It wasn't a baby, though. It was me. It was me. I was crying. And I wasn't at the mall. I was in my bed. I had woken up in a start. It had been a nightmare. I rubbed my jaw where it was so tight that it was nearly locked… a sore throbbing radiated through it. I removed the nightly mouth guard that I had been wearing for years due to grinding my teeth since adolescence and took a deep breath. It had been a nightmare. But, yet, it was reality based.

***

"Have you and Finn talked since the party?" Nola asked, but I believe she already knew the answer.

It was now a couple weeks after the party and Wyatt's actual, real birthday. After helping out in her son's classroom, Finn's sister had come into my office while Wyatt delivered his baseball themed cupcakes to some of the staff. I suspected she was on a mission of her own.

"Yeah, he called that day after he got back to Tennessee," I replied. "He said he would send me a picture that he had of a bunch of us from college," I continued. "But he never did. I texted him but got no response. Haven't heard from him since."

During that conversation, Finn never mentioned what we had talked about on the cement ledge at his sister's place, which was kind of a relief. I really hadn't wanted to go there again. I was embarrassed that I had dumped it on him in the first place. Now, as distance once again stretched between us, he was probably thinking he wanted no part of a renewed friendship with me. Why would he? Why would anyone? I was a screwed-up mess. Hence, his faded correspondence, for sure.

"I guess he's busy," I offered instead of what I really thought.

"He is," she sighed. "All the time. I don't know how he manages, but he does. Will is like that too. I'm just fine with being a stay-at-home mom."

"You're doing a good job," I said legitimately after witnessing her both inside and outside the home.

"Thanks." She tucked a loose, long bang behind her

ear. "Anyway, Finn knew I was coming here today. He wanted me to ask you if you had time to get together. He's going to be in the city. I told him I would relay the message."

"Um…" Okay, maybe I was wrong. Was there another reason for his silence? "Ah, when?"

As soon as I asked, though, another theory raced into my brain. Did he just feel obligated to ask since he knew Nola was going to see me? I mean, he would figure, wouldn't he, that I would inquire about him.

"The twentieth? It's a Saturday," was Nola's reply.

I bought some time as I pretended, with an almost cartoonish back and forth rolling of my eyes, to mentally go over my social calendar. There was no need, though. I didn't have a social calendar. I had a work schedule, and I had empty moments filled with reading novels and watching movies in between. But on Saturday, October 20, I could pretend to be busy. It wasn't necessarily that I didn't want to see him. I just knew that, because of his lack of correspondence and the fact that he had his sister do his bidding, it might not be legit.

"Uh…I don't know. I don't have my stuff in front of me."

Would she believe that? God, the whole world did things on their handhelds, and I worked in technology. I hadn't seen a paper calendar in years. And there wasn't anything I couldn't access via my phone.

"Well, check and see," she replied casually.

"I will. But he doesn't need to hold up any plans for me. You know, I doubt—"

"I'm sure he—"

"If he wants," I interrupted because there was only one way of getting to the truth and knowing the legitimacy of the invite. "He can call me."

"Yeah. Of course. I'll tell him." She looked toward the door. "I better go find that son of mine. He's already super hyped because of his birthday and now sugary cupcakes…?"

I laughed as she left. Wyatt, like most kids that age, was very active on a regular day let alone on "his" day. It made me think of Finn and the energy he had when performing. God, why hadn't I just said yes? I did want to see him. But did he really want to see me? That damn fictitious nightmare still stung in my memory. Only time and a telephone call would tell.

***

I was in that state right before pure, uninhibited sleep when my phone notified me of an incoming text. I scrunched my eyes and regained focus before turning on the soft lamp next to my bed. Picking up my cell, I first read that the time was just before eleven p.m.

I then read the text. It was from Finn, but all it said was: *Hi*.

Huh? I stared at my phone's screen. I hadn't heard from him in weeks. He never followed through with his offer to send the photograph. And now? Now, I get just a "hi"?

Regardless, *Hi* I typed back.

There was a minute or two of silent no reply before he texted again. *Did Nola ask you about getting 2gether that Saturday I'm in town?*

Well, at least I now knew his offer was legit. *Yep.*

And?

I can probably make it. Still need to check. I don't know why I typed that. I guess maybe I just wanted to keep the same stance I had with his sister. I mean, the twentieth was only about two weeks away. Surely anyone would know their plans. *I'll need to talk with U later. Was sleeping. Early work alarm tomorrow.*

There were a good few minutes where I waited for him to reply back, and he didn't. I turned off the light and legitimately tried to sleep. But now I was awake, and not just a little. It was like I had eaten three of Wyatt's cupcakes. Ugh!

His text came in then: *G'night, Lara. Don't let the bed bugs bite.*

I smiled at the glow of the screen in the otherwise dark room. It was what he had said to me that night he had kissed me on the sofa so many years ago in college. Did he remember that? Or, was it just a Finnism?

***

"Lara Faulkner," I answered my work phone professionally. It was the next morning, and I was busy downloading new photos and articles to the website.

"You said you'd talk with me later. How about now?"

Halt. Freeze. Stop the hands on the keyboard. What was Finn doing calling me at work?

"Hi," was all I could manage.

I looked down, pointlessly, at the caller ID. I knew there wouldn't be a direct number. They were all routed through the main line where the caller had to dial either an extension or talk with the secretary who would send them through. I needed to see about getting a new phone system. Knowing the caller would definitely help someone—me—prepare.

"Sorry I woke you up last night. I sometimes forget about the hour difference."

"Especially when you are on rock star hours," I retorted with a quick comeback. "There must be an app or something for time difference."

"Probably." He laughed. "So, what's the scoop with the twentieth? I'd like to see you."

More refreshed in the morning and glad that our friendship seemed to be back on track, I replied with, "Yeah. I can maybe make it."

"Maybe?"

"What do you have in mind?"

His voice seemed to ease a little. "Dinner at my uncle's restaurant in the city?" When I didn't answer as fast as I guess he wanted me to, he added, "I have a few friends who might join us."

Friends? Hmmm…Please, please don't tell me he was trying to set me up. And did that include Iva?

"Lara? How does that sound? Can you break any plans?" Was it just my imagination or did he say that as if he knew I wouldn't have any?

I kept it simple. "I can."

"Good. Well, that's good. I'm glad you can make it. Really. Do you want me to pick you up?"

"No. I'm a big girl. I can manage to get to the city all on my own. Just give me an address and time. Besides, it's not like this is a date," I teased.

"Whew!" He exhaled dramatically. "Don't have to bring flowers and chocolate then?" He had such a natural, easy-going way of talking with others. He always had. It was what, I was sure, helped him succeed in the entertainment industry, as well as the friendship department.

I laughed. "No. And if I recall, I got the chocolate last time. Damn Penguins!" I referenced our coffee shop/hockey bet.

"That you did, Rox. I'll text you the time and address soon. I gotta run. I'm late, but it was worth getting the answer I wanted."

It was worth answering the phone. It was worth knowing that his invite was legit. It was worth taking a possible jab or two from him and getting that opportunity to see my friend again.

***

I arrived a few minutes early and just as the sun was threatening to set. A hostess stand in the foyer greeted me upon entrance. There was a Please Wait to be Seated sign but no hostess. So I stood a few minutes, soaking in the atmosphere of the dimly lit restaurant, done, from what I could see, in a mostly wood décor. It was rustic yet elegant. A bar stretched along the left side of the establishment, but I couldn't see beyond it without venturing farther into the place, and I obeyed what the sign said.

A thin, sharply dressed woman greeted me as she stepped behind the stand. When I explained who I was, she yelled into the restaurant, "Eoin, your guest is here," and then turned to me. "Can I take your coat?"

"Ah, no. If you don't mind, I'm going to keep it. I'm still a little cold from the walk."

"Sure. No problem. So, you know Eoin's nephew?"

"I do. We went to college together."

"Lara," Finn's uncle interrupted, grabbing the menus from his hostess. "So nice to see you again."

"Hi," I answered back glad to see a familiar face. "You too. I feel honored to be at your place."

"Ah, flattery." He semi-chuckled. "Wait until you actually try the food. Then you can bring on the accolades."

"Oh, I'm sure I will."

"Junie, can you take her coat?"

"I offered," the hostess, I now knew as Junie, explained. "but she wants to keep it."

"Cold?" Finn's uncle questioned me.

"Yeah, but I'll warm up—had to walk a few blocks."

"New York weather is so unpredictable. Let me take you to the table. Finn's actually already here," he said with a tone of what sounded like disbelief.

Eoin directed me through the restaurant. There was a scattering of patrons at the tables, booths, and bar. Finn, seated alone at the corner booth, stood to greet me with a hug. As we went to take our seats, me sitting across from Finn, Eoin asked what I wanted to drink.

"I'll have a beer." I surprised even myself. But I needed something to drink as I was nervous about seeing Finn again because of our last in-person conversation. Plus, I was going to be meeting his friends.

"Which?" Eoin asked.

"Something light on tap?" I said thinking I wanted something cheap. I had looked up the restaurant's website beforehand, but it was very simple. There were limited photographs and no prices listed next to the food and beverage items.

"Get her what I'm having," Finn spoke up. When I looked at him inquisitively he said, "It's a seasonal pumpkin beer. You'll like it."

"Okay." As Eoin exited, I took off my light black jacket and slung it over the back of my chair. I was suddenly warm and now appreciated the short-sleeved, gray, sequined T-shirt I was wearing. I figured it could go either way if the restaurant was fancy or casual.

"You look great," Finn acknowledged.

"The top was actually—" I was about to say inexpensive when Finn cut me off.

"Well, sure, the top. But I mean your whole…you." He looked me up and down. "You know what I mean."

Did I? Is it what I thought? Or was it just my overactive imagination combined with not knowing how to take a common compliment? Whichever, I tried to disguise an emerging blush by putting my hands up to my face and saying, "It's been a while. You haven't seen me for a few years. But I've worked hard. Pilates."

"But you know, it's more than that." He paused, still not letting his eyes lift from mine. "It's your presence. You're more confident or something."

"I blame that on my job. Can't let them see you sweat." I smiled. "And part of it is a mask."

"Sort of like music videos?" he said in a way that thankfully allowed the subject to change off me and my physical and non-physical attributes.

"Probably." I chuckled, playing with my black glass necklace and thinking that we all put on acts. "Where are your friends?"

"Eh, they couldn't make it."

"What?" I felt instant relief knowing that I wasn't going to have to put on one of those acts for potential suitors.

"Both of their wives had made other plans."

"Wives?" I blurted before realizing it was coming out.

"Yeah. You know, when a guy gets married, the person is usually called his wife." Finn teased.

"So, just you and me?"

"Yep. Is that all right?" He took a swig from his bottle.

"Sure," I said and then asked, "What about Iva?"

Finn took another sip of his beer. "Iva's not happening. She…no. That's…done." He stopped himself, pulled out a printed photo that must have been sitting on the side of his chair, and handed it to me. "Sorry I never sent it."

I smiled and lightly laughed at the picture of a bunch of us pre-graduation, placing our hands on top of one another's and vowing to keep in touch. "That's a great picture. What happened? Why didn't you send it? Or call?"

"I had some things to figure out…work out." He said it slowly and vaguely and then said nothing more.

What? What was he talking about? But before I could question, Eoin placed a bottle identical to Finn's in front of me.

"If you don't like it, I'll switch it out, whatever y—" He stopped mid-sentence noting that I literally jumped in my seat upon his unexpected, sudden presence at our table. "Sorry, I didn't mean to—"

"No. That's… Thanks." I immediately began to twirl the bottle in my hands—confidence façade for sure.

"Geez, Lar," Finn noted. "You nearly jumped a mile."

"Yeah," I said. "I just didn't see you coming." I looked at Finn's uncle who had approached me from behind. "Sorry."

"No. Sorry I startled you."

"Really, I'm fine." I insisted again not liking the attention on me or my psychosis.

I hated where I was sitting because the only thing I could see was the wall behind Finn. The rest of the busy restaurant was behind me. And if I had one OCD trait, that was it. I needed to see what was coming. I didn't like sudden loud noises or someone materializing out of nowhere. But I wasn't about to tell Finn that. He had already heard enough of my messed-up life.

"So." Finn's uncle, thankfully, changed the subject. "Have you kids decided on what you want?"

"We haven't even looked yet," Finn answered for us honestly.

"I can give you some more time to talk or whatever, but I'd really suggest the pumpkin ravioli. It's the chef's special and one of my favorites."

"Lara?" Finn waited for my input.

"Sounds good to me," I answered not only because it did sound delicious, but because I knew I wasn't going to be able to concentrate on a menu with Finn talking right across the table from me.

"Okay, Uncle Eoin, make it two."

"Salad?" Eoin looked at me.

"Uh, sure."

"Dressing?" was his next question.

"Surprise me with the house. I'm sure it will be delicious." Again, I didn't need any more choices than necessary.

He knowingly looked at Finn. "Ranch?"

"Yep. Won't change."

"I'll put your order in and bring you out some bread."

"Brown?" Finn asked.

"Just for you, Munch." As Eoin left, Finn shook his head at his family's nickname for him.

Dinner was, just as Eoin predicted, absolutely delectable. I ate every single ounce. That wasn't like me. I was usually a doggie bag kinda gal, but I couldn't resist.

Even better than the food, perhaps, was the ease in our conversation. Finn and I slipped so naturally back into our friendship from college that our banter back and forth was effortless and without awkward pauses. Neither of us mentioned the revelations I had made the last time we had seen one another. But I realized there was no need. That had nothing to do with the two people we were now.

CHAPTER SEVEN

A bill never came to our table for the meal. Knowing we were getting set to leave, I questioned Finn's uncle. He shrugged it off.

"Lara, my dear," he said. "Your money is no good here."

"Oh, no, Mr.—"

"Eoin. Call me Eoin. And don't say it. The meal is on me."

"Geez, Lara," Finn interrupted. "He always makes me pay. I'm gonna have to bring you with me more often." Finn stood up, hugged his uncle the way guys do, and put on his black, trimmed with white, jacket.

I put mine on also, thanked Eoin, and followed Finn to the front door. I noted a few patrons turning their heads to look at us, well, Finn, as we passed. He didn't seem to notice. I silently wondered if he had just become immune to his recognizable star status.

Outside, Finn pulled a gray knitted cap from his jacket pocket and secured it snuggly on his head. While I was wondering if it was for warmth, decoration, or fan camouflage, he said, "There's a bookstore-slash-coffee shop just a few blocks away. Might not be as good as your place. What was that called?"

"Java Mug."

"Yeah. Whatcha think?"

"Sure." I wasn't ready for the night to end so I was glad, by Finn's question, that he wasn't either.

"Let's go then." He looped his arm through mine so that when we started to walk, our hips bumped.

I instantly stopped. When Finn's naturally gray eyes minimized to get the most direct look into my blue/green hues, the awkward feeling intensified. It was the first time since reuniting with him that I felt it—truly felt it. My feelings for Finn were starting to swell beyond friendship. And it was a strange, weird, new feeling. But I was pretty sure it was a one-sided one.

I resorted to my wise-cracking self. "What? Are we off to see the wizard?"

Finn immediately started skipping down the walkway taking me right alongside him. He sang a few lines of the *Wizard of Oz* song, making me laugh and forget about whatever awkwardness there might have been. "I can do 'Ease on Down the Road' too, if you prefer the other version," he said, slowing to a normal walk.

Still laughing, I managed to get out, "Do me and the rest of the world a favor and don't put either on your next album."

"'Hillbilly Oz,' I can see it now."

We wound our way through part of Central Park—a place I almost always made a point of going to when I was in Manhattan. It was the perfect eye of the storm scenario—so peaceful in the midst of the pounding, chaotic city. And, somehow, I loved them both. I told this to Finn as we entered the bookstore and sat down with our coffees and biscotti.

"I know exactly how that is," he agreed. "I need, even thrive, on that type of contrast. I love performing and being on the road. But when it's over, I don't know if I want to ever go back on stage. That is until I'm back again.

It's the best of both worlds scenario. Here," he said almost abruptly. "Switch."

"What?"

"Switch seats."

He stood and walked over to my chair, reaching out his hand. Allowing him to take mine, I got up. Finn sat in the seat I had just vacated, and I went to his up against the wall.

When I looked at him, puzzled by the Chinese fire drill via bookstore chairs, he said, "I don't want to be seen and you…you already look more at ease." When I softly smiled to acknowledge my gratitude and his understanding without being told, he smiled back. "I was hoping it wasn't me."

I shook my head. "No. Of course not." Although, his presence, this scenario, heightened my nerves. I wasn't sure exactly why because, at the same time, I felt more at ease when I was with him. It was definitely another case of those "friendship versus more" contrasts that were exploding all over my body.

We continued to talk about life on the road, life in suburbia New York, life in general, until Finn noticed me looking at my phone's clock. When I told him I was just mentally thinking of the train schedule back, he told me not to worry. He would make sure I got home. I started to protest that public transportation was just fine when he made a phone call securing a car to meet us at the bookstore. The car would take me back to the train station at home where my car was. Finn was within walking distance of his penthouse in the city. I decided to let it drop because the nice gesture actually did make my life easier. But even more so, I decided to let it drop because I didn't want to waste any more of those minutes arguing about something so silly. I wanted to spend that time just as we had been…harmoniously.

***

But like all good things, those twenty minutes seemed to go quicker than regular time. And it made me sad. Every time I had seen Finn since reuniting with him, I was being drawn more and more in. I didn't want to part. Yet, I knew it was best. Distance would help pacify the emotions I was feeling just as it had all those years before.

While Finn was taking care of disposing our cups and napkins, I told him I would wait for him outside. Because it was a side street and a weekend evening, I was able to soak in the crisp, October air in rare Manhattan silence. It allowed me a moment to think back to the first time I had realized my feelings toward Finn weren't strictly that of friendship. It was after that kiss on the sofa right before his graduation. But, no, not immediately after. It was when it was too late. It was when I had purposefully tried to look nice and went to see him play at his gig in Pittsburgh and then found out he and Audrey were engaged. And it dug in even deeper at Sam and Olivia's wedding festivities when he was being so kind, so "Finn" with me, but still was with her. I think he knew something was up with me back then, but he didn't know exactly what. He had even questioned me about why I was acting weird—being short with him, not dancing, cutting my hair. But I had given an excuse and vowed to stay friends instead. I wished I hadn't copped out. I wished I had said something back then. I wished, like a lot of things in my life, that I had made different choices sooner.

I looked up stunned to see that Finn was standing next to me. Either he had a very silent approach, or I had truly been transfixed in the past. I didn't have time to think about it though, as I was instead taken in by the look on his face. God, the way he was watching me…with those stunning gray eyes. I could swear he was reading my mind. I could swear he was mirroring my thoughts.

But for Finn, it wasn't just a thought. He turned it into an action. He leaned in, kissed me on my cheek, paused momentarily to look around, and then kissed me softly, gently, beautifully on my lips. It was the kiss that I wished I had returned all those years ago. And because I was, once again, stunned by its existence, I almost didn't react the way I wanted to or should have. Almost. I made sure, as he was about to break our lock, that I put my hands up to his cheeks and held our lips in place for an extra second or so.

With a renewed twinkle in his eyes, Finn said, "Would you be all right with chocolates and flowers next time?"

Still stunned that I was actually living out the scenario, I stared at him a second before responding. And then, almost robotic, I replied with, "I could do chocolates. Flowers—depends. Some of the really strongly scented ones I'm allergic to."

Surprised but relaxed, Finn questioned, "Are you really? I mean, I knew about the cat thing."

I smiled recalling how allergic I was to Olivia's damn cats in college. "Yep—candles too, anything perfumy," I answered honestly. "You want to torture me? Put me in one of those bath and body wash places."

"Good to know," he said with a little bit of devil in his voice.

Ignoring the tone, I continued, "Next time?"

Finn shifted his feet. "A couple weeks from now there's a little thing in Nashville."

"Nashville?"

"Yeah."

Okay, I had heard him correctly. "Finn, I can't go to Nashville."

"Yes, you can. You'll probably need to take a couple days off work, though. I'll get you an airline ticket. I'm performing, but then I'm in the audience the whole time, unless I win something, but I doubt it."

If the whole scene wasn't surreal to start off with, I felt like I had to take two steps back just to comprehend what he was most likely referring to. "Are you talking about the

CMAs? Are you inviting me to the CMA awards?" The commercials advertising the show were being broadcast non-stop over the past couple of weeks.

Finn answered in a matter-of-fact tone. "Yeah."

"What!?"

"Lara, c'mon. There's no one else I would rather go with."

Still taking it all in, it took me a moment to speak. "I—"

"I graciously accept, Finn. That's what I heard," he finished my sentence the way he wanted it to end.

"Finn…." How was I going to go to Nashville? I'd have to take off work, figure out the money situation, make travel arrangements…. It was a little overwhelming, especially since the invitation came completely out-of-the-blue.

"Finn, I'd love to go. Thank you," Finn finished another sentence for me.

"Fi—"

"I can keep this up all night."

I couldn't help it. I laughed, shaking my head. And then I gave him an honest answer. "You know, I would love to go."

"Then you are."

"Let me check with work, but uh, that would really be pretty cool."

I started feeling the excitement of the last few minutes catch up with me. Giddy school girl Lara I was not used to even back when I was supposed to be a giddy school girl. Lost childhood be damned. I was living it now.

"It sure would." Finn smiled back. "I'll get someone to send you your plane info."

"I can do that," I stated.

"Do you have to argue about everything?" Finn half-teased. "The check, the car…. My date—my ticket," he insisted. He had said, "my date." And he had kissed me. Before I could get my mouth to verbalize again, he continued, "I'm so looking forward to showing you the city, and you getting to see me perform on a bigger stage than a school auditorium or a college bar."

"I have."

"What?" His response was immediate.

"Yeah, not this summer but last. When you were here. I won tickets off the radio. They were up in peanut—"

"What?" he repeated in an even more shocked tone.

"Get this," I continued. "The question I had to answer was what college you went to. If I didn't get those tickets—"

"Lara, you were at the show and you didn't come see me?" He seemed offended.

I shrugged my shoulders. "How would I have done that?"

"You could have said who you were. I would have gotten you backstage."

"Finn, no one would have given me the time of day. I'm sure there's billions of people who try that."

"Aw, man," he said, and I could tell he probably realized what I said was true. "Well, from now on…." Slight frustration crept into his voice. "Geez, I can't believe you were there and I didn't know. This…. I could've…."

The two of us had been so engrossed in our conversation that neither one of us realized the car had pulled up. But when the driver shut his door upon exit, it broke our conversation. He stepped around the car and made his way to Finn.

"Mr. Murphy," he spoke plainly.

"The lady will confirm the location." Finn handed him something from his pocket and then said, "Give us a minute."

"Yes, sir." He got back in the driver's seat.

"See ya, Lara." Finn looked around and then kissed me quickly between the mouth and cheek.

"I'll talk with you soon."

"Let me know you got home," he said as he opened the back door for me.

"It'll be a little while," I cautioned while crawling in.

"I know. Just let me know," he reiterated. "I'm gonna get working on making sure you have your tickets—plane and backstage." He smiled, still shaking his head upon my innocent revelation, and then shut the door.

I made polite conversation with the driver for a little while before being able to slide back and enjoy the comforts of a luxury car versus the trials and tribulations of public transportation. I literally closed my eyes—an indulgence I didn't dare give myself on a nighttime train in New York City—and replayed the night's events in my mind from walking into the restaurant, to skipping down the sidewalk, to the bookstore, to that kiss. I already missed Finn. And now I didn't think the feeling was one sided. A smile escaped my mouth. I silently thanked his sister for being the messenger who got me to eventually accept Finn's invite, and I silently thanked his buddies who failed to be good friends. If they had showed, my evening would have taken a completely different path. Sure, it would have been fun, but probably the later part would have never come to fruition. Finn and I would have never had the private time to get to the point that we did.

I tried to resist, but I couldn't. I texted Finn even though I wasn't even half way home yet: *Glad your buddies didn't show.*

Instantly, he texted back: *Yeah. Glad you could change any plans.*

I shook my head at his call-out of my fib. *Sooo good to see U. Your uncle's restaurant rocks! Food was delish. Tell him thanks.*

U looked beautiful. And before I could text back, he sent a second one. *And I don't mean the top.*

My body warmed. *Too sweet.*

Mean it. He replied. *CMAs are going to be so much fun. Call me when U R home.*

I texted him a smiley face in response. That, to me, said

it all. It was definitely a smiling kind of night.

I texted Finn again once I got back to my quiet apartment. We went back and forth a few times while I was changing out of my clothes. His final text told me to call him. He thought that texting was fine when you needed a quick question answered, but sometimes you should hear a person's voice. And then after an hour-long conversation, we said good night with our real voices.

***

When I woke the next morning, I felt a little like Cinderella. First, I was the Cinderella at the ball—dreamlike dancing with the prince. But then, as I woke up a little more and let myself become ragged-on-the-edges Lara again, I started to second guess everything that had happened.

It wasn't so much that I doubted Finn's intentions or feelings. It was more that I doubted myself. It was maybe one thing for us to sit in a coffee shop and reminisce, or on a concrete wall and speak honestly as friends. But it was another to be beside him in front of all his colleagues and important business contacts. And it was a whole other thing to be staying at his house.

What it came down to was, I was scared. And I knew it. I was scared of how much that kiss meant. I was scared of how much Finn was beginning to mean. I had never wanted to feel that way and had successfully walled myself off from those emotions years before. But I did now. I did. And it terrified me. I was so afraid I wouldn't be able to handle them or know how to act. I didn't want to ruin the beautiful feeling, but I didn't want to get hurt ever again.

With my heart and mind swirling with emotion, I decided it would be best to call Finn and vocalize my concerns about coming to Nashville. I knew he would be on a plane that afternoon and didn't want to prolong my agony until after he touched down. So I picked up the phone, all the while wondering if the glass shoe would have to wait for the next princess.

He answered on the first ring, "Hey, I was just thinking about you."

"Yeah?" I questioned. "Obviously, me too."

"Good."

"Finn," I dove right in, not needing my stomach to fester any longer. "I'm not sure about Nashville."

"What? No. No. We went over this. Don't worry about the money, Lar."

"It's…it's not that."

"What then? Don't tell me you have other plans," his voice was sugary with skepticism.

No, I wouldn't or couldn't do that again. But how could I explain? "I don't know anything about award ceremonies, and I don't want to be a burden." That really wasn't it, but there was some truth to it.

"Is that what you're going with?"

"What?" I asked a little stunned by his boldness. But I shouldn't have been.

"You told me, and I have seen it, how much you have changed and…." He stopped and restarted, "Lara, don't back out. I want you there with me."

His words encouraged me, but I was still unsteady. I breathed in and out. "Really?"

"Yes. Didn't you get that last night? I had such a nice time. Didn't you?"

"Yes." I didn't hesitate at all to answer that time. "Yes." Maybe one of my best nights ever. Why was that a problem? It should be the solution.

"Listen, you've gotten too used to hiding. I get it. But don't. You don't have to do that."

He knew me. He knew me so well. I think he always had. But having that new bond between us of knowing everything there was to know heightened his expertise on both me and my idiosyncrasies.

"*You've* gotten very used to getting your way," I said a

little more relaxed but still nervous about what a big leap I would be taking.

"Doesn't seem like it right now."

"I'm sorry."

"You're sorry because you nearly crushed me with your opening line or you're sorry that it was even a thought and you *are* coming?"

"The second?"

"Lara…." His exhale was strong even over the phone. "No backing out allowed. I'll call you every day if I have to just to make sure."

"No. No." I laughed. "I'm coming. I'll be there."

"I think I'll call anyway—just because I want to."

"Well, that…that would be…nice."

During those next couple of weeks, he kept his promise. If he didn't call, he shot me a text. And, admittedly, it did help. It helped in the sense that I didn't think he would stop our correspondence like he had the last time or all those years before. It helped by hearing the enthusiasm in his voice when we talked about me coming to Tennessee. It didn't help, though, because it made me miss him.

CHAPTER EIGHT

A tall, broad man with a whiskery face held up a sign with my name printed on it. This driver, who Finn had sent because he would be in rehearsals, was my welcome to Tennessee. And I couldn't have been more excited, nervous, or intrigued by the wonderment of it all.

Everything went as planned. Finn's home, on the outskirts of Nashville, was isolated without a neighbor in sight. There was a gate and a winding driveway that led to the house, which the burly driver, I now knew as friendly but cautious Hawk, had a code for. He took me to the front door, unlocked it, placed my bags in the hardwood foyer, and told me that Finn would be there momentarily, to just make myself at home. And with that, he left.

It felt weird being in Finn's house without him. But I couldn't just stand in the foyer until he arrived. I followed the hardwood a little to the right and into the two-story great room complete with floor-to-ceiling gas fireplace made out of stone. Next to it was a luxurious dining room with wall of windows adjoined by a beautiful stainless steel, contemporary kitchen done in a sky-blue palette. On the oatmeal-colored granite center island, I found a ceramic bowl full of fresh apples and pears, a bottle opener, two wine glasses, and a box of coffee flavored chocolates. Next to them was a note from Finn that read:

Hope wine is a good substitute for flowers. Didn't want to risk anything. Pick a bottle of red or white from the wine cabinet below. Please start without me. See you soon.

I smiled, left everything as it was, and walked back toward the foyer. I remembered seeing a powder room to the left of the entry door. As I passed the front door, I noticed that the car and driver were still out front. Not my business. I went into the powder room, ran my hands through my hair and reapplied a little eye shadow, gloss, and blush that I always had on standby in my purse.

I sat on the sofa in the great room to wait for Finn, but that didn't last too long. The house was too quiet. It was making me nervous, and I was already jittery from the plane ride. For some unknown reason, I liked flying almost as much as I liked getting blood taken or sticking a fork in my eyeball. I thought about calling work and making sure everything was running smoothly, but I decided I didn't want to know. There wasn't much I could do about it.

So I took Finn up on his offer and opened a bottle of white wine and the chocolates. I found the TV remote in a metal bowl on the expansive coffee table and flipped through a few stations before landing on HGTV. I left the volume on low as I remembered what Finn had said about the station and Iva. Did he really watch *House Hunters*? I had three chocolates eaten and a full glass of wine nearly done when I heard the garage door open.

"Thanks, Hawk." It was Finn's voice, but I didn't see him. And then there must have been a reply I didn't hear because Finn said, "Yep. Totally. See you tonight." It was a couple minutes after the garage door closed that Finn entered the great room via the kitchen. The open bottle of wine was in his hand. "White. I figured. Such a girl," was his greeting to me as he poured himself a glass.

"I drink red too," I protested. "Just prefer white." I stood and met him with a hug.

"You're really here." His natural eyes seemed to sparkle.

"I am."

"No second guesses?"

"Just about being airborne."

And that was the truth. I was still a little uncertain about what everything meant between the two of us. But I put it aside because it didn't matter. Just seeing him made me glad I had made the decision to journey to Music City.

"You weren't kidding when you said you don't like to fly. That's another thing I never knew about you."

"Well, we didn't have any occasion or money to fly anywhere in college." I gulped the last swig of wine just thinking about being in mid-air. "Let's change the subject."

"Here, you need more." He took my glass and refilled it before flopping down on the sofa done in a blue southwest motif. Finn was dressed most casually in worn jeans and a white, practically see-through, V-neck T-shirt. They accentuated everything that needed to be in just the right way.

I sat down next to him. "Who's Hawk?" I questioned. "He kinda acted like your bodyguard."

"Ha!" Finn replied. "Yeah, he's a little protective. He's part bulldog, part driver, part friend, part jack-of-all trades. I think you're already on his good side, though."

"Really?"

"It usually takes a while, but with you, it doesn't surprise me."

Having the not-being-able-to-receive-compliments problem, I sarcastically said, "So, I passed the inquisition?"

"The inquisition? What did he ask you? Do I need to talk with him?"

"No," I practically screamed. "I was kidding. We just basically talked about how you and I know one another. Although, I think he already knew most of my answers."

Finn took a semi-gulp from his glass. "Hmmm. Well, I'm glad rehearsal is over."

"How did it go?"

"You can tell me tonight," he spoke of the actual CMA awards. "At least you'll have better seats than that summer concert," he joshed, not letting the fact go that I had seen him in concert before.

"I'm sure."

"We're opening tonight."

"Wow. That's kinda a big deal, huh?"

"I don't know. I like that it's going to be out of the way." He put one arm around my shoulders and reached for a piece of chocolate with his other. "You mind if we just chill out here for a little while before heading out this evening? I can order something to eat if you're hungry."

"No. I'm good. Unless you want something. It's your day. Whatever you want. I don't want to get in your way."

"You're not." He gently touched my nose with his fingertip. "I'm glad you're here. Chocolate and wine—everything's perfect."

He then took both of our glasses, placed them back on the coffee table, and began kissing me. The intoxicating mix of his kisses and the wine had my world spinning most gloriously. I was relaxing in a whole new way, lost in the repetitive soft sensation of his lips meeting mine.

That was until I faintly heard the television announcing that a *House Hunters* marathon was coming up next. Not that it was that funny, but with the encouragement of the wine and nearly nil to eat, I began to giggle. And, of course, it broke the spell.

"What?" Finn laughed in a light, inquisitive kind of way. "What's so funny?" His lips left mine.

"Nothing. Vavoom," I said and tried to kiss him again.

"Vavoom?" This time, his laugh was much more robust. "You're drunk, huh?"

"No. Maybe buzzed or tipsy," I admitted.

"Maybe we should get something to eat."

"No, I don't want you to miss your TV show."

"My TV show?" He looked at the screen and started

laughing even louder. He pulled me to him wrapping me into his chest. Kissing the top of my head, he said, "Yeah, let's watch this. I want to see what's going on."

***

"Lara…. Lara…. Hey, Lara." It was Finn's voice, and I assumed him gently shaking me. "Wake up."

I was still on his chest, but he had me cradled in a much more comfortable position. "Finn, hmmm…. I'm sorry. I didn't realize I fell asleep."

"You did. I didn't want to wake you. But I don't know how long you need to get ready."

"What?" I sat up a little straighter trying to nonchalantly flatten my hair, only then realizing that I hadn't just dozed off for a few minutes. "How long was I asleep?"

"About an hour. I learned a lot on *House Hunters*. I think it might actually turn out to be my favorite show." With that, he confirmed my suspicions that he had only been teasing before in reference to the television program.

"What? I slept that long?" I looked at him for the first time. "Geez, I didn't drool or snore or anything, did I?" Mortified.

"You looked beautiful."

"Get real!" I exclaimed in horror and disbelief. "I'm sorry. I didn't sleep well last night because of the flight. And a couple glasses of wine is all it takes to make me both silly and tired at the same time."

"I'm glad you could relax and make me laugh. I never realized *House Hunters* was a sit-com."

"It is now." I giggled.

"Listen, I'll give you my room. There's more space up there for you to get ready."

"Uh, all right," I agreed. "Whatever works best."

Finn grabbed my mini-suitcase, and I picked up my dress bag from the foyer. I followed him up the stairs. We passed a bedroom and entered another area. It was as big as my bedroom, but it turned out to just be a sitting room. Sliding doors opened to what was Finn's bedroom topped by a two-story ceiling. Finn opened another door to expose the master bath. There were dual sinks, a walk-in closet, bathtub, and separate enormous shower.

"Use the shower—whatever," he said, taking his ensemble hanging in the walk-in closet and slinging it over his shoulder. "I'll be downstairs. I'll see you in a little bit."

***

My hair was the last thing I did before I was finished. I decided to do something easy, casual, and country. I pulled the strawberry blonde locks back on both sides and cascaded a braid down the length. When I was finished, I noticed French doors in the master bedroom that led outside. I stepped onto the two-story covered porch and looked out and down. The back yard seemed vast but there was also an entertainment sized deck and separate hot tub area. Finn was standing in the middle of the deck. Debonairly dressed in stylish black pants, a black tie, and a green shirt that made his fake eyes shine, he was talking on the phone, but I couldn't hear what he was saying. He didn't notice me on the princess-like balcony. So, I took a few seconds longer to soak the moment in. Two months before, it would have been so far from reality, you might as well have said I was a pre-teen boy with black hair and tattoos. It would have been easier to believe. I watched as Finn made his way back inside before I also re-entered the house and started down the stairs.

Standing before him in my teal strapless dress, accentuated with fake diamonds along the bust line, I started to panic when he didn't say anything. "Finn, what? Is this good? Too dressy? Not enough? I didn't know. I tried to look online at past shows before I bought this."

I didn't want to embarrass him. With every step I had

taken going down that staircase, my nerves had gone up one. I was going to a major, televised awards ceremony on the arm of one of country music's biggest stars. And it was Finn. It was so surreal.

"Say something," I urged.

Finally, "I'm speechless." But the warm smile across his chiseled, freshly shaved face told me that his word-fail was in the most positive sense.

I relaxed enough to tease. "Well, that's not good. You're gonna need a speech for when you win tonight."

"You…turn…." After I obliged doing a 360, Finn put his hand on the small of my back and put his cheek up to mine. He whispered in my ear, "You look lovely…. Breathtaking."

Much better, I decided. If anyone was to be speechless, I was sure it was going to be me. I let him take my hand in his, lead me to the door, and into the magic of CMA night.

***

Overwhelmed couldn't even begin to describe my first few moments as we stepped out of the decked-out town car and into the chaos that encapsulated the CMA experience. There were people everywhere. Every…where. I thought I had known somewhat what it would be like by watching feed of other award ceremonies on *Entertainment Tonight* and other similar programs. The glamor…the glitz…the fans…the press. But it was so different when you were the one right in the center of it. Granted, it wasn't really me. It was Finn. But by the tight grip he had on my hand, it felt a little like me too.

"How you doing?" He turned to me, perhaps feeling the instant perspiration of my hand in his.

"I'm, uh, wow."

He got in a smile before a reporter approached us, starting a camera rolling dialogue without even asking permission. "Finn Murphy, three-award nominee tonight, multiple past winner." The blonde with an abundance of makeup spoke to the camera, "Good to see you."

"Good to be seen," he replied, and I clutched on tighter.

I hated even having my picture taken. Now there was a moving camera documenting every eye movement and head nod. And was it live? God, could we edit?

"Which award are you most excited for tonight?" she prompted.

"Not so much the awards. I'm more excited about getting on stage and performing. That's what the night is really about—the music." The way he said it, I truly believed.

"You're first up we understand?" She tilted the microphone back toward him.

"That's right. So, we need to get moving." And as he took a step, I went with him.

"First though…First," She stepped with us. "Who is your date tonight?"

"Just a friend." And he managed to completely walk us away. He squeezed my hand then and said, "Fun, huh?"

I eyeballed him. "You are being sarcastic, right?" When he managed a laugh, we saw another reporter approaching, and I spoke up, "Finn, you do your thing. I'll just stand over to the side, all right?"

"Well, here we have Finn Murphy, one of country music's hottest stars." This guy also just started into his spiel without an introduction.

I squeezed Finn's hand hard and released. Strolling off to the side, I could hear the reporter comment about "Finn's date," and Finn redirecting the conversation back to his music.

He could see me, and I could see him. It was fine. It was better. And, yes, it was wild.

After that second reporter, Finn walked us with a little more determination toward the building. There was a photo booth thing going on. A number of celebs were waiting to have their picture taken in front of the official backdrop of the CMAs. They stood with their singing partners or with their significant others.

Finn turned to me. "Want to skip?"

"Like nothing else." I let out a sigh of relief.

"All good," he agreed. "But we're definitely doing a selfie inside."

If I thought there was a lot of commotion outside, inside was an absolute madhouse. The hallways had people moving in every direction—personnel with name lanyards, other country music artists, some plain clothes people, security guards. We walked a foot or two and would be stopped. Finn this time did not let go of my hand, for which I was glad.

There weren't the hordes of photographers or videographers back there, but there were tons of people and stars alike taking personal photos on their camera phones. I thought it was an experience for me. But then I realized how truly jazzed up all these big entertainers were too. This was their special night. Finn, himself, seemed so genuinely happy and smiled so much it made me smile. And it was in that moment that he ambushed me with the selfie I had promised. And, admittedly, it was cute.

During the times when we didn't stop to talk with the seemingly trillions of people backstage, I would hear the rumblings. It was kind of funny that people were so vocal about it. Maybe they didn't realize how loud they were talking because of the sheer volume in the venue. Or maybe they just didn't care. The buzz around us was, "Who's with Finn?" "Who is Finn's date?" "Is that his sister?" "Is she an agent?" "An unknown model or actress?" That one cracked me up. And when we *would* stop and chat, Finn would simply introduce me as a longtime friend.

But when we got to the place backstage where his band had gathered, I instantly felt more comfortable. Maybe it was because I was already getting used to this crazy world.

But I think it had more to do with just how, when Finn introduced me that time as Lara, they all genuinely took me in. The drummer, the guitarists, that Hawk guy—everyone was beyond courteous and welcoming. They were southern charm personified. They talked with me and asked a few questions. It was almost like I was speaking with Finn's family again. But, then again, in a way, I was.

And then the evening seemed to just steamroll. I was left in the audience in phenomenal third row seats to wait for the show to begin. That part was maybe the hardest. Hundreds surrounded me, but I knew no one. Before scurrying off, Finn had introduced me to Danny Roth, another singer, and his fiancée, who were sitting next to me. They both seemed lovely, and I tried to make conversation, but ended up resorting to the old standby of checking my phone.

I had missed a text from Vanessa. *I just saw you on the flippin red carpet! OMG!*

I texted back: *OMG for sure. Yikes! Supposed to have turned this thing off. Hope my hair looked all right.*

Girl, you looked gorgeous. Have fun. Want the dish soon!

I placed my phone back in my small purse as the lights flickered and the audience started doing their excited screaming. And then, there he was, now changed into ripped jeans and a gray T-shirt, singing, and just wowing the audience. I was numb. I couldn't even digest all that was going on.

It took a while for Finn to get back to our seats after that, but then we were together the rest of the evening. I noticed how he had a protective hand on me during most parts of the night. But I also noticed too, how not once, not one time, even at the after-party, did he kiss me.

CHAPTER NINE

When we got back to Finn's place, which he commonly called "the ranch," it was pretty late. But we were both wide awake due to the excitement of the evening. Despite being nominated in a few categories, Finn hadn't won anything. But he explained that was to be expected. He had already won all the New Artist and Breakthrough Artist categories in previous years. Now he would be nominated in the elite categories and, hopefully, might win one or two in the near future. I asked to see his awards because they were obviously not on display in the great room or in his bedroom. Off the garage entrance, next to the laundry room, there was a family room that Finn used more as an exercise room. Besides a sofa, there was a large screen television, a rowing machine, treadmill, elliptical, exercise ball, weights, etc. And there was a cove area—almost a separate room—where his awards were displayed. I thought it was an odd place, but he was modest enough not to have to flash everything out in the open. He said they gave him incentive to keep in shape for performing and videos.

We then made our way back into the great room. Perhaps it was the after-party's champagne still flitting around my body—I did have a couple. Or perhaps it was the pure longing. I suspect it was a good combination of both. And then there was the fact that everything was so dreamlike. I reacted like another person because that was how I felt—transported into another world.

The thought that had been weaving in and out of my mind for a good part of the evening was suddenly emerging from my mouth. "I know this is kind of a big thing, but—"

Oh, God! What was I doing? Geez, I needed to get it under control. I needed to stop and think.

When I started to chicken out, Finn prompted me in a teasing way. "What? Do you want to watch more *House Hunters*?"

"No." I laughed, breaking the immediate tension that had landed in my head. "I don't know what I was thinking. Never mind."

"What?" he asked more seriously and not letting the subject go.

Instead of actually verbalizing my palpitating thoughts, I acted on them. I tipped up slightly on my heels and met his lips with mine. Silky and smooth, we played with each other's mouths for a few seconds. When his soft peck signified an end, I refuted by pulling in tighter and easing my tongue onto his. My body internally raced as he groaned and reciprocated the power of the kiss. We both knew where this was going. Or at least I hoped he did.

"Lara...," he partially breathed, partially said and released our lips to look at me. "I...uh...."

"Please," I said before he could say anything else...before he could voice a rejection. "Finn, I want to trust again. I want to feel again. I haven't since...since back then." My eyes dipped then. It was kind of humiliating this scarred up past of mine. But if I could let go with anyone, it was the man standing in front of me. It was because of our friendship. And after a night of "just a friend" comments, I realized it was obvious that was what we were, if nothing else. "I know—"

He kissed me, quieting the words that I was about to say on the matter. It was sudden and it was quick. But I realized by the way he took my hand then and silently led me up the stairs that I had his answer.

Upon entering his bedroom, Finn turned on the dimmer of the candle-shaped wall accent lights. He started kissing me again in the most sensual, tantalizing way. Our mouths were making love before our bodies could catch up. At the same time, I felt his hand guide down the zipper along the back of my dress.

"Okay?" he asked, breaking for a second.

I didn't want him to stop. I was afraid that any pause might make him or me rethink the situation at hand. "Don't ask," I answered. "And don't stop."

On my directive, Finn let my dress fall to the floor leaving me in just my black and white strapless bra and coordinating panties. I felt self-conscious as he stopped and openly gazed at me in an admiring way. When he started quickly taking off his shirt and tie, I removed my necklace. In a nearly simultaneous motion, he tossed the bed's throw blanket and luxurious velvet pillows onto the ottoman and pulled down the sheets. He began kissing me again and gently eased us both onto the bed. While he was working his belt, I kissed his beyond six-pack abs—he must use that exercise equipment a lot—and started to feel a little more relaxed. Finn took my hands in his and guided them down to the manliness growing inside his boxers. God, it turned me on.

With both of our breathing getting heavier, I knew I had to ask the question. "Do you have something?"

Obviously knowing that I referring to protection and what that meant to me, Finn caressed his hand gently along my cheek. "Yeah, I got it. We're good." While kissing me a little sweeter this time, he reached into the glass and iron nightstand for the condom.

Things started to pick up even more as Finn's hands

traveling up my thighs caused an inner-body sensation that I had nearly forgotten about. I was a helpless captive audience as he worked my panties down and then removed my bra. I know I was audibly moaning when he started caressing my breasts. I couldn't help it. But when he started butterflying kisses all over my body while moving my legs in position, I thought I might actually….

"Finn, c'mon, I need—"

He was inside me then just as I wanted him to be. But almost immediately and unexpectedly, I tensed. I was hoping he didn't notice, but his voice told me otherwise. "Hey, you know it's me. You're safe." His voice was leading just as his body was—slow, steady, and reassuring.

"Finn." I'm pretty sure my legs were shaking.

"Yeah. Lara."

I was in his arms—this man that I had known since we were just becoming our own individuals separate from families and K-12. This man who I so easily shared laughs and tales with. This man who I trusted with my secrets. I trusted him more than anyone in the world. He gave me the confidence to have that trust back after so many years.

"Finn," I said with much more assurance this time as I relaxed and matched my pace with his pulling him closer if possible.

"Oh," he screamed out as I felt his need grow faster. "Oh, God."

Our bodies reacted to one another succinctly, as if they were made for each other. Our lovemaking wasn't just different from the last time I had sex. It was as if I had never had it before.

Afterward, Finn brought both of our arms up above my head and finished by kissing my neck and lips. I folded into his chest melting. I was emotionally and physically spent. Finn and I had made love. It almost seemed like a dream. I could feel him as if he were still in me. His strength…his touch…his compassion. He made me feel whole again.

I wanted him to know how much it meant to me. So, I mumbled a "Thank you" without lifting my head.

"Thank you?" Finn's voice was inquisitive but light.

"Yeah," I said. "Thank you for taking pity on me. I know I probably shouldn't have—"

"What?" Now much more alert and a touch upset, he brought his chest up so that I had to lift my head from it.

"C'mon," I spoke honestly as we both adjusted our bodies so that we were slightly separated and looking at one another. "I know why you…why…it was just because—"

"You think I made love to you because I feel sorry for you? You think this was a pity fuck?" Finn was sitting straight up now. The anger in his voice made me back away, pull the sheet up, and get into a less prone position too. "Jesus! Maybe I did it just to get laid then, right? I just wanted to get some."

"Finn!" I was shocked and certainly didn't mean what he implied or for him to get that angry.

"God!" He swung his legs out of the bed, put his boxers back on, and grabbed some clothes from an upper drawer in the cabinet.

Before I knew it, he was out of the room and tearing down the stairs. I remained frozen; frozen like I had been before Finn re-entered my life. What had I said? Why did he get so upset? God, it was all such a mistake. Why did I have to push him to make love to me in the first place? I was happier than I had been in years, perhaps my whole life, and I blew it. I began to cry. No. It was more like an uncontrollable wail. That's when I heard a door slam. And with it so did my heart.

I laid there for a while, feeling sorry for myself and feeling sorry for what I did to Finn. This was not the night at all that he was expecting. This was one of the biggest music nights of the year, and I ruined it for him. Now, here I was in his house, in his bed, with an airline ticket a whole day and night away. I didn't know what to do.

I knew there wasn't much to be done in the wee hours of the morning, but the least I could do was get out of his bed. I rummaged through my suitcase that was still where I had left it earlier—back when excitement and possibility had existed. I put on my gray yoga pants, our college hoodie—I packed it thinking Finn would like it—and a pair of black socks. I sluggishly made my way down to the great room. Maybe I could watch a little TV and fall asleep on the sofa, leaving Finn his bed for whenever he returned. That was the game plan.

Surprisingly, though, I found him sitting in the great room's modern, lime-colored chair. He looked almost trance-like as he stared at me entering the room. It was like he had been looking that same exact way since he left the bedroom.

Unsure whether to walk forward toward him or back away, I planted myself still. "I thought you left."

"No." His voice was void of any emotion. Was that better or worse than the anger that had been on display before he stormed out earlier? "I went outside for a bit and then came back."

"Why?"

"Because I'm not someone who leaves." There was a sense of spite in his voice that time. "And, contrary to popular belief, I'm not a bastard."

"Finn, I didn't say that." I still hadn't moved and neither had he. I felt like I was on a tightrope, and I hadn't felt that way since I was a child teetering on which direction my father would decide to swing. "I'm sorry if it came out the wrong way. I am. I shouldn't have even suggested that we…" Geez, all of this was so wrong.

"You didn't need to. God, Lara, you didn't need to suggest or ask or anything." I saw him start to soften but yet he remained still and staring. "I wanted to. God, I wanted to. I wasn't sure if you…." He stopped and stood. "Listen, what we did? That meant something to me. And for you to think that it was pity—"

I took a step closer to him when he cut his own words short. "I'm sorry. You're such a good friend to me." God, I internally pleaded, please forgive me.

His exhale sounded like pure frustration. "I don't want to be…." He paused, and I could see in his tired mind that he was either contemplating how to say something or if to say it at all. "I want to be more than your friend."

"I'm not 'just a friend'?" I echoed the phrase he had recited earlier in the evening.

"What? No. I care about you so much, Lara."

I should have just told him the same. I certainly felt the same. And those words he just declared meant everything. But I needed him to know why I reacted the way I did. Why we were standing there feet away from each other in the middle of the night having such a gut-wrenching conversation.

"Then why didn't you kiss me?" I asked.

"What?" A mixture of bewilderment and exasperation crossed his face.

"At the awards, at the party," I clarified. "You didn't kiss me at all, not even a quick—"

"That's what brought all of this on? That's why you thought I was just having sex with you as what, a favor?" He ran his hands through his brown hair, turned around, and then once again looked at me. "Geez, Lara. I'm just not one for public displays of affection. I've gotten burned one too many times in the press. That's the only reason for the friend comment. It's not their business. And it certainly wasn't that I didn't want to kiss you. I didn't even want to go to that stupid after party. I wanted to be back here with you. But I needed to be there because of the label." He stopped talking and urged me with his eyes to say something, because it was obviously my turn. "Lara?"

He wanted to be with me. He wanted to kiss me. It wasn't just a friends with benefits kind of thing. It was more. I was so wrong—happily so. But I didn't know if I had ruined everything before it even began.

"Let me rewind."

"What?" Confused.

"Let me start again and say what I meant to say upstairs and was too stupid, too insecure, to say." Finn's silence gave me permission to continue. "Thank you."

"Lar—"

I interrupted him before he would think that we were going to repeat the whole "thank you" scenario again. "Thank you for caring about me as much as I do you."

He closed the gap between us in less than three swift footsteps. Without a word, he took me in his arms and securely wrapped me into him. I could feel his heart beating strongly, securely beneath his orange T-shirt.

His head resting on the top of mine, Finn said, "I do, you know."

***

I woke up once around 5:45 a.m. and saw that Finn was sound asleep next to me, back in his bed. I was relieved but still emotionally spent. It had only been a couple hours since our conversation in the great room. I was just glad that both of us were able to get to sleep. The fact that it was in each other's arms made it that much better. I carved myself back into him, creating a soft, secure setting. Hearing him murmur, I fell back to sleep.

***

The next time I woke, it was a little before nine a.m. Finn, still in bed next to me, was gulping a swig of water. I started to sit up.

"Hey," he said acknowledging my awake status. He put something in the nightstand and turned to me. "Morning."

"Sorry if I ruined things last night." It was still at the forefront of my mind.

"Good morning," Finn reiterated.

"Morning," I relented, propping myself up against one of the soft, copper-colored, silk pillows.

"I'm pretty sure I overreacted," Finn continued the train of thought I had begun. "Lara, it's just when you told me you hadn't since…since…that night, well, I felt added pressure to make sure you were all right. And then when you said what you did, I just…I lost it. That's not at all why….You know that now, right?"

"I do. I'm sorry. And the pressure thing? Sorry, I didn't think about that."

"Why would you? You're not a guy."

"Glad you noticed." I smiled.

"Oh, I noticed." His smile back was quick, though, as he turned serious. "You are…you're all right, though?"

"Finn, I was scared. I was. I admit it. But it turns out, it really wasn't for the reason you think. I mean, my past, well, it's hard not to think about. But when it came down to it, I was scared because it was you. It was actually you." I verbalized out loud what I had only before self-acknowledged. "And because of that, I knew it was something different, and it made me nervous how much it mattered. Yes, I'm fine. You made me forget all of that, because it was you. You made me feel wanted. You made me feel beautiful."

"You are beautiful, Lara. I don't know why you don't see that," he said obviously heartfelt. And then, trying to lighten the conversation, he added, "But you would have had a hard time getting lucky in this combo," he said referring to my yoga and sweats attire. And then he threw the hoodie over my head.

"Probably." I laughed releasing it. "It looks like a college walk of shame outfit, huh?"

"I'm gonna have to try to remember to kiss you more too," he noted.

"Oh, I'm sorry if that is such a task. I'm not going to have to wait another seven years for you to do that, though, am I?"

"Seven years? No. I don't even think I can wait another seven, ah—" He kissed me. "Nope, seconds."

"I get it about the PDA, Finn. But can I ask—" I was about to say "a favor" but then decided to change my words. "Can I make a request?"

"I guess."

"No more Mr. Green Eyes. I want you."

"Your me?" he asked, remembering what I had said in the coffee house in September.

"Yeah." I smiled.

"Well, I happen to like *your* eyes. They're like a brilliant turquoise."

"Thanks."

"I have to have the contacts in for our first stop, and then I promise you'll have regular old Finn for the rest of your trip."

"The many sides of Finn Murphy."

"Yeah, something like that." He spoke quietly and then grabbed for my hand. "C'mon, girl, let's get going. I know I'm gonna be later than usual for that meet-and-greet session."

***

With a quick energy stop beforehand at a local coffee shop, we made it to the meet-and-greet session that was helping support the Country Music Hall of Fame. I got to meet more of Finn's staff and take in another aspect of his career. I watched, off to the side, as he greeted what seemed like an endless line of people. He graciously accepted markers to sign all sorts of items, bent down to hug children in cowboy hats, and took smiling selfies with fans. Most of whom, I noted, were women, of all ages, including a couple who were brazen enough to reach for his behind.

Afterward, Finn did exactly what I asked of him. The moment we were alone in his sporty, metallic blue convertible, he removed his colored contacts. "Well, that's an hour or so out of my life that I'll never get back," he lightly complained.

"What? You looked like you were having a blast."

"God, no. I hate those things. It's not real."

"You sure fooled a bunch of girls in there," I stated, trying to disguise the sting of jealousy that surfaced despite not having a right to it.

Finn kissed me then with determination…with possession. "But I didn't even think about doing that with any of them." Caressing my cheek before resting his finger on my lips, he said, "This is real."

Touched by the sentiment, I kissed him softly back. Then just as quickly, in order to protect all the founded or unfounded emotions bubbling inside me, I added a touch of sarcasm. "And I didn't even have to stand in line."

Finn shook his head and started the car. He asked if I wanted to drive south an hour or so and find where I was born. My family had moved around a lot during the first ten or more years of my life because my father couldn't hold a job. It was my mother's stability as a nurse that had eventually kept us grounded near Pittsburgh. Although Finn's offer was thoughtful, I had no inclination to do such a thing. I didn't remember being there and, if I had, I am sure it wouldn't have been good memories. Instead, I wanted to make new ones.

CHAPTER TEN

Our Nashville sightseeing adventure was a relaxing day of learning even more about what makes Finn Murphy so special. We started out at an oriental café. Everything was take-out. We ordered three things to share—tempura, noodles, and egg rolls—and then took them to eat at a park near the Parthenon. He next brought me to the Ryman Auditorium. It was the first major gig Finn had played in Tennessee. As we stood on the upper balcony near the colorful, church-reminiscent windows, he beamed with pride, telling me the story of how it felt to be on that stage for the first time and to think that his dreams were just beginning.

Drinking milkshakes, Finn played tour guide, driving through Music Row before we headed off to our next destination—a farm on the outskirts of town. It was there that we went on a hayride. When I joked that it wasn't quite a roll in the hay, Finn tossed me down and kissed me. I joked about the PDA, but there was just a driver, his horse, and an open field. We weren't in much danger of paparazzi or a fan's camera phone for at least a few hundred feet until we returned to the farm. We bought two pumpkins and some dinner items from the market before leaving. More accurately, Finn bought, since he insisted that the entire trip was his date. I learned not to argue, although it was hard.

Despite it being past Halloween, once we got back to Finn's home, we carved our pumpkins. We couldn't decide if we wanted mean, silly, scary, surprised, etc. pumpkins. So, we chose no faces at all and simply carved Finn's name in one and my name in the other. Finn, admittedly, did most of the carving, though. He even convinced me to take a joint selfie of us and our pumpkins so he could send it to Nola.

I had the seasoning salts out, the entertainment-sized oven pre-heating, and was cleaning the seeds on the butcher block while Finn was on his phone discussing something with his agent or producer or videographer—who knows. He might not have to report to work Monday through Friday at given times, but he seemed to always need to be accessible. I heard him say goodbye as he was walking back into the kitchen. He held out the phone to show me the text that Nola had sent regarding the pumpkins photo.

Cute! Thanks for sharing. Sorry U didn't win. She had written.

Finn started texting something back. He wasn't going to let me see it but relented right after he pressed send: *Did U see the pic I just sent? Who says I didn't win?*

As I smiled, stepping closer, he backed up with a similar grin, "Don't touch me with those pumpkin goo hands." Before I could get to the paper towels, Finn looked at his phone's text message. "Jesus, Wyatt wants to video chat with you."

I swung my head left to right to signify "no," feeling that if I actually verbalized it, Wyatt would be able to hear me. I might have been overly cautious, but I felt like I needed to set student-school employee boundaries. Finn understood and started texting back when Nola sent a text telling us not to worry—she already told Wyatt no. She would try to talk with him about the fact that his uncle's relationship with Miss Faulkner was separate from his, and he needed to respect that. Relationship—hmmm, I liked that.

***

After showering in the first-floor changing room with separate sauna, I put on my bathing suit and cover-up and stepped outside to Finn's adjoining entertainment-sized deck. I found him sitting on a sofa near the fireplace in the outdoor living area. He was watching something on the flat screen TV when I approached him from behind.

"Hey," I said as Finn used the remote to switch the television from video to stereo music. "You don't have to turn it off."

"Wasn't really watching anything —just relaxing, thinking, waiting for you," he said while standing to meet me. "I mixed up a pitcher of margaritas. Is that all right?"

"Uh…." I started.

"I didn't make it strong."

"Okay," I agreed, permitting Finn to pour the beverage into a large cowboy-boot-shaped glass. "That's classic." I laughed.

"Yeah, right?" He smiled, handing me the glass. "Sadly, I can't blame someone else. I saw them and thought they were hysterical." After I took a sip, he asked, "You like? I could get you water or whatever."

Not too strong or too tart, I thought it was… "Perfect."

"Could you grab the chips, veggies, and dip?" He pointed to the food located on the nearby table. "Bring them to the hot tub. I'm just going to get the kabobs and pot stickers from the grill and I'll be right down."

"We're eating in the hot tub?"

"Yep. Is that all right?"

"Sure, I guess." It just hadn't occurred to me. I didn't

have hot tubs and saunas and outdoor televisions at my home. I carried the food down the deck walkway until I reached the hot tub. After setting the items on the cushions near the tub's edge, I took a sip of the margarita. I was glad I had it. I needed a little liquid encouragement to take off my cover-up and strip down to my bathing suit. Of course, Finn had seen me in much less, well much, much less, but, somehow, I was still self-conscience in my aqua and white tank and separate boy-cut swimming bottoms.

"No bikini?" Finn asked, approaching me and setting down his portion of the food.

"Ha! No—not a bikini girl," was my response.

"Why not?" He lifted off his shirt revealing those damn distracting abs, extended his hand, and eased me into the hot tub. "Seriously," he said, sitting down next to me. "Why not? You certainly have the body for a bikini."

Taking another sip, I answered, "Finn, you've seen them."

"Seen what?" he said and genuinely sounded oblivious.

"My ugly reminders." I looked down and then back up at him saying the whole truth and nothing but. After all, I figured, he knew all there was to know, anyway. "The stretch marks from…the pregnancy. They're like my scarlet letter to hide."

"No."

"Oh, Finn." I didn't need him to be my protector then. It was a reality. It was *my* reality. "You wouldn't understand."

He set his drink down. "You don't think I know about personal demons and wanting to cover them up?"

His question slammed me head on. Of course he knew about having things in your past that you would rather keep in the past. I wasn't the only one with a history meant to be hidden. It was insensitive and self-centered of me to think so.

"Tell me what happened." I touched my hand to his

under the bubbling water. "I want to understand. I couldn't believe back then what I was hearing, and you had stopped talking with me."

After a deep breath and a drink, Finn said, "Lara, I was so messed up. There was a time I didn't know up from down or wrong from right. I lost touch with you because I lost touch with myself. You're lucky I didn't pull you into that."

"Maybe," I admitted.

"I didn't let anyone in," he continued. "I didn't want anyone."

When Finn grabbed a kabob to munch on, I encouraged him to tell me more. "Why? What happened?"

"Well, the break-up with Audrey," He looked at me almost guiltily and said, "crushed me. Absolutely crushed me. It came out of nowhere. I mean, we were planning our wedding. This was the girl I was supposed to spend my life with."

I didn't want to, but I looked down. I couldn't help it. Those feelings I had when finding out that Finn and Audrey were engaged all those years ago came flooding back. I had no right then to feel the way I did, and there was certainly no reason to feel jealous now. But, yet, I did. And like my stretch marks, I wanted to cover those feelings up. If Finn didn't realize how I felt about the situation years ago, there was no need for him to know now. Somehow, though, by the way he stroked my hand right then, I knew he had at least a strong suspicion.

"You didn't like her, did you?" he asked.

"I actually did."

And that was the truth. It was hard not to have liked Audrey. The fact that she had Finn hadn't made her a bad person—just a coveted one.

"Really?"

"You were happy. She made you happy. But I guess I was wrong."

"Tell me about it. I mean, in hindsight, I know it was

all for the best, but I didn't then. It just felt like suddenly everything was gone. Audrey was gone, college was over, I was in a new city. I was lost." He looked toward the food. "Eat something, please."

I crunched on a pot sticker. "It's good."

Softly smiling, Finn's hand found my thigh. "I'm glad you're here."

"Me too." I leaned into him, feeling the motion of his body as he munched on some food.

"You don't have to tell me more if you don't want to."

Finn kissed the top of my head before continuing, "No, you should know." He took a sip of his margarita, and I lifted my head so I could look at him more directly. "So, I was pretty bad off dealing with all those emotions when suddenly, almost simultaneously, the pendulum swung and swung hard. There was a record deal and agents and gigs and there was no medium ground. I couldn't handle the contrast of the highs and lows. I needed some sort of escape."

"I know exactly how that feels."

"I know you do."

When he didn't say anything, I filled in the blanks. "So…drugs?"

Finn was silent for a moment and then quietly admitted to it. "Yeah. I'm sure you know the rest. You read it somewhere."

"Yep."

"It took a while for me to accept help. My family, if it wasn't for them…." His voice drifted off.

I made a point to look at him dead-on almost as if I was speaking to an errant child. "You're lucky. You know that, don't you?"

"I do, Lara. And I try not to forget it." He sounded truly remorseful.

"My dad? He never got over his addiction. It ruined him, and it nearly ruined the rest of us."

"Lar, I want you to know…." He held both of my

hands in his and looked at me directly. "I want you to know that is all in the past. I know now what caused it. I got help. It is something that is going to be forever with me—a constant reminder."

"Good," I said seriously. "I couldn't be with that other you." I let that soak in for a minute before saying, "And I want to be."

With passion, and I'm sure a dash of relief, Finn kissed me then for an extended moment. We sat quietly for a few more minutes eating, drinking, and intertwining our feet. But we both felt it. The jovial mood that had encompassed us throughout the day had mellowed a bit due to our serious, albeit needed, conversation choice. Our emotions in that hot tub had changed to become more melancholy.

I thought about suggesting a change of scenery when Finn, obviously thinking the same, spoke up. "Let me light the fire pit, and we can have some s'mores."

"That sounds great," I concurred. "I'll clean everything up."

Finn got out of the hot tub first, grabbed a towel, dried himself off, and threw his T-shirt back on. He then reached out his hand to help me up and out. I certainly didn't need help, but, admittedly, playing the girl card and being pampered felt good. He wrapped the towel around me, rubbed my shoulders, and then pulled me toward him. His kisses were soft and delicate and reciprocated.

"Okay. Focus. Light. Fire," he said in an almost caveman tone, causing me to giggle like that helpless girl.

Finn whipped the towel at me and grabbed our drinks to take to the fire pit. After putting my cover-up back on, I took the rest of the food items back inside to the kitchen. As I was exiting the French doors to make my way back outside, I could see Finn at the fire pit just another short wooden walkway away. The fire was already ablaze. I was almost there when he asked if I could grab the blanket from the back of the deck sofa.

Thinking how good he looked with just the light of the

fire illuminating him, I said, "If there's anything else we need, you know with the blanket, maybe I should get it now." God, why didn't I just say, where the heck are your condoms? I want you. I want you now.

Finn's voice was softer but serious as he obviously knew what I was referring to. "That's up to you."

"And you. Last time I checked, it takes two."

"Lara, there's not a question on my end. At all."

"Me either. Tell me where they are."

"I got them." He smiled confidently. "Wallet." Finn tilted his head to his wallet and phone resting on the end table near the fire pit.

"Really?" I jokingly sneered.

"I was hoping. Put them in there while you were in the shower."

"Let me get that blanket." I turned and smiled the whole way back to the sofa.

When I returned, Finn was grilling the marshmallows. "On fire or lightly toasted?"

"I think I'm both right now," I said, taking another sip of the re-filled margarita and starting to feel it.

Finn shook his head. "Get the graham cracker and chocolate ready, Cowgirl."

Once Finn placed the marshmallows on the chocolate and cracker combos, I smashed graham cracker lids on both and handed one to him. As he took a bite into his treat, he sat down on the cushioned bench surrounding the fire pit, propping his back against the numerous pillows. He then patted the space in front of him, suggesting that I sit with him. Spreading his legs, I eased my back up against his chest. He wrapped his arms around me as we continued to eat our s'mores. When we were done, Finn put his finger near my lips as there was some extra marshmallow hanging on. My mouth captured that finger and I let my tongue slowly, methodically massage it.

"Geez," his voice was a near whisper next to my ear. "Turn around."

I did so, and he immediately brought me in for a deep, deep kiss. His tongue was searching mine like it needed the other to exist. I didn't know how we were breathing, but if we weren't, I didn't care. Finn took his shirt off. So I started on mine.

"Let me do it," he nearly pleaded.

I stopped and let him. He seemed to take pleasure out of slowly, seductively lifting my cover-up and then my bathing suit top. I took pleasure out of watching him enjoy it.

It was November, though. And we were outside. So I couldn't help, despite the fire, despite the alcohol, to shiver a bit. Noticing, Finn pulled the blanket around my shoulders. He cupped my breasts in his hands and then buried his head and lips in between them so that they warmed to his touch. He gently laid me down and started rolling my swim shorts off. Then he did something that stunned me. He was kissing me, but purposefully, and in a specific place. He was kissing my pregnancy stretch marks. I couldn't help but gasp.

Finn stopped and looked at me with those gorgeous eyes mixed with gray and sincerity. "I told you this. But I'm going to say it again. I don't want you to ever feel like you have to hide with me."

I sat up, pausing our actions momentarily. "Finn?"

"Yeah?"

"I don't know how I'm going to leave tomorrow."

"You have no idea how hard I am trying not to think about that." He took my hands and put them up to his lips holding them there for an extended time.

Our lovemaking that night at the fire pit was just that—uninhibited desire, trust, and adoration for one another. There were no pretenses or worries or questions. It was sweet, it was sexy, and it was us—the way we were meant to be.

***

His body was right behind mine as we stood and waited for Hawk to make his way up the long, winding driveway to Finn's home. Just as he had been my original escort to the country star's abode, the tall, stalky right-hand man was going to be my chariot away. Finn couldn't drive me to the airport himself because he had an important conference call scheduled. And this way, it allowed us to say goodbye in private. I leaned a little more into his taut chest and sighed. It was going to be rough leaving. I had already gotten used to this little world of escapism. I had already gotten used to him.

I felt Finn's large hand apply pressure to the back of my head, smoothing and stroking my hair in a calming way. We had both been silent since coming outside. But it was time to say something while it was still just the two of us.

I turned to face him. "Thanks for my chocolates and flowers, um, I mean wine." I cringed when I spoke the word "Thanks" as "Thank you" had almost instantly become taboo for us.

But Finn ignored it, instead mimicking my sentiment. "Thanks for finally agreeing to go on that date with me."

"Finally?" It came out partially as a question and partially as a whisper.

"Lara," he seemed to softly admonish. "It's one thing that you didn't know Sam and Olivia were setting us up that first time. But you had to know later. You had to know when I asked you to go to other things with me back then." When I didn't reply because I was seriously spinning my brain trying to remember those days of friendship in college, he continued. "Like that special movie premiere thing...?"

"We went as a group...all of us."

"Because you made it be that way!" He said in a louder, more exasperated tone.

"I...I didn't know," I tried.

I think he was consciously trying not to shake his head or roll his eyes at me, but it was the truth. "And then—"

But Finn was cut off by Hawk pulling up and exiting the car. "Hey, man." He nodded toward Finn in that macho way guys do and then turned to me. "Lara, hey. Nice to see you again."

"Yeah, you too." I agreed, and a sudden swish of sadness swept over my body.

This was it. I was going home. I looked back to Finn who softly skimmed my cheek with the back of his hand. I tried a smile, but it was extremely half-hearted.

"Let me get your bags in the car." Hawk offered, surely sensing the high emotions in the air.

"Thanks." Finn said to Hawk but didn't let his eyes drop from mine. "Lara…." He breathed a long, heavy exhale from his nose as I heard Hawk putting the items in the car behind me. "God…okay." Still with the intense eye-lock, he slowly nodded his head in a way that it seemed like he was trying to actually make it okay. And then he gave me that final, heart wrenching kiss goodbye. "Call me—"

"As soon as I get in." I finished his sentence already knowing the drill.

Finn's lips curled up in a semi-smile. He saw that I got in the car, and he told Hawk to take good care of me. And then I watched as the image of Finn got smaller in the distance as we drove away…away from Nashville and that dreamlike long weekend.

***

I got his text just as I boarded the plane to New York. It read: *I miss U 2* and attached was a photo of the lipstick rendering I had left with those same words on his master bathroom mirror.

I pushed up the blind covering the window next to my seat. It was impossible to see a clear image. Seeming to mirror my sad emotions, rain spattered and sprayed consistently and with vigor on the pane.

Another text followed then. *Soon* was his solo word.

I wiped at the instant tears that filled my eyes. They were the sad variety, but they were also filled with a tiny ray of hope. That one word meant even more than the ones that had preceded it. It meant that even though the end had come for my visit, it hadn't come for us. It wouldn't be like before. We would find a way to see each other again.

CHAPTER ELEVEN

I did miss him…more than ever. But because of those magical days we had spent in Tennessee and the words we had spoken honestly with one another, I didn't resort to the self-doubts like I had before. I didn't have on my full body shield. There was a protective vest over my heart, ready just in case, but I knew it wasn't being used to its full capacity.

It helped that we talked or texted a lot during the next couple of weeks. Finn sent me a funny image reminding me to vote on Election Day. I laughed and texted him that I never did end up registering to vote. And he sent back, "Mickelson for Mayor!" There were many moments since meeting up with him again that I wondered if he remembered that night. I knew it was one that I couldn't forget, and I was assuming, by the text, that Finn hadn't either. As for Decan, he probably relished his meager campaign stop beginnings. As not only was his mayoral run successful, but Finn informed me that he was now married, living in DC, and working in the West Wing.

On another day, I updated Finn on the child, Harlan, who we had the concert fundraiser for. It appeared that he, unfortunately, needed a heart transplant. So, the school was having another fundraiser. Anyone who wanted to donate a dollar could wear their pajamas to school that day. Believe it or not, that was a huge incentive in an elementary building. Finn said he would donate to the cause but only if I would send him a photo of me in my pj's. He, instead, got a photo of me well covered in my sweats and hoodie combo. And I promised him that had I bought a few new camis. Like the wine, he could choose red or white when he came in.

***

Once he discovered that I didn't go to my mom's place in Pittsburgh for the Thanksgiving break and that my only plans were to watch the parade on TV and do some Black Friday shopping, Finn insisted that I join him and his family for Thanksgiving dinner. They were all flying in and celebrating at Nola and Will's. Of course, I was ecstatic to see Finn again. I missed him so much. But I was a little leery about spending the holiday with his family. Sure, I had met all of them at Wyatt's birthday party and they were more than nice, but things had changed. I would now be coming as Finn's what? Date? Girlfriend? That had to change the dynamic and/or the scrutiny. But I'd be damned. I was happy.

Finn arrived the day before Thanksgiving. He went straight to a fairly local veteran center to entertain the vets and help pass out Thanksgiving meals. Country music always seemed to be a hit with the military. Wanting me to meet him there, he sent a driver and car to pick me up. I told him I could drive myself. But he had insisted since it was a far enough distance and the weather forecast was formidable for the day—anything from rain to ice to wintery mix to fog. I accepted without much argument because, admittedly, I was not a fan of driving in those types of conditions… and because it was sweet.

It turned out to be a wise decision as flash freezing rain

resulted in a couple road closures and many accidents. By the time the driver pulled up to the curb and made sure I got in the building safely, Finn was mid-act. I stood near the back and admired his presence on the make-shift stage—how he commanded the crowd and had them all either singing along or cheering. I watched as he shook hands firmly mid-lyric with so many of the men and women. I could see in his eyes, albeit green, that he wasn't just putting on an act similar to the videos and award shows I had seen him in. But, instead, he was invested in what the day was about just like he had been at the benefit concert at my work place.

I was thinking about that real Finn Murphy and how he had become such an important, meaningful part of my life. I was practically lost in that thought when he caught my eyes in the crowd. It was a subtle wink, but I knew it was for me, and I smiled softly back in recognition. I don't know if it was my imagination, but it felt like he sang with even more robust energy after spotting me. If he did or he didn't, regardless, it turned me on all the more. I knew I had missed him. But seeing him again made me truly realize how much and how hard I was falling. Every inch of my body was acknowledging it—my brain, my heart, and those inner female parts.

After his final song, Finn was immediately drawn into more handshaking and autograph signing. I saw him say something to a woman with shoulder-length caramel hair who I recognized from Nashville. In turn, she walked to the back of the room to find me and re-introduce herself as Reese, a publicist for Finn. She wanted to know if there was anything she could do for me. Acknowledging that he was working and that I needed some of that brisk November air, I asked Reese to tell Finn that when he was done I would meet him at the car. The plan was for us to both take the car back to my place where we could have dinner and he would stay the night.

Seeing me approach, the driver snubbed out a cigarette

and opened the back car door for me. I slid into the creature comforts of real leather seating and a mini-bar. I had not partaken of any beverage on the ride over, but I was seriously contemplating opening something since I suddenly felt like a nervous, bumbling teenager expecting my boyfriend to climb up to my bedroom window.

Before I could decide one way or the other, said boyfriend texted me: *What's up? Why are U out there?*

I smiled, thinking that there he was, in the midst of all those rugged, strong, armed forces types, and he was concerned about a girl. I typed a quick reply back: *All good. Just needed some air. Didn't want to bother U.* Especially since I knew how he felt about public displays of affection.

Not a bother—at all. Give me 5 & I'll meet U @ car.

K was my simple response, but it was full of promise.

It was probably closer to fifteen minutes when I heard the trunk of the car open, a small thud, and then the trunk close, followed by Finn opening the same car door which I had entered. "Same place. Thanks," he said to the driver.

Sliding over to give him room in the back seat, I watched as his magnificent body folded in next to mine and the door shut behind him. "Hi," I greeted, glad that I hadn't drunk any of the alcohol. I was already on a buzz with him right next to me.

"Hey," he said with the softest voice and matching smile.

"That was amazing."

"Yeah?" His eyes, still performer green, were locked into mine.

"Inspiring," I amended as the driver closed his own door and started the car in motion. "Your performance but also how you were with those vets. It made me...." *want you even more, love you even more.* But I knew I wasn't ready to actually say those words out loud to him even if they were accurate.

"Hey, sir." Finn leaned a little toward the front seat and spoke to the driver of the car service. "Can you put up the divider?" As the darkened window started to go up, separating us from the driver, Finn called out a "thanks" and flanked my face with his hands. "God, it's so good to see you."

He brought my mouth to his for a most powerful and hungry kiss. I could feel his tongue dancing with mine. It felt so good to be next to him again—too good.

"Well, that doesn't help," I admitted a little breathy.

"It does *not* help?" he sounded genuinely perplexed.

His left hand rubbed my right leg, and I squirmed. I actually squirmed. I closed my eyes trying to regulate my heartbeat which seemed to be hammering faster and faster by the millisecond. But it didn't work. I felt like a child needing to go to the bathroom. I had never, ever felt like that. Miller and I had had sex, but it had been more or less something to do. But with Finn, I was drawn to him emotionally and physically.

"Kissing you doesn't help, Lar?" he refocused me, this time with the slightest hint of hurt in his voice.

I touched his hand still resting on the tight, white jeans covering my legs. "Not when it makes me feel…" Gosh, we had already been so intimate, and I had revealed so much to him. Yet, I couldn't say horny.

His smile seemed to explode on his face. I didn't need to say it. He knew. With a swift move, he flopped off my shoes and brought me onto his lap. Even though we were completely clothed, I could feel that I wasn't the only one having a reaction to our close proximity.

"Like this?" he asked.

"Mmmm-hmmm."

"And kissing *always* helps," he countered and laid a few magic ones on my lips. When I laid my head down on his black T-shirt-covered chest, he said, "God, it hurts to be away from you, and it hurts to be this close to you."

"Sorry," I lamented. "I could, you know, try to help you out…. Do a little temporary fix. But not with Jeeves"—I used a light-hearted name for our driver—

"right there."

"No, Lara. No." He punctuated his words precisely and with determination. "Not you. Not that. Not here. No."

When I looked up, this time he wasn't as eager to meet my eyes. I replayed his simple words in my mind. What did they mean? I could only guess that back seat blowjobs were common in his line of work. I tried to push it out of my mind.

"Real," he recited the word he had said to me after the meet-and-greet in Nashville and then brought me back to his chest so I could hear and feel his heart beating. "Stay right here…just like this. It won't be that long until we get to your place."

And we were able to do just that…at least for a little bit. Until, of course, he had to take and place a couple calls. Finn seemed to always be connected to his career. But I was also beginning to realize how much he was connected to me.

***

I was a little embarrassed to have him at my apartment and warned him that it wasn't a sprawling ranch with every modern convenience and then some. He said he would stay on a cot at the Salvation Army if I was there with him. I said he was used to reciting lines, but, admittedly, was still touched.

"Something smells delicious." He immediately pecked me on the lips as we entered my apartment and were no longer on a public street or hallway.

"I made chili earlier. Hope that's good. We can eat whenever." Picking up one of my mother's nervous traits, I had cooked like crazy that morning to keep my mind off Finn flying and arriving.

"Does it have chocolate chips in it?"

"Huh? What? No. Why would—"

"Skyline chili," he said matter-of-factly while taking off

his coat. "That's how they make it in Cincinnati."

"So?" I was confused as Finn was a native Kentuckian and resident Tennessean.

"It's still my football team." He smiled, and I had a memory of him telling me that in college—Bengals were the only cats he likes.

My belly shook in laughter. "No chocolate chips. Sorry. Here, give me your coat." I said before taking it and hanging it in the hallway closet that stretched the length of the living room because it also housed the washer and dryer.

I walked him through the efficiency kitchen with ceramic tile counter that backed to the rather spacious living room. There was also a decent sized dining room and an "I can only take one step or simply put plants out" balcony. Then we started down the hall where I pointed out the bathroom to the right and the small bedroom that I used as a work room to the left. At the end of the hall was the master bedroom complete with personal bathroom.

"Here's my room," I said as we entered.

Finn stated what would be the first question anyone would ask when entering, but I forgot because I was so used to it, "Where's the bed?"

I decided to play with him. "Bed? Why would we need a bed? I had some people take it away," I teased.

"Oh, Lara, I can be very creative, you know," Finn said in a voice that made my insides tingle.

"Promise?" I encouraged him.

"That rocking chair has a lot of potential." Finn suddenly lifted me from the ground into his muscular arms.

Before it went any further, I gave in to the ruse. "All right. All right. Hold on. I have a bed." I walked over to the wall of built-in cabinetry and pulled down the mirrored middle section of the wall unit to reveal the queen-sized bed.

Finn's smile couldn't have been larger. "You know what these beds are called, don't you?"

"Yeah," I said matter-of-factly. "They are Mur—" I stopped myself, realizing then why he was smiling so.

"Go ahead. Finish what you were going to say."

I laughed. "It's a Murphy bed."

"Why, that bed already has my name on it."

"So, it does."

***

"Good morning, Roxanne." Slightly awake, I turned to the sound of Finn's voice.

Snuggling into his side and kissing his bare chest, I jokingly replied, "You think you're going to get me to sleep with you again by calling me a prostitute?"

"If the red light fits," he jested back.

"Finn!" I playfully hit him.

He started singing the lyrics that I had never really paid attention to. And, suddenly, they weren't a college joke. They were about loving a woman since first knowing her and not wanting her to be with anyone else.

I kissed him mid-song. "You can call me Roxanne any time you want."

"And you'll still sleep with me?" He smiled a devilish grin.

"Way to ruin the moment, Murphy." I shook my head in a joking manner.

"Will this help?" He turned me and kissed me gently, yet, seductively.

"Mmmm-hmmm," I replied. "What time are we meeting your folks?"

"Talk about ruining the moment."

"Sorry. What time?"

"It doesn't matter."

"It does. I don't want to be late."

Finn sighed. "We should be at Nola's before one."

It was my turn to sigh. We had slept in longer than I thought we would. And I truly, really did hate to be late to anywhere. I had grown up in a house where things were expected to be done—done right and done on time. The fear of not doing that still resonated steadfast in my adult persona. "I guess we should get up then. Want some breakfast? Coffee? Juice? Biscotti? Bacon? Granola? Left over pie?" I had bought an apple pie the day before.

"Definitely coffee…maybe a biscotti," Finn answered in a way that I knew he did not share my concern about promptness but was conceding to it being a done deal.

"Okay, I'll start the coffee maker," I said, starting out of bed and grabbing for the silk cover-up—he had chosen the red set.

"You mind if I use your shower?"

"No, of course not. Go ahead. You don't need to ask. There are towels in there—a dark green one and an orange one. Doesn't matter. Use either."

"How about a glass for water? I need to take my vitamins."

"Aren't you high maintenance?" I teased.

"Yep," he smiled taking it.

"Look under the sink. There should be some paper cups. And vitamins? What are you? An old man?" I joked.

"Uh, no, and I don't want to be."

"I'm just teasing. I take gummy multi-vitamins myself."

"Gummies? What are *you*? Ten?" He got out of bed and traced his hands on the red silk that separated my skin from his.

Before things went any further, I kissed him quickly and turned. I heard him put on some soft, earthy tunes as I went to the kitchen to start the coffee. While Finn was in the shower, I turned on the television in the living room to watch part of the famous Macy's Day parade. Even though I lived so close to New York City, I had only ventured to see it live once and that was enough. The crowds were not worth it. Heaven forbid I ever tried New Year's Eve. I heard the shower turn off just as my phone rang. I took a sip from my coffee, sweetened with just a little honey, and, recognizing my brother Lane's ring, picked up the phone.

"Happy Turkey Day," I said, actually not feeling so alone on the day for once.

"Gobble. Gobble," was my brother's non-traditional response.

"You at McEllie's family's place?" I spoke of my sister-in-law's family who lived near them in North Carolina.

"No," he answered. "Heading out soon, though. All this fuss over a meal."

"Especially for a vegetarian. She must hate this." I turned the volume down on the television and breathed in the welcoming aroma of my coffee.

"She does fine. More for me." I could hear the smile in his voice that turned with the next subject. "Did you talk with Mom?"

"Not yet. I will. I guess she's going to have dinner with him," I said, speaking of our mother's current beau.

Lane and I were both a little leery of the relationship. Neither of us had met him, but some of the things our mother had said threw up caution flags for us if not her. She always seemed to pick the same low-lifes.

"Yeah. That's what I heard. I'm not sure—"

He was cut off by Finn yelling out from the hallway, "Hey, Lar, where do you want the towel?"

"Just leave it on top of the hamper," I called back.

"Do you have a boy at your house?" came Lane's voice from the other end of the phone.

"Huh?" I was caught between the two conversations, and I didn't completely register what my brother said.

"Is there a man at your place this early in the morning?"

I laughed, but it was more of a breath out. "Yeah."

"You go, girl."

I realized I hadn't talked with my brother in a while. He didn't even know that I had gone to Nashville. He knew that Finn had come in for the fundraiser, but we really hadn't talked since then. When my brother and I had a chance to catch up, we reclaimed our bond, but it, unfortunately, didn't happen as much as it should.

"Stop it," I urged lightly.

"It's about time."

"Seriously, leave me alone."

"What's the deal? Who's the dude? What's he like? And I don't mean between the sheets."

"I'm not talking to you about that!"

"Lara?" I hadn't realized Finn had entered the room until I heard him say my name with concern.

"Hey, I'm going. I have company," I spoke into the phone emphasizing the last word and looking at Finn.

"I'm glad." I could hear the smile and sincerity in my brother's voice. "Text me later."

"Okay," I said and hung up. "Hey," I said to Finn now admiring how his blue sweats hung ever so tentatively on his exposed hips.

"You all right?" There was that same unease.

"Huh? Yeah. Why?"

"What was the phone call about? You sounded mad. Who do you want to leave you alone?"

"No." I shook my head trying to replay my end of the conversation that Finn heard. "No. That was just my brother. He was razzing me…about you."

"Oh, good."

"Good that he was razzing me?"

"No. Good that you're all right."

"And good that it wasn't another boy that you had to beat up outside on the playground?" I teased.

But he was serious. "No one should hurt you…ever again."

I knew he was referencing my past then and all the tumultuous tales I had told—stories of me being hurt emotionally and physically from one person or another. I didn't realize he held that so close in his thoughts. But he must have since an innocent phone call prompted such a reaction. I wanted to reassure him that I wasn't that girl anymore. I wouldn't let myself get hurt. There were walls that were built to protect me from such an invasion.

"Finn, all of that was a long time ago. It's different now. *I'm* different now. I can take care of myself. I'm not made of glass." I met him in the middle of the room and placed my hands on either side of those sculpted hips.

"I know," he said seriously and then, in typical Finn fashion, added, "But, listen, you better learn two things." He tugged me even closer into him. "Your hands on my hips are going to drive me insane every time." He punctuated his statement with a solid kiss before adding the second. "And any boy on any playground won't even have a chance."

I kissed him back while letting my fingers draw circles on his hips. "Coffee's ready, Macho Man." I am sure my internal smile was even greater than my external one just knowing that I really had someone willing to protect me.

CHAPTER TWELVE

Thanksgiving with the Murphys was probably something Norman Rockwell would have envisioned only just a little more relaxed. Besides Nola, Will, and the kids, Finn's parents and Will's parents were also in attendance. Uncle Eoin was not there as he was able to be with his kids and, unfortunately, ex-wife on the holiday. Will's mother only brought up Iva once. To which Finn, courteously, but I am sure genuinely, asked how she was and at the same time interlocked his hand with mine.

We ate dinner in the middle of the afternoon which, I guess, is a tradition in most families for that holiday meal. I don't remember what time we used to eat Thanksgiving dinner growing up. I probably blocked it out like so many other holiday horrors.

When we went to sit down at the massive dining room table, Finn gallantly pulled out my chair for me. "Is this seat going to be good for you?" he questioned in a joking, mocking manner.

I widened my eyes willing him to stop. I wasn't in a crowded or noisy place. And, even if I was, I didn't need Finn to point out my nervous quirk to his family. But, regardless, it was the ideal spot around the table.

"Oh, Lara, I just thought to sit you next to Finn," hostess Nola commented while bustling in with the last food dish.

"Yes. Yes. It's perfectly fine," I said, sitting down in front of the plate adorned with a construction paper turkey with my name written on it. "Everything is beautiful," I added as Finn took his seat next to me.

I dug my heel into the top of Finn's shoe-covered foot. As he stifled a yelp, I couldn't help but smile. But, in return, he smoothly placed his hand on the inside of my thigh, which was thankfully hidden beneath the tablecloth.

Our unseen action was quickly interrupted by Wyatt yelling out, "I have homework!"

"No, Wyatt," Nola contradicted. "I don't think you do. I checked your folder. Besides, it's dinner."

"Mom, I do. It's Thanksgiving homework. It's homework for the whole family. Miss Faulkner, tell them." His declaration caused everyone's eyes to swirl to me as he bolted out of the room.

"You gave homework over Thanksgiving break?" Finn was the one who said it. "Boy, we need to loosen you up, Miss Faulkner," Finn jested rubbing my thigh.

"I didn't give homework, thank you very much." I glared at him and shooed his hand away. I never gave any type of homework. We didn't do that in the club classes. I had no idea what Wyatt was talking about.

We soon found out, though, because Wyatt bounded back into the dining room with the turkey book the students had made through a computer program the week before. Using different computer art tools, they personalized the cover to look like a turkey, printed it out, and then attached blank pages where each family member filled in what they were thankful for. It was supposed to be a family bonding, appreciate the meaning of Thanksgiving project—not homework.

"Well, since we already go around and say what we are thankful for, maybe we can write it down too, for Wyatt,"

Mrs. Jamison suggested.

"You really don't have to do that right now, Wyatt," I said.

"I think it's a great idea," Mr. Murphy chimed in. "Here, Wy, let me start."

Wyatt handed his grandfather the book and a pencil. "Here, Pop-Pop. You can either write or draw what you are thankful for on your page. Right, Miss Faulkner?"

"Right, Wyatt," I agreed.

I had to give it to Wyatt, he did listen in club even if I thought he was talking through it most of the time. It was so bizarre to be sitting there feeling as sexy as hell next to Finn but also feeling pure and innocent in the eyes of the grade-schooler across the table from me. It was a good combination that I had no intention of messing with.

After quickly penciling something on the paper, Mr. Murphy said, "I'm thankful for watermelon rinds."

I threw my head backward. Finn roared laughing. Will's parents and Nola, who weren't present for the watermelon conversation during Wyatt's birthday party, looked perplexed.

And Wyatt said, "I like watermelon too, Pop-Pop. Good one."

I tried to look at Finn's dad but couldn't. I had a hard time even looking at Finn. Norman Rockwell was probably turning over in his grave.

Finn's mother took the turkey book next and got the dialogue back to what it was intended. "I'm thankful for the fact that we are all in good health, especially that Pop-Pop's cancer is gone. We are blessed every day we have on this earth." She raised her wine glass up and everyone else followed for a silent toast. I looked to Finn, but before I could question, his mother continued, "And I'm thankful that so many of you were able to join us this year." She looked directly at me and smiled, and again I felt Finn's hand in mine.

Kelsea wanted to be next. "I'm thankful for my

drums."

"Rock on, little one!" Finn said stretching over to give his niece a fist bump.

Will snatched the booklet from Kelsea who complained that she wasn't done drawing her drums. "I'm *not* thankful for the drums," he said and scowled at Finn who smiled and took a sip of wine. "I am thankful to be off work, though, and with my family."

It was Finn's turn next. "I'm thankful for my guitar." He smiled at Kelsea and then became serious. "I'm thankful for my family—for my parents and sister who supported me through the bad times. And I'm thankful for the success of my latest album and my fans. And I'm thankful for Lara. I am blessed."

I had the feeling that was more than Finn usually contributed to the Thanksgiving tradition. Or at least he wasn't usually as serious, because the whole table got quiet and respectful. Until Nola, as only a sibling can do, broke it up.

"What? Is this the acceptance speech that you didn't get to give? Give someone else a chance already. Geez. The food will get cold. Here, Lara, your turn." Nola grabbed the book from her brother and handed it to me.

"Oh, no, it's not for me to—"

"Miss Faulkner, it's your homework, you have to do it!" Wyatt cried out and, again, all eyes swung to me.

"Okay." I took the book just wanting to get it over with. I thought for a moment and then drew a simple picture of a little boy.

Finn was peering down at it as Kelsea yelled out, "What is it?"

"I'm thankful for Wyatt," I said.

"That's it?" Finn asked, I think a little taken back.

I turned to him. "Connect the dots, Uncle Finn." And then as Nola started saying what she was thankful for, I whispered so closely in Finn's ear that my lips were touching, "No Wyatt in school, no you, no us." Looking from Finn to Wyatt, I noted that they were both beaming but for different reasons.

***

I couldn't help but notice Finn putting on the imaginary brake with his foot as I drove us back to my place. "Stop that," I casually admonished.

"What?"

"You're acting like I'm a bad driver."

"I can't decide if it's you or the car."

"It's not me," I tsked.

"Debatable." He grinned but then continued with his onslaught of my car. "Does this even have airbags?" He cringed exaggerating a grip on the door frame.

"Yes! Stop. We all can't have sporty little roadsters."

"No, but you can be safe."

"I'm safe. The car is safe."

"What about in the winter?"

"I pray that work is cancelled."

"Oh, geez." He looked down, shaking his head before looking back up again. "Lar, can I drive?"

"Finn, no. Why?"

"I like to drive. And, I don't know, it's kinda the guy's job, isn't it?"

"That's not 1950 and sexist at all, is it?" I defended with a friendly banter.

"It wasn't meant to be," he said and then added, "Honey Bun." When I burst out laughing at the ridiculous term of endearment, he smiled his contagious, gorgeous, full grin and continued his train of thought. "I mean, my dad always drove when we were growing up. Didn't yours?"

"No," I replied plainly. Knowing that Finn already knew the worst about the man, I decided to just go ahead and explain. "When he didn't have his license suspended, which happened more than once, we didn't really want to be in the car with him."

"Sorry," was his knowing, sympathetic, one-word response.

"Well, regardless, we're almost there." I managed to turn and smile at Finn and then took the opportunity to change the downtrodden subject. "Thanks for inviting me today."

"You have a good time?"

"Absolutely," I replied, honestly amazed at how fast the hours at the down-to-earth family holiday went. "How could I not? Your family is so natural…so genuine. I didn't need to worry."

"You were worried?"

"Yeah, I mean, I don't know, going to a family's holiday, that's kinda a big deal. Or no?" I second guessed myself, this time purposefully keeping my eyes on the road.

"Lara, you'd already met them."

"I know, but not since…." How to say it tactfully?

"…we've been in the watermelon rind category?" he offered a humorous ending to my trailing statement.

"My God! I will never live that down, will I?" I practically screamed.

Finn laughed. "My dad likes you. If he didn't, he wouldn't josh around like that." And then he added, "Believe me."

"I can't imagine him not liking someone."

"It's rare, but it's true. He has a stellar sense of people."

I had a sudden remembrance of seeing Finn's father at his college graduation. I had been witness to an awkward, leery interaction between the Murphy patriarch and Audrey. It was subtle, but I could tell Mr. Murphy wasn't too fond of Audrey's possession of his son. I didn't think much of it then, but it definitely resonated with me now.

"He's a great guy…like a big teddy bear," I said. "I have a feeling he would do anything for your mom and your family. You're a lot like him."

"That's a good thing, right?"

"It is." I glanced over at him. "Why didn't you tell me he had been sick?"

"It's the bear part of that 'teddy bear.' He didn't even tell Nola or me that he was sick until, well, it was around this time last year that they couldn't make it to Thanksgiving and they had to explain that he was getting his chemo. He's a private, proud man who wants to take things on himself. In that way, he's like you, isn't he?" I could feel Finn looking at me as I was driving.

Even though it was a positive comparison, I didn't think I matched up to such a strong man. So, I asked a question of my own instead of answering. "He's healthy now?"

"Yeah, everything has been clear."

"He doesn't like to talk about it, though?"

"I don't know. I guess everyone has that something that they'd rather not have the whole world know about. People treat you different when they find out you have some type of illness."

"Maybe," I conceded.

"They do, Lara."

"Well, anyway, thanks for telling me."

"Does that mean that you are thankful for me?" he teased.

"Don't tell Wyatt," I smirked.

***

The following two nights I was to spend at Finn's penthouse in Manhattan. It had the modern conveniences that his place in Nashville had but not the space. There were three bedrooms, one of which he converted into a gym/game room. The master bedroom had access to a sunny wrap-around deck with spectacular views of Central Park. The sleek kitchen, living room, and dining room were all open and stylish with floor-to-ceiling windows plus a granite fireplace in the living area.

We met the Murphy/Jamison clan for ice-skating at Rockefeller Center on Friday. Finn did fairly well not getting recognized as he was wearing a cap and scarf. Plus, Wyatt and Kelsea had been trained not to yell out his name. I wasn't as obedient, though, because every time I felt like I was about to fall, which was more often than not, I was yelling for him to catch me. Afterward, we warmed up at the eatery inside.

It was that Saturday night, though, when things came to a chilly, abrupt turn around. Finn and I were attending an anniversary party his label was throwing in midtown. I was already a little sad because it was his last night in the New York area. But sad didn't describe my despondency mid-way through the event.

I knew he could tell something was wrong. He had that sideways look at me the entire time he was talking with any of the number of people pulling for his attention. But no matter how I ached, I would not ruin his evening—at least not publicly.

I needed a break. But I couldn't retreat to the restroom. And the bar certainly wasn't a good solution. I needed somewhere where there weren't a bunch of record execs or crooner counterparts every time I turned.

I touched his hand. "I'm…I'm just gonna step outside. Out front."

"Uh…" He was torn between me and an older, shorter brunette who was talking about promos. "Just give me a minute."

I walked through the double doors and out to the bone-chilling, late November air. The Manhattan night was far from quiet, but it was better than being inside. It was better than listening to things I had just never wanted to hear. I breathed in as calmly as I could so I could begin the mourning process of what had been.

At least I hadn't gone too far down the Finn rabbit hole. Oh, right—who was I kidding? That was a complete lie. I had fallen hard and fast for that man.

Despite knowing I had things at his place and he was heading back to Nashville that next morning, I knew then that I needed to go. I needed to be back at my own apartment. The few material items would have to be lost… like I feared everything else was.

Thinking I could get a taxi rather quickly in the fast-paced, wheeled city, I texted Finn: *Catching the train—going back to my place.* And I promptly stepped farther out to the sidewalk and stretched my neck looking for a yellow cab with the center light illuminated.

Sure enough, it was less than a minute when I found myself speeding toward Grand Central. I didn't try to make conversation with the driver through the dirty, thick, clear plastic barrier separating the front from the back of the car. And I ignored the annoying mini-television broadcasting some obnoxious, loud commercial. Instead, I looked at the red flashing monitor announcing the increasing price of the ride. It seemed to be thumping as hard and as fast as my heart. And the hole in the seat next to me, exposing loose dirty white cushion stuffing, mimicked how torn up I was. I didn't want to go, but I needed to go. I knew it. I just needed to accept it.

Knowing that if I let one teardrop fall or answered the repetitive calls flooding my phone from Finn, that I would fall apart, I remained stoic during that ride. Upon arrival, I paid the driver and went into the terminal that was busy— but not to the extent of its usual reputation. I had done this route plenty of times over the years, so I moved in "Lara autopilot" as I bought my ticket and started toward the seating area. It was a good thing I didn't need to concentrate since my mind certainly wasn't into thinking beyond the basics.

I only had a few minutes to wait until it was time to board. So I briefly browsed the covers of the magazines at a newsstand shop and opted not to get anything to eat or drink. I hadn't eaten much at the party, but, regardless, I wasn't at all hungry.

It was when I was looking at the board listing the arrivals and departures and thinking my nerves were too shot to even sit and wait, that I heard my name. It wasn't loud. In fact, it was a bit winded. But I knew the voice well. Despite there being a number of people swarming around that area, I saw Finn instantly. He was a good few feet away. His head was shaking ever so slightly as he was pleading me with my eyes to come to him.

When I didn't move, he looked around. I knew he didn't want to be recognized. There were times when he didn't mind it as much, but this...this certainly wasn't one of them. And he didn't have on any type of clothing that could be used as a disguise—not a ball cap, hoodie, or even glasses. Standing there in the brown suit he had worn to the party, it was probably close to a sure bet that someone would identify him.

But I guess he was willing to take that risk, because he walked toward me. I knew then that it was inevitable that we were going to talk. I certainly wasn't going to take off running in my decorative heels and cocktail dress, after all.

"What? Where are you going?" His eyes swept repeatedly across mine.

"Home." I kept it simple.

"Why? No. Lar, please...please don't leave." There was a bit of panic when he said that last word. Before I could think any more about it, he said, "I'm sorry. I told you I hate those gigs. But it's a necessary evil." He spoke of the label's party. "You should have just told me."

He reached his hand out for mine, but I instantly retracted. I didn't want to feel his touch. I didn't want to be confused.

His look of concern upon the rejection heightened. "I don't get...Is this about the PDA thing?"

If only it was about the fact that he didn't kiss me in front of that room of fake music know-it-alls at the party. I could have dealt with that. I understood that. It was, unfortunately, so much bigger.

"No. I just don't fit in there. I don't belong. If that is your world—if you are one of those beautiful people whose only concerns are themselves and…." I could feel myself starting to get revved up, so I aborted the rest of my words.

Finn shot a good look around the terminal. I could feel his anxiety. It was definitely because of my leaving, but it was also because of the risk of being recognized. I could sense it, because I was feeling it too.

"Can we do this somewhere a little quieter?" he asked slowly.

I glanced at the board again. I was going to miss the train, but there were plenty of others running through the evening. I did need to talk to him. He deserved to know what had made our night—everything—strike a bad chord. So, I began to walk in silence. And, keeping his recognizable face down, Finn matched my strides, walking right alongside of me.

When we found a corridor where the shops were closed and no one else was around, he was the first to speak. "What's going on, Lara? What happened?"

"I don't think this," I looked back and forth quickly between the two of us. "is going to work."

"Jesus! Tell me what's going on!" His booming, piercing voice made me physically jump. Noting, he took a huge breath and exhaled, then spoke softer but with even greater concern. "Sorry. Talk to me. Please. You know you can." He nodded as a woman wearing earbuds and toting a small suitcase on wheels strolled by.

It was true. I knew I could talk with him. One of the most honest and pure things between us was our friendship which allowed us to speak freely.

"There were two women in the bathroom at the party." I replayed the scene. "They wanted to know if I had any smack or anything good on me." I watched as his eyes went from focusing on me to closing in a show of woeful acknowledgement. "They said if I was with you…."

His eyes flicked back open and he took both of my hands securely in his. "Lara," he said my name solidly and didn't deter from his stance as he continued. "I don't do that shit. I don't—any of it. I told you that. There were people in there from all genres, and I don't know more than half of them. Unfortunately, I screwed up in the past, and it is part of that all-that-is-holy public record." A twinge of disgust mixed in with his concern. "They just assume or want it to be true so they can pretend they know it all or score or something. But it's not. I don't do it. I promise you. You didn't run into any of that in Nashville, did you?"

"No."

"Not that there isn't. I'm not gonna lie to you, but not with the people I hang around with. I promise you." He searched my eyes, silently willing me to say something.

But I couldn't. I was still trying to take it all in. The evening, the fact that he was leaving, his past, his present—it was a lot to comprehend and sort through.

He dropped my hands, turned around and back again, and said, "I hate my past."

"I know how that feels."

He nodded his head ever so slightly. "Please believe me, Lara. I'm sorry that happened…that someone would say that to you…that you had to be confronted with that. But I am telling you the truth. I couldn't bear it if you don't know that."

I exhaled…hard. I did. I did know that. He had hardly even drunk that night or any time I had been with him. He certainly didn't demonstrate any signs of a druggie lifestyle. All he ever did was show me how much he cared for me. And I, true to form, built up my Lara walls before anything else and had run.

"Please," he almost begged before I could answer. "What do you want me to do?"

"Take out those damn green contacts and be *my* Finn."

I smiled, because if I didn't, I would cry and that could not happen. I was still too much in my protective mode.

"God." His exhale release was as strong as mine had been. "Yeah. Yeah. I can do that." He breathed out again. "Lar…." He wanted to do or say more, but a teenaged couple walked by. "Can I tell the driver to quit circling and meet us? I mean…the contact solution *is* at my place," he said a little more confidently.

"Yeah."

He tapped something into his phone, looked around to see that there wasn't anyone else nearby, and then pulled me into his suit-covered arms. Carefully, softly, he kissed me then. "And you are more beautiful than any of those people at that party…in this station…."

"Finn." I tsked.

"Listen, you scared me so bad when you left. I was already having a hard time knowing I have to go tomorrow. Now I really don't want to if you are the tiniest bit unsure about any of this."

"It's me," I acknowledged. "I just need to trust—"

"You can." Speaking with confidence, he touched my hand, and that time I didn't pull away.

CHAPTER THIRTEEN

A delivery of a dozen red roses and a dozen yellow roses arrived around dinnertime that Monday. I didn't have to read the card. There was only one person they could be from. But I opened and read it anyway. There were only two words on the card: *Trust* and *Real* which definitely, beyond a doubt, solidified the sender.

Trying not to get too emotional at the thoughtful, romantic gesture, I took a picture of the flowers and forwarded it to the rose giver with the attached text message*: I love, love, love, love them.* And I added a heart symbol.

While I waited for a response, I searched for the ideal spot in the apartment. They were so bountiful that they almost overwhelmed every place I put them. Finally, I decided on my bedroom. That was where I felt him the most, anyway.

Just as I had them settled, Finn's text reply came in: *& who might they be from?*

I typed back: *The only REAL person I TRUST.*
I'm glad. Got unscented, BTW.

I stuck my nose into the flowers and was amazed at not only the non-fragrance but at the consideration. *Can U talk? Can U call me?*

When my phone rang out "Roxanne", the designer ring I had programmed for Finn on Thanksgiving, I picked up and said, "Can't ever lose with roses, Cowboy."

"Good to know," he replied.

"Finn?" I turned more serious while sitting on my bed and admiring the gorgeous arrangement. "I do trust you. I just sometimes don't trust myself. I don't trust that things are real…at least the good stuff. I'm always waiting for the other shoe to drop."

"I know, Lar," he sounded a little Buddha-like. "I get it. I just don't want you to forget or doubt me, you, or us, especially when I'm so far away and can't really judge what's going on in that cycling mind of yours."

"Cycling or psychotic?" I joked.

"Beautiful," he amended.

"Geez."

"Christmas seems so far away."

"A lot farther today somehow than yesterday." It should have had the opposite feeling, but not when I was only one day removed from him leaving and a month more to go before seeing him again.

"You're for sure gonna be at your mom's place that week?"

"Yep."

"I'm gonna make it work." He spoke of his plans for us to somehow meet up since he would be celebrating with his family in Louisville during that same time. "As soon as I figure it out, I'll let you know."

"I know," I stopped mid-stream and changed the wording. "I *trust* that you will."

"Ha! Ha!" he laughed. "You good with everything?"

"I was. I am. And, if I'm not, I'll just stop and smell the non-scented roses," I teased.

"Then expect a new delivery every week."

"Don't…you…dare," I spoke slowly for emphasis.

"Hmmm, that sounds like a challenge."

"It is not. Finn!"

"Huh?" He was playing dumb on purpose.

"I love the roses, but don't send them all the time. It'll lose the meaning."

"I gotcha."

"Calling me…talking with me…that never gets old, though."

"Ditto."

***

Even though we texted or talked frequently, the night that he actually called to confirm our holiday plans, I was at our staff holiday party. It was at Yvonne's house and there were people packed throughout the first-floor, nibbling on appetizers, sipping on drinks, and having a good time. Luckily, I heard "Roxanne" sing out from the confines of my crossbody purse.

"Hello?" I answered generically. But I couldn't hear. So I said a little louder, "Finn? Can you hear me?"

A number of my co-workers immediately swung to face me. They had heard who was on the other line. Internally shaking my head, I tried to find a corner that was not so occupied.

"What's all the noise?" he questioned.

"I'm at our work party."

"Oh, sheez, I forgot about that."

"Not a biggie."

"Hey, just quick, then. Everything's set. I'll text you the plans. But keep the last couple days of your Christmas break open for me."

"Sure thing. Sorry, I can't hear very well."

"I'll text you."

"Got it," I said and hung up.

But I wasn't off the hook with my co-workers. They had heard me call out Finn's name on a Friday night phone call. And it wasn't like he had a common name like

James or Robert or Michael. So, I couldn't really get away with telling them it was someone else. But I didn't want to explain. I had, up to that point, been able to generically answer their questions after returning from the CMAs. But defining my relationship with Finn was not going to happen. I wanted to keep it separate from work and, because of that, I could understand Finn's hesitancy for PDA. So, I played off the friendship thing again and left early from the party, because I never win at poker. I am sure the love that I felt for that man was written all over my face.

***

The first thing I thought of when I saw him exiting the car in front of my childhood home was he looked H-O-T hot! Dressed in all black, his hair was slightly ruffled, and he had the most gorgeous smile spread across his face. I slowly made my way down the sidewalk to meet him.

"You look good." As soon as I said it, I realized those were the same exact words he had said to me after seven years apart. Did "good" mean "hot" then too?

"Right back at you, Beauty." When I shyly smiled at his term of endearment, he pulled me into an embrace. "You are," his voice, soft and melodic, flowed into my ear. "And I really missed you."

"I've missed you too." I leaned back, daring to kiss him outside.

He didn't refute. In fact, he kissed me longer when I threatened to break away. It was probably because we were on as non-public, rural of a country road as you could get. But I chose to think it was because he just couldn't resist me.

I looked into those striking gray eyes melting into mine. When Finn had told me his plan, I couldn't think of anything better. We were meeting a few days after Christmas. After coming to my mother's home to pick me up, we were going to spend a couple days back at our alma mater. I offered to just meet him at the college —since it was more or less in between Pittsburgh and Louisville—instead of him having to drive all the way and then halfway back again. But he insisted, claiming it was part of a surprise. Plus, he wanted to meet my mother.

I didn't like the thought of either. I'm not particularly keen on the unpredictable. And only God knew how my mother would act. Well, I knew and, while innocent, it could be downright embarrassing. But, for Finn, I was beginning to think I would agree to anything.

I took another glance at the car he arrived in. It was a red Jeep almost identical to the one he had in college, but it looked like the latest model. "The rental is a nice touch." I tilted my head toward the SUV.

"You like?" he asked, smiling.

"Yeah. I told you how much I liked your Jeep."

"Good. It's not a rental. Merry Christmas," he said, digging into his coat pocket and handing me the keys with a ribbon wrapped around them. "It's yours."

My mouth was literally, physically gaping open. It took a good minute for me to speak. "Finn, I can't afford a new car."

"It's a gift, Lara. A gift," he said matter-of-factly. "There's nothing to afford. It's paid for."

"Finn, no. No. You can't give me a car," I said resisting the keys dangling between us.

"Why not? Sure, I can. It's yours. I want to," he said like it was the most natural thing in the world.

"Finn, that's… No. That's too much. That's *way* too much. It's too expensive. It…." I was so flabbergasted I couldn't even string a complete sentence together.

"It's not. It's fine. Believe me. I can afford it. It's a Jeep Wrangler. It's not a convertible Mercedes. It's done."

We were getting nowhere. "I can't just take a car from you. Besides, I have a car."

"I know. I've been in it, remember? It's old. Plus, it

doesn't have four-wheel-drive, and I know you need that in New York and here for that matter," he said, looking at the snow that had already scattered on the grass. "I can't imagine…I don't want to imagine you driving in the snow and ice in that car of yours." He noted the instant look on my face. "I saw that cringe, and I remember what you said about driving in the winter. No arguments. The Jeep is yours." When I started to protest, Finn interrupted me instantly, "Don't try that look on me, either." He smiled so that I couldn't help but smile also. That must have been enough for him to feel like he had won. He pulled me to him and quickly planted a kiss on my lips. "Merry Christmas," he spoke with finality.

Relenting, I said, "Merry Christmas. I'll give you whatever I get for my car."

"We might have to make you write down the definition of 'gift' ten times." He smirked.

"You're getting it." I shook my head with determination. "And the Jeep is all yours… you can drive," I added, knowing he wouldn't argue that. "When you come over."

Now a little more relaxed, he wrapped his arm around my shoulders and teased, "I'm coming over, am I?"

Hopefully more often than not, I silently wished, but instead said out loud, "God, this is like seventy-five Christmas and birthday gifts put together." I don't know where I came up with that number, and I'm sure it still wasn't accurate, but it made Finn turn me to him. Seeing his dreamy smile, I asked, "What?"

"I like that idea." And before I could question again, he said, "Seventy-five holidays with you."

Wow! I hadn't meant it like that. But I did like the warm internal feeling it brought despite the chilly December air.

"C'mon, are we going inside?" Finn broke the silence lingering between us. "Is your family here?"

"Well, my mom is. Lane and McEllie left yesterday."

We were back to my reality—no longer new cars and years of holidays.

"Did you get a chance to catch up?"

"Yeah, it was good. We'll have to find some time for you guys to meet up."

"For sure," Finn agreed. "What about this guy your mom's been seeing?"

"Don't go there."

"I need to know what I'm walking into."

"He's not here. Lane and I kinda let it be known that we didn't want him here while we were here. He's not good news, Finn. My mom keeps picking the same guys over and over again. It's pure emotional abuse."

"I don't want him around you, Lara."

"He's not going to be. This is not my life anymore. I can only tell my mom what I think. I can't live her life for her." I looked him in the eyes so he could see I was serious. "C'mon, let's get this over with. She is a nervous wreck wanting to meet you. It's ridiculous."

"No sweat. I'm good with moms."

"I bet, Charmer."

But before we could make it to the door, my mother opened it and, staring at Finn, said, "My, oh my. Hello there. You must be…well, you must be…. Hello."

"Hi, Mrs. Faulkner. It's so nice to finally meet you. I'm Finn." He took her hand and then leaned in for a kiss on the cheek, solidifying his charmer status.

I think my mom was actually blushing as she spoke. "Of course. Well, of course I know who you are." There she was—embarrassing but loveable Elisabeth Faulkner.

"I hope Lara has only told you good things." Finn looked mockingly at me.

"Lara. Well, yes, Lara, of course. It's a pleasure to have you in my home."

Geez! Does Finn have to put up with this star crap all the time? It's nauseating, especially from one's own mother.

"Mom, let's actually get in the home," I grumbled.

"Mrs. Faulkner?" Finn took my mother's arm to accompany her into the house. Boy, he was laying it on thick and enjoying every minute of it.

Then again, so was my mom. "Such a gentleman. Thank you. And you can call me Elise."

"Elise." Finn actually turned and winked at me.

"Lara, make sure the door is locked when you come in," my mom directed.

"I will." I sighed, shaking my head.

"You know, I worry about my little girl all alone and so close to that big, crazy city. Please," she looked at Finn, "have a seat."

"Thanks, Mrs.… Elise." He sat down on the sofa. "You know, New York, ma'am, isn't the horrible place that everyone makes it out to be. It's actually quite quaint, neighborhoodish in areas, and there are so many people around, you can't help but feel safe in the numbers."

Sitting next to him, I concurred, "That's what I tell her all the time."

"But I know you can't help but worry. That's a parent's prerogative, right?" Finn said.

I wrinkled my eyebrows at him. What character was he playing? This was hysterical.

"You're absolutely correct—to love and to worry." My mom, sitting across from us, looked at me and back at Finn.

"I know," he said, taking my hand and slowly caressing the top of it.

"Lara's been through a lot in her young life, and I just don't—"

"Mom—" I tried to stop her. I didn't want to relive any more of it, especially in that house.

"Lara, I didn't say—" she started.

"Finn knows…everything. It's just, you don't need to fret so much."

My mother tried to look deeply into my eyes to see if

"everything" meant everything, and when I nodded affirmatively, I am sure it took her off guard. "Oh, well, good. I'm glad. I'm glad, Lara." She legitimately sounded relieved and then looked at Finn, a little less star struck and with a little more assessment and admiration. "I'm…you're good for her."

"I hope so, ma'am." I felt his hand move slowly on top of mine again.

Still a little in disbelief, my mother looked at me again. "You never told anyone before, have you?"

My parents and Miller's parents had known about my pregnancy and giving the child up, but that was it. And that was only because I needed my mom's expertise as a nurse, and I knew she wouldn't be able to keep anything from my father. Otherwise, I had kept it all hidden—literally. But neither set of parents, including my mom, knew all that Finn knew. I could have never told them about the child's true parentage and how he was conceived. For one thing, my father would have gone absolutely crazed, which he just about already had finding out I was pregnant. And, for another, it was humiliating, especially at eighteen years old.

"No. Mom, please, can we—"

"Elise, I have a little something for you." Finn changed the subject while digging into the interior pocket of his coat and pulling out a red envelope.

I closed my eyes in gratitude that we weren't talking about my horrid past any longer. But I was curious as to what he was now handing to my mom. He hadn't mentioned anything to me.

"Oh, oh my. Okay." She mumbled and took the envelope from him. When she opened it and pulled out the paper gift certificate, she said, "Well, that's not necessary…at all."

"I know a nurse's work is non-stop. I thought you would enjoy some pampering."

"I…I…yes. That is quite a nice spa. You must have

done some research." As my mom spoke, I looked at the gift card to a nearby spa and resort.

Finn smiled, looking happy that my mom was pleased. "I did."

"Well…well…thank you very much. I will enjoy this for sure. How about some cookies and cocoa?"

"We really need to get going, Mom. Finn was just popping in to meet you."

"Oh, Lara, he just got here. Let us chat for a little bit. Besides, by the time you get back, it will be time for you to leave again for New York."

"I would love some cookies. Homemade?" Oh crap, there he went with the charmer routine again.

"Of course. My personal, secret chocolate chip recipe," she bragged, but I must admit, she made some mighty delicious cookies.

"Awesome. Can I help you with anything?" he offered.

"No, no. Sit. Thanks, though. I appreciate the nice manners." And she bustled her way into the kitchen.

"What are you doing?" I smacked Finn in the arm.

"What? I like cookies." He smiled that irresistible smile. "Who doesn't like chocolate chip cookies? Do you want me to start talking about watermelon rinds like you did with my parents?"

I put my hands up to my face. I truly would never live that down. But I got my revenge. "No," I whispered, leaning into him and letting my hand rest on his upper thigh. "But I do want to be partaking in some of that watermelon action or at least some pampering of my own. That was sweet by the way," I spoke of my mom's gift certificate.

"Mrs. Faulkner," Finn called out toward the kitchen. "Maybe you can wrap up some of those cookies to go. We want to make it safely before any more snow hits."

I smirked and ran up the stairs to get my packed bag. I was ready to get out of that horrible house of memories. I was ready to escape back to the place where I had been reborn. And I was so ready to do it with that man.

CHAPTER FOURTEEN

After Finn made a quick stop to drop our bags off at the alumni center/motel, we drove into the main part of campus. It was as if time stood still. Not that we had been gone that long, but in ways, it felt like a lifetime. Probably even more so for Finn as his life had changed way more dramatically than mine in the time since graduation.

When Finn started singing the Beatle's "There are Places I Remember" song that was so apropos, I asked, "Did you have that planned?"

Quietly laughing, "No. Lyrics just pop into my head. You should be glad I don't spew them off as often as they do."

"Why? Would I be hearing a lot of lyrics about a crazy or bitchy woman?"

"No." He laughed and reached over to toss my hair. "Look, we're here." He put the car in park in front of the science building.

Although bitterly cold, the snow had stopped. So, we got out and did a quick lap of the buildings immediately in that area. The first ones that we came across were the freshman dorms. I never resided in those since I transferred in. Finn said the freshman boys' dorms were so gross that it made fraternities look like the Mr. Clean model home. Hormonal boys on their own for the first time? No doubt, I thought. Across the way was the main building where a majority of the classes were held. Finn and I had taken a couple classes together in that building. One was an English lit class that I barely scraped by in, and the other a writing class that we both seemed to enjoy. Then there was the library.

"Finn, that's where I first met you," I said almost childlike.

"The library? I don't think I even stepped foot in that library the whole time I was here."

"Oh, I'm sure you had to for some class. But, no, that's where I was waiting for Olivia and Sam to pick me up the night your band was playing."

"Yeah. Why *were* you at the library? That had to be like a Friday or Saturday night."

"Oh, geez, never mind."

He pulled me close to his side. "That," he said, turning us both around to look at the snow-covered grassy area in front of the science building. "is the last place I saw you on campus."

"You remember that?" I knew I did. It was ingrained in my brain—his graduation, he and Audrey looking so happy, so ready for their life.

"Yeah. Of course." He sounded sentimental until he concluded with, "You gave me a McDonald's gift card. Awesome!"

"When was the last time you were at a Micky D's?" I joshed.

"You'd be surprised, Rox. Those shamrock shakes come out…I'm first in line—double fisted, every year."

We got back in the car then and drove up the hill to where my old dorm and Finn's fraternity were nestled amongst other residences. Because it was the winter holiday break, there were only a couple cars in the parking lot where traditionally the lot had been packed beyond capacity. Finn parked close to my former dorm and opened his door to exit.

"We're getting out?" I asked what I guess was obvious at that point.

"Yeah. Don't you want to go inside?"

"Ah, sure. I just thought it would be locked. Do you think anyone is staying over during the break?"

"I got the key, Lar," he said, now out of the Jeep and leaning in to talk with me.

"Oh, sorry, Rock Star." I grabbed his Christmas gifts that I had placed in the back seat. "What? Did you buy the building too? The campus?"

"Knock it off. No. The manager gave me the key. You could have gotten it too. You're alum. I just didn't want you to freeze your cute little behind off any more than necessary."

"Cute, huh?" I asked, shutting the passenger door and shaking my tail feathers at him. "At least you're not singing, 'Baby's Got Back.'"

Finn laughed. "C'mon, let's go step into the past." He opened the front door with ease. We walked into the foyer of the split entry, and Finn immediately bounded up the stairs. "Aren't you coming up?" he questioned when I did not instantly follow him.

"Yeah," I said taking the steps, in contrast, at a slower pace.

The place seemed cold and desolate. I'm sure the heat was probably set at a low temperature considering no one was most likely staying there over break. I stood at the tip of the stairs as Finn peered around, looking in the living area and the cubbies.

"Same painting, huh? Same sofa?"

"Uh, I think," I responded. "Some things are different, though."

"Well, you are for one thing."

"Me? I guess."

"You weren't like a lot of the other girls. You always

seemed so realistic and pure."

"Huh!" If I had something in my mouth, I probably would have choked—the teenage pregnant slut being called pure.

"But at the same time sassy. That part hasn't changed." He smiled. "I mean, you wouldn't open up to anyone. I know why now. But your self-confidence is so nice to see. It makes you even more beautiful."

In a lot of ways, I agreed. I had grown. For sure. But I think he saw my confidence and beauty because he brought that out in me.

"What's up?" he asked when I hadn't given any conversational feedback.

"It's this place."

Finn was instantly concerned. "Should we have not come here? You should have said so."

"No, no. I guess I just didn't realize how different I was—how closed off I was. I thought I just moved on when I started school here. This was really my re-bound place, though. I think I only started feeling more at ease that last year right before all you guys graduated."

"That was a crazy time." Finn sat down on the sofa, and I joined him.

"This brings back memories."

"Mmmm, it does." He squinted his eyes at me before saying, "So, you're going to stick with the story that you didn't know I wanted to go out with you back then. Sitting here on this sofa, you are going to stick with that?"

So there was no doubt. He did remember. He remembered that night on that very same sofa in college. He remembered kissing me and what he said.

"No. I …I did, but only then…that night. Well… after. But, Finn, honestly, it's what I told you before. I didn't trust that anything good could happen to me and, if it did, I didn't think I deserved it not after…." I didn't need to vocalize it. We both knew what I was referring to. "And because of that, when I denied it, denied you, and you didn't pursue, I knew that was the case. I knew you didn't mean it, and I knew no one ever would. I was unlovable for all kinds of reasons." It was a little bit of the way I felt after Wyatt's party and CMA night, but I shouldn't have. I knew that now. I needed to believe in Finn's mantra—trust. And I did. Because of him.

"God, Lar, that's not true." He touched the side of my face ever so gently. "I was scared, too, you know. I didn't want to be rejected. If I had known then what I know now…. I wish we would have talked back then. God, it would have been so different. We wasted so much time." Perhaps realizing the conversation was getting much too serious for what we intended the whole trip to be, Finn switched topic gears while lifting his eyebrows. "You don't want to talk right now, do you?"

Knowing exactly what he was thinking, I played along. "You don't have the key to my old room, by chance, do you?"

"No." He laughed. "I did try, though."

"I bet you did."

"You set then? Want to go?"

"Sure. But before we do, I thought this would be a good place to give you your Christmas gifts."

"I was wondering how long you were going to torture me by carrying those around." He smiled reaching for the bag in my hand.

"Fine. I can take it back," I teased, shifting the bag away from his hands.

"Oh, no!"

"It's not really that big of a deal." I looked at him pointedly. "It's not a Jeep."

"Geez." He exhaled shaking his head. "Can I have it already? I love gifts," he added sounding like a little boy. Once I handed the bag to Finn, he pulled out the two wrapped boxes. "Does it matter which one I open first?"

"No. No, I guess not." I was suddenly nervous. I wanted him to like the gifts so much. I hoped that he thought the same things I did when picking them out. "One is more sentimental, and one is more practical, I guess. Take your pick."

Finn looked at me as if to gauge which one I really wanted him to open first. When I didn't react to his inquisitive look, he said, "I guess I will go practical first?"

"The small box, then."

"Hmmm. The small box. I would have guessed the other way." He took a second to smile at me and then tore through the paper in record speed.

Before he could give me any kind of reaction, I explained, "It's a dual-time zone watch. You can program it so it says the time you are currently in and another time somewhere else. I thought"—I paused ever so briefly—"it might come in handy if you were on tour or, I don't know, some other reason."

"Like telling Tennessee time and New York time?" He recalled the phone call before our un-official first date at Eoin's restaurant. "And not calling you too late on a work night."

I raised the corner of my lips in a soft smile. "Like that."

"And this isn't the sentimental gift?"

"No."

"I love you. You know that, right?"

The pitter-patters in my chest were an instantaneous reaction to his declaration. "I do know that," I admitted. "But it's nice to hear."

Those three words strung together had yet to come from either one of us. We had texted x's and o's and wrote heart symbols, but "I love you" was still out there in the vast unknown. In fact, the phrase was pretty much an unknown my whole life.

And I said it then, more freely than I ever thought possible. "I love you too, Finn."

I thought he was going to kiss me then as he leaned in. But instead, Finn rested his forehead against mine and placed my hands over his heart. We stared at each other for a sentimental, loving beat or two.

Not wanting to get too emotional, I said, "I'm glad you like your gift. Go ahead, open the other."

Finn went for the bigger box. Either because it was marked "Fragile" or because he was apprehensive on the sentimental aspect, he opened this one more slowly. When he got to the actual gift, he started to laugh openly. "Is this yours?"

"I guess we were both going down memory lane with our gifts, huh?" I replied.

"Why are you giving me your lava lamp?"

I paused for a second and then spoke with sincerity, "Because I don't have to put it on anymore. Right? It's only for you."

He put my gift on the coffee table in front of us and took my face in his hands. "You're not going to blow me off on this sofa again, are you?"

In response, and as if I were transported back in time, I shook my head slowly, in awe of him and of how far we had come to be back there. It wasn't a sloppy, semi-awkward wet, drunk, college kiss this time but a series of soft, feathery, loving movements of his lips on mine. When I looked at him, I saw that his emotions had taken hold. A couple tears trailed on his check via his sensitive slate-colored eyes. I wondered if it was a reaction to my gift or reliving my rejection all over again from so many years ago. Regardless, it was based, no doubt, on the foundation of love.

Grabbing the gifts in one hand and my hand in his other, Finn led me down the stairs. I paused to take one last look before leaving. Even though it was cold and ghost-like quiet, the old and new memories of that building brought resounding warmth to my heart. And the surprise at our next locale made it overflow even more.

***

"Close your eyes."

"Close my eyes? Finn…what?"

"Humor me, please."

I closed my eyes, but I also took his hand first. I trusted him implicitly not to steer me wrong, but there would always be that fear of the unknown embedded in me. Plus, admittedly, I just liked the feel of our hands intertwined. I heard the door unlock and felt myself being guided into the motel room. When Finn told me I could once again reclaim my sight, I discovered in front of us, yes, a bed, desk, closet, armoire, etc., but there was also a fully decorated live Christmas tree. It was beyond beautiful.

I turned to Finn who now had on a Santa hat. "What is all of this?"

"It's Christmas…our Christmas."

I went to the tree and examined the popcorn-and-cranberry string woven around the branches. I saw an ornament with my name on it. I saw the lights sparkling like the stars on the night of Wyatt's birthday party. And beneath the tree was a toy train encircling the base.

"This is unbelievable," I acknowledged. "When? Who?" I didn't know what question to ask first.

"Wyatt and I strung the popcorn, and mom had extra lights in the attic. The manager had a tree ready and set things up pretty quickly, huh?"

"That's why you had that second suitcase."

"Yep."

"I thought you were just being some kind of diva," I joked.

He laughed. "Check out the chair. There's something for you on it."

Upon examination, I found a plate of half-eaten cookies and an empty glass of what must have been milk. I smiled and then picked up the envelope next to it with my name on it.

The letter inside read:

Dear Lara,

Everyone here in the North Pole has watched all year long and agrees with me that you have been such a good girl. I am very proud of you. I know some days have been difficult, but no one could ask for a better kid in the whole world. Well, Rudolph needs to be fed. Keep up the good work.

"Yes, Lara, there is a Santa Claus," Finn said reciting the famous line from the *Times* reply to Virginia.

"This is so sweet," I barely got it out, still in awe of the scene in front of me.

"My dad wrote it for you," he smiled.

"Just like when you were kids," I recalled him telling me the fact that Nola still believed until age twelve and Finn, although younger, figured it out but didn't give up their father's ruse.

"Yep. I'm glad you like it." Finn sat down on the chair. "Come sit," he said patting his lap. "We need to get a picture of you with Santa."

"Perfect," he said. "There's always someone crying in the Santa photos."

Wiping the tear away, I said, "The Jeep was extravagant and thoughtful but this, this, this right here, is beyond words. I don't know what to say."

"You already did…when you told me you loved me."

Right answer, I thought. "Maybe Santa needs a little ho, ho, ho for all his hard work?" I lightened the sentimental mood.

"Are you being a naughty little girl?" Finn's eyebrows raised as his hand fell a little farther down on my bottom.

"Rudolph isn't the only one with a red light, Santa," I teased and, as he pressed the phone for the photo, I kissed him, never wanting the magic of the holidays and us to end.

CHAPTER FIFTEEN

Because Finn's schedule was pretty relaxed in the month of January, he decided to stay at his Manhattan residence that month, starting directly after our drive back to New York in the Jeep. We immediately got into the pattern of staying over at each other's homes during the weekends, with him sometimes extending his stay at mine. And we learned each other's intricacies, habits, and routines—the good, the bad, and the ugly.

I was a two-day-a-week exercise kind of gal. One was my Pilates class on Saturday mornings and the second was walking with colleagues after work. If it was a weekend at the penthouse, though, I would miss the Pilates class. Finn was much more diligent with his exercise and health care routines. He ran nearly every day he was at my place and did the machines when he was at his. In addition, he meditated every morning while I showered. He claimed the meditation process helped him form lyrics in his head, and he would often grab his acoustic guitar and strum a few chords while I made breakfast.

Finn was constantly on his phone or tablet dealing with something. It seemed more defined than the other times I had been with him. But he was with me. And it wasn't like he didn't pay me attention. Besides, I had plenty of my own work projects to do when he was occupied with his.

Minor things, like him getting rid of his scented aftershave and me getting used to him chewing on ice cubes, were worth it in order to enjoy the beauty of being together. A simple thing like having an arm wrapped around me when I cringed or jumped at a violent movie made me feel loved and secure. And the fact that I had someone to make the bed with or kiss me goodbye before I headed out was unparalleled. They all provided me with an inner peace I hadn't realized wasn't there before Finn.

It was toward the end of January when we got into heavier topics. Finn and I were lying in his bed dreading, once again, his inevitable return to Tennessee. I had my head on his chest just listening to the beat of his heart when he spoke my name.

"Lara?"

"Yeah?" When Finn didn't counter, I looked up at him.

He met my eyes. "I know you maybe don't want to talk about it…."

"What? What's up?"

After another slight pause, Finn asked what was on his mind, "With everything that you went through, would you ever want to have kids?"

My sigh was audible for I had thought of that same question plenty of times. But it was one I never quite had the answer to. Plus, it was a heavy topic especially on the night before he was leaving. I rested my head back on his chest so I didn't have to look directly at him.

"You know, after I gave him up, I couldn't imagine it. Never. Ever. I gave up a child. Why should I be allowed to have a kid of my own? And watching these parents day in and day out manage—try to manage—parenthood, I realize how truly difficult it is. I give them all the credit in the world. I couldn't do it—not by myself. It was definitely the right decision at the time for me," I answered, thinking that was the end. But when Finn didn't say anything, implying that he wanted more of a direct answer, I looked up at him and started talking again. "Finn, I don't know. I would have to know that everything was right." I sat up a little more after another round of silence. "Why? What brought this up?"

"Birth control," he spoke plainly but then instantly explained, because I think he could sense the terror that filled me immediately. "Don't worry…I'm with you. I was just wondering, y'know, if maybe you would consider going on the pill…if I could skip the condoms."

"Oh." I realized the implication of a commitment and other topics not previously broached that switching birth control meant.

Finn looked at me candidly. "I want to be with you, Lara. This isn't just a reunion thing. You know that, right? I love you. And," he jested, "I mean, I already conceded my side of the bed to you."

I smiled. He had. He had noticed almost immediately how I preferred being farther away from the bedroom door. It was the same feeling of the restaurant chair arrangement. And Finn, playing the macho protector role, chivalrously made the door side his side…not that we weren't basically always intertwined.

"I know," I answered honestly on all accounts. And then, because the conversation was the most serious we had had in a while, I added sarcasm, "It's…I don't think they make birth control in gummy form."

"You and those damn multi-vitamins." He went along with my teasing, probably sensing my unease. "If I could take it with mine, I—"

"I know you would." I smiled and said, "No. I'll go on birth control. I know it will be easier all the way around." And then I said what had really crossed my mind when the topic of protection came up—his past with women. "I was just thinking…we never really had the talk. You know, you pretty much know my background."

With lament, Finn replied, "You don't want to know."

"Maybe I don't. But I think I should."

"Lara, please." His face scrunched displaying his unease. "I don't know a number."

"You don't know a number?" Maybe I *didn't* want to know.

"I suppose…I could give you a number—rough. This conversation is just never a good one for any couple."

"Probably not, but only one of the two has been all around the country, playing concerts in front of all kinds of girls—front row, arm reaching, backstage girls," I challenged.

"And I rocked hard in the beginning," he admitted. "I wanted to be liked. The drugs—"

"The backseat blowjobs." I tried to sound unfazed while posing the question that had been lingering in my mind since Thanksgiving.

"Yeah." To his credit, he looked at me dead on. "All one-sided by the way. Those girls…so willing. And I never had to do anything for them. Sad." His pause was hardly long enough to register. "But you know I am not that guy and only fell for a little bit. My life now is pretty mundane."

"Ha!" I spit out.

"Okay, maybe not mundane but not rock star cliché. Would it change anything to know all the details?"

"No," I answered, and it was the truth. I loved him. Period.

"Then all that's important is that you know I was safe…always." This time the pause was longer as if he really wanted that fact to register in my brain. "If you want me to prove that to you—"

"No. I trust you." More than anyone…ever. "I respect that it's in your past."

"Yeah?"

"Were you in love with any of them?" The question came out before I had time to think it over. I wanted to know. Yet, it made me appear so jealous…which I was. I just didn't want him to know.

"No."

"No? That was an awfully quick answer."

"There wasn't anything to think about," he said plainly.

"But Audrey…."

"I thought I loved Audrey, yes. We talked about that."

We had. No need to recut into sealed wounds. No need for either of us.

"Eva?" I ventured.

"Iva?" he laughed emphasizing the long 'I' in the beginning of her name.

"Oh, Iva was it?" I joked, but was intensely interested in his answer. Audrey and Iva were the only two I had met in person and, somehow, that brought my jealousy to an elevated level.

"You know darn well what her name is. You're one of the best people I know when it comes to remembering names."

I laughed. "I-va, then."

"God, Lara, no. We didn't even sleep together. Mundane." When he saw the undisguised look of shock on my face, he smiled in a knowing way. "Not to say it wasn't heading that direction. I just got 'Hot for Teacher.'" He then broke into the lyrics of the Van Halen classic while playing air guitar.

"Okay, okay," I half-laughed, half-yelled while playfully hitting him until he stopped singing and swallowed me into his arms.

"All right?" he asked more genuinely.

"Yeah," I relented.

"So, you're my girl, huh?" A huge, relaxed smile spread across his face.

"Uh…I guess. Yeah," I answered, liking that a conversation, which had started out semi-tense, had turned into one which confirmed a new level of commitment between Finn and me. His girl. God, I loved that.

"Yep. You're my girl." He seemed to read my thoughts

with confidence. Then, after a slight pause, he wrinkled his brow and, looking at me, said, "But, you know, there might be a problem. In order to be my girl, there's a requirement."

"What?"

"My girl has to dance."

"Finn…." I tilted my head in mock exasperation. He knew my hatred of dancing.

"What? What do you have against dancing?"

"I'm not good at it. It's sort of like me running. Can't do it. I look ridiculous. I hate people watching me."

"Everybody looks ridiculous," he said.

"No. *Everybody*"—I emphasized the word while poking the master of stage presence in the chest— "does not. I'm not coordinated enough. I can't jump rope by myself. I even have a hard time doing a jumping jack." I said with exasperation, nonetheless, the honest truth.

"Really? Really, Lara? A jumping jack? You can do that."

"Seriously. I really have to concentrate and then can only do a few. If it was just hands or just feet, I'd be fine. I'm not coordinated. Really."

Finn shook his head, obviously still in disbelief. "I'm gonna get you to dance," he said with determination and, after a moment, did something about it. Sliding his legs once again into his boxers, he threw his previously discarded red T-shirt at me. "Here. Get up."

I watched as he went over and adjusted his tunes on the speakers. After a few button pressings, soft slow music filled the room. He came back over, physically put his T-shirt over my head, seeing as I hadn't, and stretched his hand out to mine. Willing me to get out of bed, he pulled me onto the makeshift dance floor better known as the bedroom's hardwood.

"No. Really. I can't," I protested but, regardless, found myself directly in front of him.

"Lara, there's no one here, and we're just going to slow

dance. You just need to move with me. I know you can do that," he said while suggestively looking me up and down.

"I hate dancing," I tried again while tugging at the bottom of his shirt that I was wearing. It hung just below my buttocks.

"Maybe you never had the right partner."

Liking that thought, I gave in. Facing Finn, I stretched my left arm out to his shoulder while reaching my right arm up for him to grasp. He had the most incredulous look on his face. In one fell swoop, he swiftly tugged me into his taut body and fixed my hands around his neck. He then placed his barely touching fingers on my lower back, tantalizingly near my bottom.

Now, snug up against him, I looked into his eyes. He smiled and softly kissed me before moving to the beat of the music. I don't know how, but, miraculously, I was moving right along with him—no stepping on feet or moving the wrong way. And we were moving. Finn was even turning me in different directions. It was at that point that I realized it wasn't necessarily the dancing that I hated. It had always been the intimacy—the trust. And with Finn, that was not an issue at all.

Dipping me dramatically at the end, he said, "Definitely a dancer."

"It was nice. But club dancing is still out of the question."

"We'll see." His words sounded like a challenge.

"So, can I be your girl?" I placed my hand over his heart.

"Definitely a dancer and definitely…definitely my girl."

***

"It's your brother." I showed her the caller ID on my phone.

Nola, who I had coincidentally run into in the grocery store parking lot, said, "Give him hell."

I pressed the button on the phone that would allow me to receive Finn's call, but I did not vocalize a response. Instead, I paced back and forth alongside the Jeep. That action was creating a purposeful frenzy-like state.

"Lara?" His voice carried across the line when mine hadn't.

But then I started. I tore right into him. And I didn't let up. "Your girl? Your girl, right? Isn't that what you said? Or are you living up to that rock star thing—a girl in every city?"

"Lar—" he started.

But, nope. I wasn't done. "She's the one that is beautiful. Younger. Prettier."

"Lara, stop!" he belted.

"You told me you loved me." I looked at Nola whose eyes grew wide and a little misty.

"Lara, shit!" I swear he was next to me the way his voice was right there in my ear. "Listen to me. Let me explain."

"No. I think those articles say it all." I referenced the entertainment feed that Nola and I had just seen on our phones—Finn kissing a blonde on her cheek at a club the night before. "Who is she? Some starlet? Maybe I should just go and take a kiss selfie with Ben Winthrop," I spoke of the television star.

Nola couldn't help it then. Sitting on the bumper of my car, she burst out laughing. It was a good thing, because I was nearly doubled over trying not to laugh myself. Plus, I really felt bad for Finn.

"Ben Win—" He was upset. "Who is that laughing?"

"It's your sister."

"Well, Nola knows very well—"

I let him off the hook. "I know it's a picture of your cousin, Finn. Nola told me she and her friends were in Nashville to celebrate her birthday. We were just messing with you."

"Ah, Jesus." He exhaled. "That is not funny."

"Sorry." But I laughed, anyway, as Nola's giggles got even louder.

"Where are you?"

"Grocery store parking lot."

"Well, you tell her she better stock up on snacks because she owes me big time."

When I relayed Finn's message to his sister, she yelled toward the phone, "Luv ya, Munch."

"And you?" His voice threatened me in a sexy way. "Ben Winthrop? Really? That's what does it for you?"

I smiled. "I think you know what, or who, does it for me, Cowboy."

Nola waved and walked toward her car as Finn kept talking. "You better know that's a right back at ya, Rox."

"I do."

"Lara, seriously, we might need to talk about this." His tone changed now to a subdued one.

I hit the release lock and climbed into the front of the Jeep. "I got back in the car. Your sister left."

"Tell me," he said in a calmer tone. "Tell me what you really thought when you saw it."

"My heart sank," I admitted that much, but not the part of how it reminded me of seeing Miller with that blonde all those years ago.

"Ah, shit." He exhaled. "Is that why you didn't pick up my call before?"

I did a quick glance at my phone. There was a missed call. But I hadn't seen or heard it.

"I had my phone off during Pilates class and then drove straight here. I just turned it back on and did my normal…."

"Your normal what?" he prompted when I stalled.

"Morning internet search of your name?" Did that come off a little stalkerish? I didn't mean it that way. I was just always thinking of him.

"Uh, right," he said as if he suspected. "Don't do that. I learned not to a long time ago." He paused ever so slightly. "And then you saw the photos?" he continued.

"Yeah. Right here in the grocery store parking lot. That's when Nola came out of the store." And saw me upset, but, again, I didn't add that. "So, she quickly explained."

"And you concocted your evil plan." I swear I could hear his head shaking. "But if Nola hadn't been there, and you didn't know it was Iriss," he spoke of his twenty-one-year-old cousin. "what would you have done?" He didn't wait for my reply, though. "Because this stuff happens. They just post without checking facts." I could hear the frustration regarding his chosen career and the lifestyle that went with it. "I don't want you to doubt anything. I want you to call me. I know that's hard."

"Trust," I said out loud, knowing he had nailed my normal go-to behavior. "I will. I might have a few choice words," I said in an easy manner, but there was some truth to it.

"I suspect you might—that you did. Just don't—" He stopped his sentence mid stride and then said my name. "Lara? I will *never*,"—he emphasized that word like his hand was on a stack of bibles—"ever cheat on you." I knew his own history with Audrey had a part in him saying those words, but I also knew he was just that kind of guy. "And even though I'm not into PDA and having the press up into my personal business, I don't want anyone second guessing who I'm with. I want them to know I'm with you. But I will protect your privacy like… well, even more than mine. Are you good with that?"

"So, you're saying I can be your girl but no paparazzi 24/7?"

"Yes."

"No deal, Murphy. I want the flashbulbs. I want to be a YouTube sensation." I tried a little levity in a conversation that had gotten very serious. Otherwise, when I eventually got into that food store, I would have looked like a tortured POW. "I want fakey people hitting me up on social media because I'm with you. I want—"

"You are impossible." He growled his laugh.

"No. You know I don't want any part of that. I want you," I said more seriously. "But I don't want anyone second guessing that, either. It's getting pretty hard to deny it at work, anyway."

"Then don't." I smiled at his answer and listened as he changed the subject. "Do you want to hear some good news?"

"You mean there's better news than you snuggling up with a younger chick in a nightclub?" I wiped at a damn solitary tear that had managed to find my face. I determined it was one of relief, though, and not a sad one.

"Yes!" he bellowed even though he knew I was joking. "Real news."

"What?"

"It's not that big of a deal, but the ACM noms were announced. I'm up for Male Vocalist of the Year."

"It's not that big of a deal!" I exclaimed, knowing this was a first for him and a major potential award.

"I mean, sure, it's an honor. But so is just getting to do what I do—sing my songs and have people enjoy the music."

"It's a big deal," I refuted.

"So is talking with you."

"Oh, brother."

He ignored my sarcastic reply. "I know it's only been a week, but I miss you."

Instead of just repeating the same truth back to him, I continued the lightheartedness. "And all my dance moves."

"And *all* your moves." I heard the seductive undertones in his voice. "I gotta go. The phone is burning up. God knows if it's about Iriss or the nom."

"I hope it's the latter."

"Eh, who cares. Just so you know the truth and are by my side, nothing else matters."

CHAPTER SIXTEEN

The doorman I was familiar with, Graham, was not at his post at the building that was home to Finn's penthouse. Another gentleman, with a uniform identical to Graham's, sat in his place. Needing him to key me up to Finn's private floor, I approached his desk and explained that Finn was expecting me.

The man pierced his eyes at me with intense scrutiny. "And you are?"

"Lara," I answered shifting my slumping bag more properly back onto my shoulder.

"And what's your business?" When I'm sure my face took on the puzzlement of my brain, he rephrased, "How do you know Mr. Murphy?"

"I'm…." I stumbled, not only because I wasn't used to an inquisition, but because I realized I had never said our status out loud. "I'm his girlfriend."

The doorman's eyes pierced again and looked at my bag. "I'll have to call Mr. Murphy and check."

"That's fine. Sure." I'm all for security.

"'Lara' you said?"

"Yeah. He'll know."

The man got on the phone, and looking at me the

entire time, dialed a number, waited, and then spoke into the phone, "Good evening, Mr. Murphy. I'm sorry to bother you, sir." He was so much more formal than Graham. "There's a Lara here to see you. She says she is your girlfriend." I could hear the doubt in his voice as if this was a ploy other women had tried, and then it dawned on me that it probably was. He listened for a minute longer and then before hanging up said, "Yep. I got it. I'll tell her, sir. Good bye." Topher—his name was embossed on his nametag—directed his next comment to me. "Mr. Murphy says you are not his girlfriend."

"Wha—?" I couldn't even manage to get the one-word question out it stunned me so much. Isn't that what we were classifying each other as? We had said we loved one another. He said he wanted everyone to know he was with me. I was his—

Before I could get any more distraught, I managed to refocus on Topher's continuing words. "He says you are his one and only love and that you are welcome any time."

I didn't realize how much Finn's relayed words had affected me until the elevator reached the top floor and I saw him propped against his door frame waiting. Upon seeing me, he immediately brought his thumb up to the corner of my eye. A tear must have pooled in the spot where my scar met my lashes.

"Beauty, what's wrong?" he asked now literally holding me at arm's length away.

"It's Valentine's Day, Finn. And there are weeks on end when I don't see you. I'm already a sure thing. You didn't need to have Topher say that."

Finn's belly shook in laughter more than his voice. "I wasn't trying to seal the deal. I just find 'girlfriend' so sixth grade. I want you to understand how much you mean to me."

"I think I do." I smiled up at him. "But I did kinda like when you called me 'your girl,'" I admitted.

"For sure," he replied. "'My girl' most definitely. That's

so much better than girlfriend." He brought his hands up to flank my face and kissed me. "Happy Valentine's Day, Lar. I love you like no other."

Geez, make me swoon, why don't you? "I love you too." I touched his face. "I'm so glad you're here. How was your flight?" I asked as he shut the door behind us and we moved farther into the penthouse.

"Fine." I felt his coarse fingertips put their talent to use as they rhythmically strummed all the way from my shoulder to my hand. "Are we really going to talk aviation or are we going to get to that sure thing comment?"

I couldn't help but burst out laughing. It had been a long day at work and an hour commute into Manhattan, but I was energized upon seeing him, especially knowing I had the next day—Friday—off and the whole weekend to spend with him. "You aren't even going to feed me?" I teased.

"Reservations are for later."

"Can I take a shower first? I like to put work away." Especially with all the winter sniffling going around in the building.

I could tell he was disappointed at the delay but relented with a tease of his own, "I'm just going to get you dirty again." A little jittery, he started pushing me up the staircase toward his master bedroom. "Hurry up, girl!"

"Okay, keep your pants on." I laughed.

"I'll try." He raised his eyebrows.

"I knew as soon as I said that…." I shook my head.

"Then why did you?"

I tucked my hands into the sides of Finn's casually loose, charcoal slacks so that I could purposefully feel his hips. "I'll just be a couple minutes."

"Good God. Go! Go!" He exhaled, urging me into the master bath.

I was no sooner in the shower than I heard movement on the other side. I slid the shower door open to see Finn in the bathroom shirtless and taking down his pants to expose his boxers. Finn caught my smile in the reflection of the mirror and turned to face me.

"I'm feeling a little dirty too. Maybe I can join you and hurry you along?"

"Somehow I don't think that will hurry me along," I said, gathering my wet hair away from my face.

"Okay by me." He nodded with a smirk, pulled down his boxers, and stepped into the shower next to me.

"Finn…" Damn I was hot, and it wasn't because of the shower water.

"God, I miss you when we're apart."

He took my face in his hands. We were both beyond ready. There was no foreplay needed after being with each other so often before and then being away from each other for so long.

"Me too," I agreed.

"Oh, shit."

"What?" I asked slightly alarmed.

"I…I need to get a flippin…." He was starting to back away, and I realized he was referring to a condom. In response to me pulling him closer, Finn cautioned, "Lara. Lara, no."

"Finn, it's fine," I soothed. "I've been on birth control for a couple of weeks. It's my Valentine's gift for you."

"For real? We're good?" I could hear the tension immediately drain from his voice.

"Yep. We're good," was all I could get out before he took me ardently against the shower wall.

"Oh, God," I cried out.

"Beauty, I can't get enough of you," he said as I purposefully grabbed onto his hips.

After rocking passionately for an extended time, Finn kissed me. And then we both collapsed onto the shower floor. I couldn't help but look at him for a minute or two in wonder and awe of our extremely hot, intense, love making. I was cradled in between his legs as he methodically and repeatedly continued to stroke my body.

I turned and kissed him gently. "Well, that was something."

"Yeah," he breathed out. "Thanks for my Valentine's gift."

"It was kinda for me too, wasn't it?" I admitted. "We can definitely do without those condoms."

Finn smiled. "You got the real deal now, Baby. All of me…real."

"That's all I want."

As cliché as it might have been, we actually went out for a fancy dinner on the holiday. I'm pretty sure Finn did it just for me as he knew I'd never had that experience. He reserved us an intimate table at an Italian restaurant. It was an attempt to keep our evening private—i.e. away from the media or fans. It worked for the most part. There were a few onlookers including two young girls who were bold enough to ask for an autograph and a selfie. I was surprised when Finn denied them. He was always good to his fans no matter what. But that evening he was curt insisting that some nights were sacred.

And then he had to leave again. He went back to Tennessee to do, among other things, a Make-a-Wish benefit and more prep work for his upcoming summer tour. It wasn't any easier seeing him leave, but with each time he did, I was more certain that we were solid. I was more assured of his love and commitment to us.

**

I'm, in general, a cautious person. Life had kind of made me that way. So, a knock on my apartment door a little before ten p.m. on a Friday night in the beginning of March made my pulse quicken and my bad thoughts radar go up.

I lowered the volume of the television set and then turned it off completely, trying to remain as quiet as possible. I was hoping whoever it was would go away.

After all, they couldn't see me. The door was solid and there were no windows. But the knock happened again. And I froze again.

When "Roxanne" suddenly came blaring out of my phone, I both jumped and swore because it had scared me so much. But that song meant the caller was Finn. So I was happy to pick it up and talk to him while I silently willed the stranger at the door to go away.

"Hey, Cowboy," I spoke quietly into the phone.

"Hi, yourself. Why are you whispering?"

I debated whether to tell him or not. I didn't want him to worry miles and miles away. His protectiveness would probably have me calling the police.

"I'm not." I semi-lied but, nevertheless, didn't speak up any more.

"So, you're not trying to avoid the person at the door? The person who just flew in to see you?"

"What?" What! "Finn?"

The knock at the door came again. This time, I practically ran to it and opened it up. Even all covered with a knitted baseball cap, jacket, and scarf, he was alluring.

"Surprise," he rang out and encapsulated me into his body.

"Seriously," I said, rubbing my cheek up against his five o'clock shadow. "What's going on?"

"I was missing you something fierce. So I tried doing meditation, but I just couldn't concentrate. I decided there was only one thing to do about it." He took my hands in his.

"God, what it must be like," I said, thinking how us mere mortals couldn't simply hop on a plane at any given moment.

"Missing you? It's downright unbearable."

"Finn, you know what I mean."

"You surprised?" He grinned his contagious smile.

"I should say so."

"Happy surprised?"

"Of course. Ecstatic surprised."

"Then are you going to let me in?"

The moment we were inside, not in a public hallway, he pulled me into his arms and kissed me. It was a fantastic mixture of hunger and comfort. And it was what I thought epitomized our relationship.

"I missed you too. And I'm so glad you're here," I said as he took off his outerwear and we made our way to my sofa.

"It's kinda hard. I have so much going on right now. And I have to leave tomorrow night, but it's already worth it." He smiled softly and noted my pajama attire. "You look like you're ready for bed."

"I am," I said simply and waited for his response.

"How 'bout sofa?" His eyes widened and narrowed quickly.

I leaned back length-wise and he planked above me. He made love to me in a quick, needy, powerful way. It was a little different than ever before. But not necessarily in a bad way—just definitely different.

Afterward, with Finn's lips resting on the top of my head, I said, "Wow."

"Uh-huh."

"Now I really am ready for bed. C'mon." I pulled gently on his arm, ready to get up. "Let's get some sleep."

"I'm still pretty wound."

"You're not tired?" I asked, astonished.

"No," he said. But when I looked, his appearance didn't quite mirror his words. "I'll hold you for a while. I don't want to let you go," he spoke close to a plead. "I want to hold you like this all night and maybe a repeat performance in the morning?" On the last two words, he skimmed his hand along my side.

I was amazed that he could still have that energy. Finn had been going non-stop with his career…with his life. I hadn't asked him to fly up to see me, but I had welcomed it whole-heartedly. Perhaps, though, I was being selfish at his expense.

"Make sure you are taking care of yourself," I spoke up. "I know you love me. You don't have to fly back all the time. I don't want you to burn out."

"Okay," he burst out loudly and then added a little more softly, "I'm fine. I'm fine, Lara."

I wanted to believe those words. After all, when he toured, he had to be constantly on the move and up late all the time. But he wasn't on tour, and he shouldn't need to feel like he was. I decided to trust, if not his words, the security of his arms wrapped decisively around me and close my eyes.

***

Finn was back in the New York area by mid-March. He spent the first two nights in the city doing work related things, which I guess involved going to a private event at a night club the first night and then hitting the scene with friends the following night. He had texted me that evening, wishing that I was there with him. But that wasn't even remotely in the realm of possibilities on a work night and miles away.

He was at my place on St. Patrick's Day and really wanted to go out since he was brought up in an all-Irish family. I was absolutely, completely exhausted from an exceptionally tough week at work due to a power outage and a cold front that had everyone cooped up indoors. So, I told Finn to go out by himself. There was an Irish bar not too far from my apartment where he could hang. I told him if he wanted to drink, he could call me, and I would come pick him up. But, instead, he persuaded Will to go along with him.

Luckily, Will drove because it was around one in the morning when I heard Finn use my key and stumble into the apartment. His entrance was not graceful nor, consequently, quiet. Therefore, I was awoken from my slumber.

"The drive-thru would have been open. I just wanted a Shamwalk Shake," Finn slurred to Will as I entered the living room.

"Sorry, Lara." Will tried meeting my eyes and not my innocent, non-suggestive, full length pant pajamas. "I was just going to try to get him settled on the sofa."

"Beau-ty!" Finn started stumbling in my direction.

I laughed not having seen Finn drunk since college. I had noticed how he seemed to engulf black coffee like it was going out of business, but, for the most part, managed his alcohol. It made me wonder if that was a part of his drug recovery. Certainly, that particular moment wasn't the time to ask, though.

"Baby, you have a good time?" I said instead.

"Beauty," he repeated while sloppily pushing my hair away from my face.

"I'm going." Driver Will was, thankfully, a sober contrast to Finn.

"We'll see you tomorrow," I said referring to Kelsea's birthday party.

"Yeah. Won't expect you too early." Will chuckled and exited.

"Beauty," Finn said draping his arm around me. He was a one-word man.

"Finn, c'mon, let's get you to bed." I laughed.

"Lara, oh, Beauty, I love you. I really do."

"You are so drunk," I said as we made our way to the bedroom.

"Lar, Lara, when am I ever going to see you drunk?"

"Well, it's not going to happen tonight," I said referencing the same phrase I had said all those years ago on the college sofa.

"You are such a tease." He smiled a huge smile and sank onto the bed.

"Finn…." It was my kind, warning voice.

"Roxy." It was his playful, sexy voice.

"That's not going to happen tonight either." I climbed under the covers.

Finn joined me. "C'mon."

"You need to get some sleep." I pecked him on the lips. "I love you," I said, turning and curving my back into him so we both could get some rest.

***

It wasn't exactly a restful night, though. At three a.m., I felt more than heard Finn come back to bed. I hadn't known when he had left it in the first place.

"What's wrong?" I murmured.

"Nothing. Bathroom. You awake?"

"Not really."

"Okay," I swore he sighed before I drifted back to sleep.

***

But it was just a couple hours later when I woke again to Finn kissing my neck. "Mmmm." When I adjusted my eyes to the dark, I turned to face him. "What time is it?"

"I love you, Lara."

Now, glancing at the bedside clock, I said, "Finn, it's like five in the morning."

"I couldn't sleep. I tried."

"Finn, Baby, are you all right?" I brushed his face in concern, not realizing that he would actually be warm to the touch. "You're a little warm."

"I'm fine. It's the comforter. And you always think I'm hot with those damn cold feet of yours." Before I could rally a comeback, he said, "Just be with me. Please. You're what I need. I need you. I want you. You are my reason…." His voice faded on purpose and he kissed me like he was taking my breath from my body to resuscitate his own. He lifted my top, placed his lips right between my breasts, and cupped his hand in between my thighs. He knew that drove me wild. He knew I couldn't resist. And knowing that was what he needed for whatever reason at that moment, I met his desire and we made love.

CHAPTER SEVENTEEN

The pattern of his behavior continued the next few days minus the extreme drinking. Finn, who decided to stay at my place for the remainder of his New York stay, seemed to be suffering from insomnia as he was up nearly all night every night. I would wake to find him playing a game on his tablet or writing lyrics. When I asked him if there was something he was worried about, he said there was just so much going on inside his head that it was keeping him awake.

As loved and as wanted as he made me feel, having Finn stay with me that week was exhausting. Finn at least got to sleep in during the day while I was at work. Although, I don't know if he ever did. He would text me periodically throughout the day saying he was just checking in. And he always seemed to be energized and working on something when I would get home.

That Wednesday, after work, we headed into Manhattan. We were staying at Finn's place in the city, and the following morning we were off to North Carolina. Finn had a concert there that not only coordinated with my four-day spring break, but it was also fairly close to where Lane lived. So I was able to go with Finn and visit with my brother. Seeing Lane and having him and Finn get a chance to finally connect couldn't have thrilled me more.

"By the way, when did you become such a clean freak?" I joked as we walked along Central Park having just finished a delicious dinner at Eoin's restaurant. Hand in hand, I couldn't help but think how far we had come since that similar October stroll.

"What are you talking about?" Finn replied.

"My place. I come home and don't know where anything is. Couldn't even set the lunch bag down for a sec without you cleaning it out and putting it away."

"I don't know how you can stand it. It was driving me crazy."

"I can keep one thing organized and right now that is work. Maybe if I wasn't so busy entertaining you"—I bumped my hip into his so he would know I was joking—"I would have time to clean."

"You do entertain me, Beauty." He brushed his lips on my hair.

I let go of his hand and, instead, wrapped it around his opposite hip, drawing us even closer as we walked. He smiled at my touch and we continued in silence for a couple blocks until we reached Finn's building. He said he just needed to go in and grab the tickets in the lobby. Finn had arranged for Broadway seats, and we had just about enough time to pull it off. I decided to wait for him out front just to soak up the fresh night air. Brisk, yet still, the weather was on the brink of deciding whether to finally turn to spring or not.

The millisecond Finn entered the building via the glass revolving doors, a woman approached me. "Lara?" she asked.

I hadn't been making direct eye contact but, with her acknowledgement of my name, I, of course, did. "Yes?" I had no idea who this woman was and was desperately searching my brain for recognition when she identified herself by name and position—a reporter.

"I know you've been seeing Finn Murphy and was wondering if I could just ask you a few questions."

Wow! That was a first. When I had been out with Finn, there were instances with press and a few pictures of our hands intertwined. But if there were ever any questions, they were always directed at him, and that didn't even happen that often. Finn wasn't a TMZ fav, thank goodness. Fans, yes. Press, not so much. They remained at press junket-like events for the most part. Finn didn't give them reason to branch out. So, therefore, I never had to deal with it either.

I told the reporter that I really didn't want to talk with anyone. The music industry, and all that went with it, was Finn's thing, not mine. To her credit, she wasn't pushy. I've been in numerous retail stores where the commission-focused salespeople had been far, far worse.

"I understand," she continued. "It's just, it's not music industry exactly. He's been spotted around town, hitting the clubs—not like him. And we couldn't help but notice you weren't there."

Oh, boy. Here we go with the same scenario as when they took the picture of him with his cousin. I knew better, though.

I laughed, not wanting anyone or anything to distract me from my man or our nice evening out. "Not with a 5:30 wake up call," I started only to be interrupted by Finn entering the scene.

"And you are?" Finn looked at the woman as he asked the question. But I suspect he already knew the answer by the way he protectively positioned his body in front of mine. Before she could even fully announce her credentials, Finn's gaze turned to a glare. "You need to back off."

"We were just—" she started.

"And now you're not." He seemed suddenly icy.

"Finn," I tried while reaching out for his hand. "It's all right. She really wasn't—"

Pulling the keys from his pocket, he interrupted me and said, "Meet me in the penthouse."

I searched his eyes wondering what had happened to the jovial man who had just been walking down the sidewalk moments before. I needed him back. "Come with me," I urged.

"Lara," I heard the warning in his voice. "Go." He pinned his eyes on me while fitting the keys and not his palm in mine.

Not wanting to cause a scene, I did as I was instructed. But I was far from being happy about it. As I went through the rotating door, I heard Finn start to tell the reporter that she had no right stalking his place of residency or, for that matter, his girl. I looked back only once while I stood waiting for the doorman to key me up on the elevator to the private penthouse.

Because the elevator arrived and traveled quickly, I was up and unlocking Finn's door before I knew it. I immediately walked out to the wrap-around deck, needing the air. I needed to breathe.

It was only a matter of minutes until I heard the front door open. But it was enough time to let the steam in my brain rise to the top. It was enough time to replay in my mind what the reporter had said and how Finn acted, particularly toward me. I listened as I heard Finn close the door and sigh. I walked back indoors to meet him in the living area.

"Lara? Are you all—"

It was my turn to interrupt. "If you want me to go," I said, referring to his demand downstairs. "Then fine, I'll go." And I proceeded, pissed, to walk past him toward the door.

He reached for my arm clearly confused. "What? What's this about?"

"It doesn't matter."

"Obviously, it does."

The way he softly touched my hand made me at least

stop and decide to continue. "What matters is the way you reacted down there."

"What?"

"You should be used to that—the press and the fans. What happened?" I admit it, the sad tiredness suddenly in his eyes was breaking me down a bit.

"I am. But you aren't, and you shouldn't have to be. I told you I wanted to protect you from all that. You don't need your life totally under the microscope like mine."

"It's all a part of being with you. I've accepted that. And pretty well, I may add. I accept staying in and not going out as much because of the fan recognition. I accept that, when we do, there will probably be photos taken and you have to ward off girls. And I accept that because I love you."

"And I want them to know that I love you too, but then draw the line." He exhaled. "I know it's hard being in my life."

"It's not, as long as it's a life I know about, right?" I didn't mean it to sound as accusatory as it came out, but it did, anyway.

"Lara," he said slowly as I heard the anger start to creep back in. But it wasn't directed at me. "What did she say?"

"Nothing. Really," I answered honestly. "She wanted me to tell her…tell her what is going on with you. Why you were out…and without me."

"What? Christ! Is that what she said?" His hands wrung through his hair, mirroring the frustration in his voice. "See? You shouldn't have to put up with that. None of my personal life is their business. You know I've always felt that way."

"I know how you feel about kissing me."

"Lara…." Exasperated. "Please. I love kissing you. If you're really upset about the PDA thing, tell me that. Christ, we can go to Times Square, and I'll make sure it's all Kiss Cam."

I couldn't help but do a one breath laugh. He wasn't trying to be funny. He was worked up and so was I, but, regardless, it was kind of funny and sweet.

"You know you have open access to me," he continued. "You know where I've been, where I go. It's not their business. Even if you're not with me, you're in here. Always." He placed his hand to his heart—part hurt, part concern, part upset.

"Finn, I know that. That's not it."

"What? What then?"

"It was your reaction. You got so…." I paused trying to pinpoint what I had been witness to. But because I was upset myself, my scholarly vocabulary words failed me. So, I settled on, "Different."

"No. No, I didn't. Yeah, I was upset. But…." His voice drifted off, most likely because he knew he couldn't deny that I was speaking the truth.

"Finn, you were mad. You still are. You're like bouncing and your fists," I said, looking at them clearly clenched.

"Jesus, Lara, I am upset, and I think I have a right to be. I don't want you hurt." He unballed his hands, but I could see it was a struggle.

"You're the only one who can do that. Treating me like an insubordinate child. Shutting me out like that downstairs."

And, just like that, one tear turned into a downright rain storm. I was bawling. I couldn't handle someone being suddenly angry with me and not giving me an explanation as if they didn't care. I knew it was because of my inner demons, but it couldn't be helped.

"God. Oh, man. I'm sorry. Don't…don't cry." He secured me so tightly in his arms, I felt like he would go right through me.

But that only made me sob that much harder. I knew Finn cared. And it was because of that, that I think I cried the way I did. Because crying wasn't something I usually allowed myself to do. I didn't like people seeing that vulnerable side of me. And Finn was seeing it. And it scared him as much as he had me with his anger. He probably had every right to be mad at that reporter. But he also needed to understand things from my perspective.

"Don't be mad," I said in between tears which were surely soaking his fitted shirt. "Or, if you are, I need to understand why. I need to know what you're feeling. Talk with me."

"Baby, I can't help but want to protect you." I felt his hand slowly, calmingly stroke my hair. "I won't apologize for that. That would be like not loving you."

"Finn, I'm just concerned. I want to make sure you're all right."

"I swear to you." He stopped for a second, and then confirmed, "I am."

We didn't go to the show. We were both too exhausted emotionally and, because of that, physically. Finn held me in his arms for the entire night until I fell asleep. Those arms were still tense but better than they had been when I left him on the sidewalk. I hoped the touch of my body leaning into his made him feel as secure as his did for me. And I hoped, more than anything, that whatever funk Finn had been in since coming back to New York would dissipate once we were away.

***

His built-up energy helped, of course, during the concert. Finn rocked that beach town location with vigor. Lane, McEllie, and I watched backstage and went out for drinks afterward. Finn was very affectionate, and Lane was very protective. It was a bizarre scene, but they both had my best interests in mind and became, if not the best of buds, something close.

Finn and I were staying at a rental on the beach. The day after the concert we spent walking around the local area with Finn trying his best to stay incognito. After dinner, we went beach combing to find shells and beautiful pieces of sea glass. As the day went on, Finn seemed more and more relaxed and more himself. We made love that night and it was he who actually fell asleep first.

I woke up in the middle of the night to hear the sound of a guitar being played. I followed the distant chords through the living area, out to the porch, and finally onto the beach. That's where I found Finn half-humming, half-singing a song I didn't recognize. He seemed mellow even if the pattern of sleeplessness had continued.

He must not have heard my approach due to the soft effect of feet on sand. When I knelt down and stroked his back, he immediately stopped playing and turned to me. "Hey," he partially whispered. "I didn't wake you, did I?"

I sat down next to him intertwining my one foot with his and digging the other toes into the sand. "I'm not sure. But it doesn't matter. I love listening to you play. What was it?"

"Just messin' around."

"Don't stop." I rested my head on his shoulder. "Sing something for me."

He looked from me to the water and began singing a Kenny Chesney tune. It was one I recognized from the radio. It was an oldie but a haunting goody about a woman who saves a man from himself.

***

We took separate flights out from North Carolina. I went back to New York and work. Finn went back to Tennessee for about a week before heading to Las Vegas for the ACM awards.

I tried to stay awake that night to find out if he won Male Vocalist of the Year, but I was fighting a terrible sinus infection that had just worn me out. He called to tell me that he didn't take home the trophy and immediately apologized for waking me up. But I didn't mind. His voice was so soft and serene, and we were talking about him coming in for my birthday that was just a few days away. So, an interruption of sleep was well worth it.

On my birthday—Saturday, April fourth—he made it just in time to pick me up and drive us to Wyatt's baseball game. During the event, though, he couldn't stay still. He alternated between helping Will coach and simply walking the adjoining gameless field and talking on his phone. That's where Nola caught up with him as I remained in the stands with Kelsea, cheering on Wyatt's team. I watched the game with one eye while the other was on the Murphy siblings. Too far away to hear, I could, nonetheless, see their very animated body language and wondered what drama was unfolding.

Finn returned to our seats before Nola. He sat down next to me putting his hand protectively and a little roughly on my thigh. He kissed the top of my head and tried a not-so-believable smile.

"Everything all right?" I asked.

Ignoring my question, Finn bounced Kelsea onto his lap. "Hey, Buttercup, Lara and I have to go."

"What?" I squinted my eyes at him. The game wasn't even half over.

Again, he ignored me and spoke to Kelsea. "Be a good sister and support your brother."

Nola, upon hearing Finn's comment and seemingly sensing the underlying meaning, approached. "Finn, you don't have to leave."

"It's Lara's birthday. I'm sure with a career in the education field, this is the last thing she wants to do on her birthday." He was being civil, but the tension between the two was undeniable.

Even though what Finn had said was fairly accurate, I would never have verbalized it. "Finn, it's all good. It means something to Wyatt to have everyone here."

Finn stood taking Kelsea up with him. He gave her an

Eskimo kiss, causing her to giggle, oblivious to what was happening around her. "See ya, Firefly."

"Bye, Uncle Finn."

While Finn walked over to say his goodbyes to Will and Wyatt, I stayed with Nola, not knowing if I should question the scenario or not. I decided on the obvious. "I guess we're leaving."

After a beat, Nola said, in an almost accusatory tone, "He sure does love you." Before I could react, she continued, "Thanks for coming. It does mean a lot to Wyatt. And happy birthday. Have fun."

"Yeah." And then just as I decided to question, "Nol—"

Finn interrupted, "C'mon, Lara. Let's go."

He put his hand in mine and gently but decisively started leading us away. We walked in silence to the car. And we remained that way until we were on the main road.

"Finn?" His name was my only question.

"I love you," was his quick answer.

"I know that." And then after a moment, I furthered my investigation. "What? What's going on?"

Because there definitely was something going on. It was obvious by our abrupt departure from the ball game. But there were also the other recent incidents when he had seemed stressed and not the jovial person I had always known him to be.

"I love you," he repeated his statement as if that clarified everything.

"I love you too." I echoed before trying another approach. "Finn, you know you can talk with me about anything, right? I want you to do that. I want you to know that. If something is bothering you, or if it's something that Nola—"

"Sibling shit," he said, still looking straight at the road ahead. His tone became more agitated as he spoke, and it was one I wasn't used to. "That's all that was. Pain-in-the-ass sister crap. She needs to mind her own business." And he end-tagged it with a firm, "just once."

"About what? I'm sure—" I started only to be bypassed.

"Lara!" His outburst of my name was sudden and strong. It startled me so much I physically jumped and subconsciously inched toward the passenger door. Obviously noting, Finn took a moment and then said with much more kindness, "I'm sorry." He paused. "I'm just being selfish wanting you all to myself on your birthday."

Relieved that the conversation didn't continue on its slippery slope, I truthfully agreed with his comment. "Okay." I inhaled and released a calming breath, choosing to take him at his word even though I was still a little concerned. "That does sound kind of wonderful."

As much as I adored Finn's family, I was, indeed, looking forward to the rest of the day just with him. We drove in silence for a bit longer. Finn looked over at me again, and then methodically rubbed my leg surely as a way to reaffirm his apologizes for shouting.

"Wy isn't going to be the next Babe Ruth any time soon, is he?" He tried a new line of conversation.

"Nope." I laughed with just a twinge of unease left. "He'll get a hit one of these days. I just hope he's having fun."

"Kelsea was, anyway."

"She's a baby doll. I love her."

"You really would make a great mom." He left the sentence sit there a moment before turning and meeting my eyes with a look that was a mix of hope and melancholy.

***

The rest of the day, thankfully, turned out to be everything that I wanted it to be. It was peaceful. It was serene. It was just the two of us.

When I opened my gift from Finn, I discovered

stunning diamond earrings that just exuded simple elegance. Studs dangled ever so slightly from a rope-like pattern. I had no idea how much they cost, but if they weren't a thousand dollars they were pretty damn close.

"Finn!" I exclaimed right away and then realized I shouldn't start off with an admonishment regarding the price. "They're beautiful," I said most honestly.

"They reminded me of the dress you wore at the CMAs."

"Yeah, but those weren't real." I fondly recalled the neckline and that special, life-changing night.

"Well, now you got the real thing."

"I told you, the Jeep was my birthday gift."

He had the audacity to laugh. "You never said that."

"I most certainly—"

He stopped me. "You said it was *like* seventy-five Christmases and birthdays."

My internal thoughts damned him and his insanely accurate memory. "Well, I'm saying it now."

"Aw, Lara, I'm not *not* getting you gifts."

"A card. A card is good. You're allowed to get me a card."

"A card?" He laughed. "You are impossible."

"Finn."

"I hear you," he said, but I knew the semantic difference between "hear" and "listen." Before I could tell him so, he said, "I have something else."

"What!"

"Relax." He actually touched my arm. "It didn't cost a thing."

I looked at him with doubt. It was then, though, that I thought he seemed a tad bit nervous. It was subtle and probably not noticeable to someone who didn't know him. But it was to me.

"What?" I asked more softly.

Without a word, he materialized a pair of earbuds and had me put them in my ears. "It's called 'Lara's Song.'"

I tilted my head ever so slightly to this man in front of me. He pressed play and then, uncharacteristically, he shyly looked away. Even before the first note, I knew it would be something special. But then I heard his magnificent voice and the heartfelt words that detailed everything we were together and how he felt about me. It was the most beautiful, romantic gesture I could ever possibly imagine. And I fell even deeper in love, which didn't seem possible.

I pulled the buds out. He looked at me with uncertainty scripted across his face. I had no idea why. But I wanted to erase all of that and whatever concerns I had earlier in the day. I bracketed my hands on his cheeks and kissed him as tears started rolling down my face.

"That was worth ten thousand birthdays and Christmases," I said after wiping the tears.

"Oh no you don't." He laughed with relief. "I'm glad you liked it. I meant every single word, and it still doesn't say how much I am in love with you. Happy Birthday, Beauty. C'mon," he smiled as he lit the candles on my cake. "Make a wish."

I closed my eyes, thought, took a calming inhale in, and blew. The flames flickered and sputtered and then went to black. I thought, sadly, that the image was most likely a mirror of my wish. I wanted my birthday and the happiness that I was feeling to never end. But I knew that wasn't possible. It never is.

CHAPTER EIGHTEEN

I had to rely on simply listening to that beautiful recording and not the live version for twenty plus days until Finn could come back to New York. But when he did, what I had been afraid of for a while seemed to be happening in full force upon his return. He was just visiting for a long weekend because, with his tour ready to begin in a little more than a month, he had a lot of preparation to do. And he looked worn…beat…weathered. He wasn't all jittery and wound up like he had been before, but he also wasn't calm, cool, and collected. He wasn't Finn…at all.

Because of this, we decided to spend his first night back just relaxing at my place. I made some popcorn, pulled up a movie, and we sat on the sofa in each other's arms. The movie wasn't so good, though, and we were both losing interest. It had been three weeks since we had last seen each other and, naturally, I wanted to be with him. I wanted our bodies as close as they could be. Assuming, of course, that Finn felt the same, I began kissing him with purpose while moving my hands to his waist. Even though I felt him back away slightly, I continued to pursue my intentions.

"Lara…." His voice seemed to border on a warning.

"What? You have a headache?" I teased still wrapped up in my mission.

"No, I'm just…tired," he replied.

"Tired? You never sleep. The rock star finally has his limit. I don't believe it."

But when my hands started on his pants button, he was much more adamant…much more insistent. "Lara, I said no! And stop it with the rock star shit." Finn was definitely not joking around. He was off the sofa in an instant. "God!"

"Okay," I spoke so quietly it was nearly softer than a whisper. I looked at him surely with the proverbial deer caught in the headlight gaze.

He was wound up now and it had come on so quickly. "Why can't I just be Finn? I thought if there was one person I could just be me with, it was you. Why can't I be enough?"

"What?" How could I take this back? How could I reverse the last couple of minutes? "You're enough—more than. I'm sorry." I got up off the sofa to meet him. "If I did—"

Finn cut me off with his words just as I felt tears threaten to emerge. "I just…." He took an extended breath and then more calmly said, "Look, it's not you, it's m—"

"Oh, God, please, anything but that." I couldn't help but feel instantly hurt knowing where those words always led. "You're not really going to say it's me, not you, are you?"

Where was this coming from? No, please, no. I didn't see this coming…at all.

"Lara, please…," he said with an exasperated, frustrated look in his eyes. "It's not like that. I'm trying. I'm trying so damn hard to be the guy you need." The more he spoke, the more his voice started to rise again. "You've got to give me a break. Christ!"

Despite his agitation, I was a little more at ease believing that he wasn't trying to break up with me. "Finn, what are you talking about? I never told you…. You are what I need. What's going on? What's this about?"

"I think I should probably go." He looked down then.

"No. Don't. Stay." I took another step toward him. "Just stay. We can talk."

"No. I don't think that's a good idea."

"Finn, c'mon. I don't know what's going on. I don't want you to be angry."

As I reached out for him, Finn, without warning, abruptly chopped down my arm with his own, grabbed it, and restrained it behind my back as if I were a criminal and he the cop. He seemed determined to keep me away from him. Having flashbacks of my father, I quickly, and with determination, wriggled free and backed away. In fact, I not only backed away, I stepped so that the smaller of the two sofas was now between us. And with that, I couldn't help but think of the irony. The soft piece of furniture, known as a love seat, was now acting as a barrier between me and my love. But at that moment, I felt like I needed the protection…the wall. And it hurt.

"Lara." His sad, glossy-eyed gaze lasted for an extended moment, like he wanted to say something more. But then, without another word or kinder touch of any sort, he grabbed his keys from the kitchen counter and walked out.

I stood there long after the front door had shut just staring—staring and wondering. What had just happened? God, I had been looking forward to him coming into town so much. I missed him so, so much more than I thought Miss Self-proclaimed Independent Woman ever would. I was in his arms and then those arms were cruelly tossing me aside. Why was he so angry? What had I done? And it was obviously me this time. There wasn't a reporter in our midst. Where did this come from? And where had he gone?

I hadn't realized I'd sunk to the floor in the same spot

where he had left me until I noticed I was playing with a random piece of popcorn. It had fallen to the floor surely just as confused by the scene that had suddenly erupted as I was. I flicked the puffy, yellow snack into the air. I was angry with it, myself, and, yes, Finn. It was so out of character for him to act the way he was. Of course, on our first night together, he surely had flashed a level of frustration. But somehow that had been different. He hadn't left and not returned. And it was obvious…this time, he wasn't coming back.

I sat there for more than an hour and then eventually managed to pick myself up and sit logically on the sofa. My cell phone, sitting innocently on the coffee table, seemed to beckon to me. I had to reach out to Finn. Yes, I was angry that he had left and how he reacted in the first place. But, more importantly, I loved him and had to find out how he was—what was bothering him so much.

I picked up the phone and was suddenly nervous. I was nervous to talk with him. Maybe "nervous" wasn't the right word. I was afraid that his reaction to me would be the same or, God forbid, worse. And I didn't know if I could handle that. I wanted it to be all right. So, I decided on the safer route by thinking out a carefully scribed text message.

Text or call me please. I didn't mean to upset U. I love YOU, Finn. -- Roxanne.

And no response. None. None. None.

Never, never, did he ignore me. Even if he was in important meetings or rehearsing, he flipped back a quick text or got back to me within a few minutes or so. Now it had been more than forty-five minutes since I had pressed send. I had been pacing and then bawling uncontrollably. And my reasons why ranged from anger to fear to worry.

When my sobbing slowed to a nearly normal breathing scenario, I decided to try another text. I didn't know why a second one would make a difference, but it was killing me not to do anything…not to hear from him…not to know why.

Please please let me know U are all right. I'm worried about U.

This time I sat and stared at the phone willing it to respond to me. He could call or simply text back. I didn't care. After about ten minutes, I had myself so worked up that I had the sudden urge to pee. So I went into the bathroom.

Just as I was washing my hands, his text came in. *I'm not worthy of you.*

It was simple, but I felt so relieved. I was relieved that he answered. But at the same account, his actual message was concerning.

I'm calling. Please pick up. I pleaded via text.

This time, I hit his speed dial number and took in a deep breath hoping that he would answer—hoping his mood was different than the one he had left with. The nervous pit in my stomach returned. Would he pick it up?

I heard his voice after two rings. There was a noticeable sadness and tiredness in it, but he sounded more like the man I knew than the one who had been in my apartment earlier. "I'm fine, Lara. Let it rest for the night."

"Where are you?" was all that I could think to say having not thought out what I really expected from the conversation.

"I'm on my way home now," he spoke in simple syllables.

I took note of the final word and questioned, "Now? Where were you?"

After a moment, Finn answered, "I was trying to clear my head."

"And?" I asked softly…cautiously.

"And I need to sleep now." He wasn't giving me much.

"You're still mad." I stated what I thought was the obvious.

"At myself…not at you." That definitely sounded like the Finn I knew. After a slight pause, he asked, "Did I hurt you…your arm?"

"No."

He hadn't. But I couldn't help but to look at it as if he had. It wasn't my arm he hurt.

"I didn't mean to be so rough. I was just—"

"You scared me," I interrupted still wrapped in my previous thought.

"I'm so sorry, Lara." He sounded broken.

"Finn, I…." God, I couldn't fall apart too…again.

"I know," he said when I couldn't continue. "I didn't mean to. Forgive me."

I regained my composure. "I love you. Tell me what's going on…please."

"It's late. Can we please maybe talk about this tomorrow?"

Because he sounded more himself, even if exhausted, I agreed. "Yeah. I'm glad you're all right and that you answered."

"Good night, Roxy."

His sentiment brought a smile and an emotional tear to my face. "Yep," was all I managed to get out before I had to hang up in fear that I would choke up.

***

But we didn't talk the next day. I waited for him to call. And I waited some more. When he didn't call, I started yelling some not very polite words at the walls in lieu of at him. Of course, I could have just been the one to call him but, somehow, I deemed it *his* turn even though at that point in our relationship, we were far beyond those childish games.

I got on the internet to browse top stories but more importantly to get my mind off Finn and what was turning out to be the exact opposite of the weekend that I had been dreaming of and waiting for. That was when I found out. The entertainment feed was speculating about Finn's recent behavior just as I was. They seemed to be documenting Finn's moves over the past few months—in Tennessee, at award shows, and in New York. This would not be out of the ordinary but would rarely make any kind of news. But what the press was speculating made my whole world spin and yet become perfectly clear. It was what that reporter outside Finn's penthouse building just over a month before had originally questioned.

The pattern of Finn being bouncy, jittery, and sleepless versus quiet, reserved, and mellow apparently happened not just around me or had been noticed just by me. Music industry followers had taken note too…and they knew the reason. I don't know why I hadn't put it together. I should have. I knew better. I just didn't want to see. Finn was back to using drugs.

It was the second time in two days that I broke down and wept. I found myself clinging to the chair as if I were clinging to life. How could I have been so stupid? All the signs were there. They were alerting and cautioning me to stop, think, and look, but I blindly went on believing. No—loving. And that was what threw me off. That was what had done me in—love.

Now it was my turn to act irrational. I wanted to throw something…smash something…cause pain to something like you see in the movies. But I didn't. I walked in circles around my apartment never realizing until then how truly small it was. My mind was so angry… so hurt…so battered. I couldn't keep an unblurred thought inside it, let alone come to a conclusion on what I should do about the situation at hand. Anyone watching me would have believed *I* was the one as high as a kite—that *I* was the one on drugs.

I picked up the phone. I put it back down. I picked up the phone again. I put it back down again. It wasn't time. Not yet. I didn't know what I wanted to say or at least if I could do it and make any kind of sense. I tried to calm myself down with yoga-like breathing techniques, and it worked…a little. At least I got to the point where I slowed my pace as I circled the apartment.

Then I started straightening things up around my place. I found the wilting plant and tended to it like I had never tended to it before. I thought of my mother and how she always took refuge in her garden. The meticulous pruning and gentle watering was her escape from the madness. She could nurture when she wasn't getting any herself. She would try to make the world more beautiful than it actually was.

The knocking on the door jarred me from any alternate world I had hoped to be in. I was glad right then that Finn did not have his own key to my apartment—the super was strict about duplicate keys and only made them for names on the lease. I wanted to face Finn on my own terms, but I just wasn't sure what those terms were. I wasn't sure about anything… at all. But while I wagered in silence, knowing without a doubt that it was, indeed, Finn, he knocked again and again.

"Lara? Lara, c'mon, let me in," came the voice that would normally soothe my very being. "Lara, please, you know I'll stay out here until…you know I will."

From his words and the devoted inflection in his voice, it was obvious he knew that I knew what was going on. He *would* stay out there. I knew he wanted to try to explain whatever he thought could be explained, even though it wouldn't make a difference.

Taking a deep breath and letting out an even larger sigh, I walked to the door and opened it. He looked as beat as I felt. I met his eyes but only for a split second. Purposefully, before he could reach out to me, I turned and walked solo into the living room. I heard the click of the door and knew he had followed me even though I didn't turn around.

"Lar?" The touch of his hand on my shoulder made me flinch.

I took a step away and finally turned. "Don't," I said plainly.

"Okay," he spoke tenuously as if knowing that I was more upset than he had ever seen me.

Every feeling that had been mixed and stirred since he left the apartment the night before exploded. "I told you that was the only thing I would not put up with. How could you, Finn?"

"Lara—" He barely got my name out before I interrupted.

"Who are you?" I bellowed.

"I—"

I was on a roll. My blood pressure was so high, I could hardly hear him even try to answer me. "I don't want to believe it, but I'm living it for God's sake. I must be the biggest fool there is, huh? What do you do all night? I mean besides, obviously, when you're not out carousing and getting high? What? Make fun of me, I'm sure. Thinking what a pathetic idiot Lara is?"

"C'mon, I'm not doing this with you again." He was trying to remain calm. "I don't think you are pathetic or whatever you—"

I toned it down just a notch in order to try to get some sort of rationalization for this madness. "Finn, where are you? I know this isn't you. I know it. All those years ago…the cocaine…." He looked down as I spoke that ugly word. Guilt was written all over his face. "I know it was true. But the Finn that I met again in September? That was the Finn I knew…before all of this…before all of the fame and the accolades and the drugs. God, I was so glad to see him. God. God, Finn. What? What happened? Why did you go back to that?"

Tears were readily flowing down my face. I couldn't help it. I couldn't stop them. I wanted an answer, but he just stared at me. I could see he was tortured. I knew him so well that I knew he wasn't even worried about answering my question. All he wanted to do was wipe the pain away for me. But he also didn't dare take a step closer.

I looked at him and asked the question I feared the most. "If it was me…if I led you back to that life…to the drugs."

I couldn't even continue. I knew that was the truth. I knew it was me—not on purpose, but it was me. The pressure of being with me, especially distance wise, caused him to relapse. I knew it.

"Okay, are you done?" Even though he was calm, I didn't appreciate the tone of the question.

"Don't be condescending to me." I wiped my tears. "Don't."

Finn waited a moment, probably so both of us could sustain some self-control. "Look, I was…I did. I got caught up in it all. I told you. I was doing coke back then. It was easy. It was an escape. It was all that they say it is and more. I needed it. I craved it."

"Well, good for you." My sarcastic tongue escaped. "I'm glad your craving is fulfilled again. You obviously need it more than you need me."

"I need you," he said immediately. "God, I need you. Don't you know how much you've made my life better? You're my whole…my reason I…." He almost stuttered with emotion.

My inner volcano was about to erupt again. Was he seriously going to blame me? I didn't give him the chance. "Oh…God. I didn't want to believe it, but I have to. I have to face that you are a drug addict. You have really—" I couldn't even keep my train of thought on track. "You're a drug addict, Finn."

"I'm not, Lara. I'm not taking drugs—not now!" His voice was starting to elevate if even just to overpower my tirade. "I told you not to listen to—"

"You liar! You're a liar! I grew up with an addict. I don't know why it took me so long to see it. God, the least you can do is be a man and fess up to the truth." I struck him in the chest causing more tears to flow. I had never felt heartache so bad.

Finn didn't react to my physical altercation. "Why can't you believe me? Why can't you just believe me? I'm telling you the truth." Since I was closer now, he took the opportunity to grasp my shoulders with his hands so that we were looking square on. "Look in my eyes."

"Your eyes?" I almost laughed as I shook him off. "No. They're just another fake part of you. All of this is a façade, isn't it? All of it. Even us."

That got him. "Christ! What do I have to do?" His voice was on the rise. "Why can't you just fucking believe me? Why can't you believe me?" He raked his hands through his hair.

"You're crazy. You're high right now, aren't you? Leave me alone. Go! Don't come near me. Go! Leave! Don't call, because I won't care." It all came out before I had a chance to edit.

"Why can't you believe me? You told me you would listen to me if someone said something. But you're not. You're not. Why? Why can't you trust me?"

"I did. I did believe you months ago, but I don't now. I can tell the difference. And trust? God…I trusted you more than anyone in the whole world. You know how much that took? Look where it got me," I answered back, surprised that the tears had dried. I guess a well only runs so deep. "I don't want to see you, Finn. Never…ever. We're done. Do you understand?" I looked at him with a determined stance braver than I actually felt.

With a defeated look in his eyes, he turned away, took one step, and then turned back around. "This…this…" He swept his arms out in a dramatic fashion. "This is why I never reached out to find you again. I wanted to. I almost did…a few times. You probably thought I hated you or forgot about you. But that wasn't it. I thought of you…what you were doing…how you were. But I just knew. I knew I wouldn't be good for you. I'm messed up, and you didn't deserve that. But, God, seeing you…you swept me back in. I couldn't resist. I tried. Do you know that? Do you know that's why I didn't call you after Wyatt's party?"

"No." I whispered recalling my doubt of his actions back then. I had just figured it was my drama that had held him back.

I'm sure he didn't hear me say that little word though, because he was on a verbal roll. "But it was you. You were Lara. I should have. I should have resisted."

I stood stunned. He had revealed so much. Yet it didn't excuse him from taking drugs and standing in front of me and continuing to lie. I didn't move. I didn't say a word. I vowed to stand strong.

"I'm going to leave for now. But I *am* going to call you, Lara."

Yeah, try in another seven years. Maybe, just maybe, I will have cooled down by then, and maybe he will be successfully through twelve steps. I adverted my eyes when he took a step closer to me. He knew then not to even think about one more. I could feel as much as see him turn and then walk away. Despite being so infuriatingly mad, a part of me instantly thought, God, were those the last words we would speak to one another? I hadn't paid attention to them seven years ago when I didn't realize the finality of the situation, and those words were nonessential. This time I did, and the words were so, so painful.

***

Finn did call me the next day. Well, he called twice. The first time he called, it was 1:23 in the afternoon. I noticed because I always considered that a lucky time, and he knew it. But I didn't give in. I didn't pick it up, and he didn't leave a message. He waited until 8:10 to try again. Nothing special about that time. He probably just couldn't wait any longer. Again, I didn't pick it up.

This time, though, he left a message. "I love you. You

have to know that. I'm no good without you. Call me back. Please."

The weird part was, I wasn't even tempted to call him back. Something had snapped in me. The sound of his voice, which normally would have made me goofy like a teen girl, made me slightly repulsed. I was so mad and felt so betrayed. There was nothing he could say. No "I love yous" or pleading would even begin to chip away at the anger field surrounding me. The body armor was back on and the wall of Lara was definitely built high.

***

I don't think I had ever been so thankful for Monday and work to arrive. I hadn't gotten much sleep that weekend, and I was exhausted when the 5:30 a.m. alarm went off. But, at the same time, I needed to focus on something besides my anguish. I went through the motions of my job and tried to put on a good act.

But it was hard, especially when Vanessa, who was single once again, popped her head into my office that morning and declared, "I see Finn got nominated for an award!"

The CMT award announcements were that morning. Prior to our arguing, Finn had mentioned that he would know if he was nominated for video of the year just hours before flying back to Nashville. I glanced at the clock. He was probably taxiing off at that very moment. What was he thinking…feeling? God, what was I thinking? Why did I care?

***

May first was just a couple days after Finn left. It was like pouring salt on the proverbial wound. I didn't know how I was supposed to handle all of it at once. I had ignored Finn's "Love you" text the night before. But when

I heard his ring on my phone on the first of May, I was tempted to pick up. I needed to talk. I needed to talk to someone who knew—someone who would understand. And he was one of only two people in the world who would. My hand was on the phone, but my stomach was in knots. I let it ring enough times so that it eventually went to voice mail. The decision was made.

Before I could over think it, I called my mother and let her, as she had through the years, talk me through the day in history of when I gave up my child. We didn't actually talk about the baby, who, by now, was a young boy, more than to say that we knew the day was hard. My mother rambled on about pointless things, and I blew off her questions about Finn. I chose to make her believe that everything was fine and status quo with the two of us. I didn't want her opinions on the matter, especially knowing how she dealt with addicts in her personal life. It was good to talk with her, though. It was soothing. It was normalcy.

When I got off the phone with my mother, I noticed the phone alert. I had a voice mail message. I breathed in deeply and listened.

"Lara? Baby? I just wanted to let you know I'm thinking of you. No matter what is going on, I want you to know that. I know what today is. God, Lara, please, please, talk to me. Please. God! Call me. Talk to me. I want to be there for you. I can't bear this. Lara? Please."

So, he had remembered. It didn't surprise me. Finn was nearly neurotic when it came to details. He truly listened when someone spoke, especially when he cared for the individual. And, if I were honest, I didn't doubt that love for me. That was one thing he had promised and kept true to—his love and the fact that he would never cheat. Unless you counted his toxic love for drugs as his mistress. And judging from how his voice changed from sounding jittery to upset to sad in a less than a minute recording, it appeared she was still in his bed.

I was glad that I spoke with my mother because the

conversation did what I had needed it to do. It let me acknowledge the past so that I could, once again, place it back there—in the past. I needed to recognize its place in my personal timeline, lock it securely back in the baggage vault, and move on. It was exhausting and draining, but it was also freeing. And because my mother was my sounding board, I didn't have that need, that urge, to talk with Finn, which I knew was best. I knew the longer I went on without talking with him, the better chance I had of being free.

Free but, admittedly, not happy. I knew I would probably never be happy again. I hadn't realized until it was over, but I had subconsciously been waiting for Finn to return all those years. Somewhere, deep inside, I knew he was my destiny. And now, my destiny in ruins, I could not see a future at all. I had been all right during those seven years being single, strumming along. It should have been no different since breaking up with Finn. But, yet, it was. It was so different. It was truly an end. There was no hope for my happiness. Finn was the one. I knew it. I knew it the second he re-entered my life. And now it was over.

Apparently, Finn had come to that realization, also—the "it's over" part. After leaving that voice mail message and me not returning it, he didn't make any more attempts to contact me. I should have been relieved, but I was sad and a little bit shocked. I hadn't expected him to give up that easily. But, in a way, he was no longer in charge of his own decisions or his own life—the drugs were. I feared for his well-being and hoped that he would find the strength to rebound again. But I knew I could not be a part of it.

CHAPTER NINETEEN

About a week later, I left work only to find Finn waiting by my car in the parking lot. Pacing, he looked down right pissed, even though I couldn't quite see his eyes beneath the low riding baseball cap. I would have normally found that look casually sexy on him. But certainly not then.

Of course, I wasn't expecting him. So the sight of him caught me completely off guard. I froze. Only a few steps or so from the door, I contemplated slinking back inside because he had yet to see me. In the moment that it took for me to watch him and ache just a tiny bit for what had been, he spotted me. He stopped and looked at me. His eyes did not take on the natural softness of the color of gray. They were dark and seemed ablaze. I had no choice but to continue toward him and the car.

"Wh—" I started but was not allowed to verbally get any further.

"You're taking this out on Wyatt? Really?" Not even a semblance of a kind greeting, his voice was as dark as the navy-blue V-neck he was wearing.

"Finn, you shouldn't be here."

"This," He pointed vehemently from me to him. "You

and me? It has nothing to do with my nephew."

"What?"

I didn't know what he was talking about. Probably because *he* didn't know what he was talking about. The statement itself was false, and he seemed out of his mind delivering it.

Wyatt had been acting up a little in class over the past couple of weeks, both for me and his teacher, Gwen, but so had other students. It was nearing the end of the school year and, just like the weather, behaviors changed too. Nola had made Wyatt write an apology note to both of us, and she had attached a side note saying they were talking about it at home. In my opinion, it didn't even warrant a note. Wyatt was just getting warnings in class—no consequences—and mostly for talking. But Nola and Will were good parents and were teaching him right.

"He's a little boy, Lara. You can't treat him differently because…I thought you were better than that."

I turned the tables deciding to make him feel what it was like to be accused. "And I thought you would never hurt me."

I could see the sting register on his face, but he didn't wait for more than a second or two to retaliate. "You. You're the one who left me. You. You…left…me. You wouldn't even listen."

Immature and inappropriate for a school parking lot, I did not sensor my response. "Fuck you, Finn."

"You used to." At least his voice was a tad softer, more reminiscent.

Determined not to give in, I remained steely. "And I'm trying really hard right now not to regret that. Get out of my way."

"Don't be a bitch. It's not you."

"I guess we really never knew each other then, huh?" I was proud of myself. No matter how much I was tearing apart inside, I remained stoic outside.

"Lara." When he reached out to me, I noticed he was

wearing the watch I gave him for Christmas.

But before sentiment could creep in, I also recalled him swatting my arm away when I had tried reaching out to him just a few weeks ago. "Don't. Don't touch me."

"I—" Finn started but was interrupted as Calette, a teacher's aide, approached.

"Lara, is everything all right? Do you need help?" she asked, appropriately sizing up the situation.

"Finn?" I challenged looking directly into his eyes. "Do I?"

"Of course not." Displaying a mixture of anger and sadness, Finn placed his arms back at his sides.

"C'mon," Calette encouraged me, looking at the two of us with slight apprehension. "I'm parked right next to you."

I hit the lock release to the Jeep as Finn said, "Lara, damn it!"

I stepped around him and got in the car. He had no choice but to back away from the Jeep as I pulled out. Only once did I look, and it was via the rearview mirror. The image of Finn, with his hands shoved in his pants pockets, slightly shaking his head, watching me leave, haunted me the entire ride home.

***

Once again, I thought that would be the last time I would hear his voice—in that parking lot after work. It was nearly another week, but I heard from Finn again. He left an absolutely heart-wrenching voice mail in which he was audibly, and without humility, crying and claiming how much he loved me and how sorry he was. I sobbed practically in unison. How I believed in the sincerity of his words yet couldn't trust him to tell me anything else with an ounce of truth. I knew he was hurting, and everything inside me, every ounce, every molecule, wanted to reach out to him. But I couldn't. I wouldn't. I had learned the hard way—the school of hard knocks way. I couldn't be around someone who abused any type of drug. It was too dark and too unhealthy—not just for that person, but for me, and I could not sacrifice my life again to someone who chose that life over me. No matter how much I loved him, I couldn't do it.

"C'mon, aren't you going walk—?" Vanessa startled me with her abrupt entrance into the room. When I jumped, she said, "Jiminy," and leaned against the table to face me at my desk. "What's wrong?"

"Nothing," I denied and placed my phone back down. "I'm not really up for walking with the group today."

Vanessa took her phone and texted something before turning to me. "Me, either. Just cancelled. It seems more like a thirsty Thursday. What do you say? Let's get out of here."

"Neh."

"Then talk to me here. I know there's something up. It's Finn, right?" When I nodded my head in agreement, she continued, "And this isn't just that you miss the guy because he's in Music Freakin' City. I know *that* Lara. She still has that lost, hopeful, romantic glimmer in her eyes. This is different."

"It is," I admitted, but to nothing else.

"You're not going to tell me?"

"No." No one really knew what had gone down with Finn and me, and the media coverage about his reckless behavior deescalated as quickly as it first appeared—just enough for me to see but not enough for those not totally invested to take note.

"Well, I don't think you really have to tell me. It's written all over you." Her mouth curled down in a quick sad motion. "Look, I know he's a hotshot and a God to look at." She winked, and I almost laughed. "But he's not worth you being this miserable. No guy is." She paused and then said, "Unless he is…because on the flip side, I have never seen you happier than you have been since Mr.

Murphy came on the scene."

But that was the problem—Finn was on the scene. I saw him everywhere. And not just via the various forms of media that I was purposefully trying to avoid. I saw and felt him personally everywhere I went. If I was at work, I saw him singing for the benefit. If I was at Java Mug, I saw him smiling with the chocolate pretzel rod in his mouth. If I stayed at home, I saw him in my bed. Of course, he wasn't really in those places, but he had been, and he had left a visual imprint of them in my brain.

I needed a break. I needed to be free—to free myself like I had in the past. And cutting my hair wasn't going to do it this time. I needed to really escape. I couldn't even lose myself in the hustle and bustle of New York City which was normally one of my regular mental outlets. Memories of Finn were there now too. But I did need to go.

Before I left work, I called off the next day and then phoned, ironically, a friend of mine from college. Haylie owned a bed-and-breakfast just a couple hours or so north. It was the perfect getaway. And she told me it was a great time for me to visit. Her husband was away on business. So, if I could help her with some of the chores—she was in her final trimester of her second pregnancy—she would let me have a room for free.

It was an ideal couple of days. Playing with her little daughter Sienna and cleaning the barn area kept me busy and active and my mind off Finn. And, without saying a word, Haylie noted right away and respected the fact that he was not a subject I wanted to discuss. It was exactly what I needed. I felt good. In fact, I felt better than I had in a while.

And then it happened. I was on the highway driving home. I felt refreshed going slightly above the speed limit, having the windows down, my hair up, and singing right along with the radio. I had found an eclectic to almost oldies radio station, purposefully not wanting country. But, of course, right after the Chili Peppers, the next voice that was broadcast was Finn's. And, of course, it was my song. I hadn't heard it on the radio before. He had actually asked my permission on my birthday to release it as a single before his next album came up. I couldn't understand why he needed my permission, but he had insisted that it was my song. And, if it was all right, he wanted the whole world to know how he felt about me. I wondered if he regretted it now.

Cars were whirling past me on the highway—some with horns honking, some with hands waving, and some with words yelling. I didn't realize what the issue was until I looked at the speedometer and realized I was only going around thirty miles per hour in a seventy zone. I put on my turn signal and pulled over to the shoulder. I then finished listening to the song, bawling my eyes out like I was a kid and my dog had just died.

How was I going to live without him? I reached into the back of the car for my phone. Truly wanting the weekend off, I had thrown it back there two days before and hadn't looked at it since. But now, when I swiped at the screen, the battery, of course, had run dead. I laughed a downright hysterical laugh, looked at the ceiling of the Jeep, and said, "Really?"

Luckily, the ceiling didn't answer. But there was my sign. I was not meant to call him. I was meant to drive on and on and on.

***

With just a couple weeks left of school, the building had another fundraiser for the young third grader's battle with cardiomyopathy. He was responding well to the transplant but still had a lot of rehabilitation. The local McDonald's agreed to contribute half of all their proceeds during a two-hour time span. Of course, families from all grade levels packed the booths and drive-thru that evening.

It wasn't as big of a turn-out as Finn's concert, but the kids sure did have fun. And it was another place that reminded me of the man who was never far from my thoughts—the booming indoor playground was reminiscent of a rock concert and, of course, McDonald's was the gift card I had given Finn for graduation.

But the biggest reminders were Finn's nephew and sister sitting in the fast food restaurant begging me to join them as they ate their meals. I hadn't seen Nola since Finn and I broke up, but I knew she was aware of our status if for no other reason than Finn's parking lot tirade about me treating Wyatt differently. It would be extremely difficult to eat my salad and iced coffee standing up. I should have thought of that when ordering and gotten a sandwich or yogurt parfait instead. But, alas, there I stood with no other seats available and Nola calling out my name.

"Hi," I said sliding next to Wyatt into the red, end booth. "You sure you don't mind me joining you?"

I had a hard time looking across the table at Nola. I knew I shouldn't. No matter what accusations Finn threw at me, it wasn't me who caused our split. It was him—him and his sadistic habit.

"Of course not." God, how had I never noticed the sibling similarity in their voice inflections?

"No Kelsea and Will?" I tried to remain focused.

"Nope. Had to split parenting duties. Wyatt's my date."

"What a nice date." I smiled and, before I could miss mine, I continued, "Whatcha eating, Wy?"

"Nugs."

"Nugs." I laughed. "Gosh, everything is an abbreviation now-a-days, huh?"

"It appears so," Nola agreed.

"What's the toy?"

"It's a little sand bucket." He turned the container around, showing me that he had already adorned it with McDonald's sponsored stickers.

"That's pretty cool. I wish the adult meals came with those. I'm jealous," I offered in a hopefully not noticeably fake voice.

"Yeah, right?" Nola agreed. "The meal actually came in the bucket—dual purpose."

I took a couple bites of salad as students passed our table and shyly giggled out a "Hi, Miss Faulkner."

"Hi," I said while waving back.

"You're quite the celebrity," Nola acknowledged.

"So not used to it being me." As soon as it was out of my mouth, I wanted to take it back. Of all people, to say that to Finn's sister. I knew it was an open invitation to the topic that I absolutely did not want to approach.

"No, I—"

"Mom, can I go play now? I'm finished," Wyatt interrupted, practically bouncing in the seat next to me.

"Yeah." Nola smiled at her son. "Say 'excuse me' to Lar—Miss Faulkner."

"I know your real name." Wyatt smiled at me but not in a bratty sense—just proud.

"I know yours too," I joked back.

"You don't know my middle name," he tested.

"Hmmm...maybe not, Wyatt William Jamison."

"Hey!" he exclaimed surely shocked.

"People in school know everything, Wyatt. Don't forget that." Nola mockingly preached knowing that the middle name knowledge was compliments of Finn and had nothing to do with my occupation.

"We're like parents," I said letting Wyatt out of the booth. "We've got eyes in the back of our heads."

"Ewww. That's gross." He cringed but nonetheless took a glance at the back of my head. "And it's not true."

"Kids can't see them," Nola tagged in with me.

"Mom!"

"Go play, Wyatt. And be kind and...careful." Nola watched her son enter the visible play area as I sat back down. "I'm glad we have a chance to talk."

I took a sip from my coffee and resorted to sarcastic, defensive Lara. "How can you talk in a place like this? It's so loud. But I'm glad there is such a good turnout."

Nola didn't give me the pass. Should have figured. Her brother wouldn't have either. "I know what he did at school." And then, just so there wasn't any confusion as to the "he" she was referring to, added, "in the parking lot."

I shook my head thinking *here it comes*. "This is not the time to do this."

"He didn't have a right to do that," she forged on. "I know Wyatt is acting up. But it shouldn't have anything to do with what is going on between the two of you. We've tried to keep him sheltered from that…from everything." She closed her eyes in a long, respectful blink to the dark topic surrounding her brother.

"I know. He's a good kid. And you know I certainly wouldn't say anything or treat him differently."

"Yes. We absolutely know that." She continued, "Finn was just trying to find a way to keep in touch with you."

"There's the phone," I spit out.

"And would you answer it?" Nola defended her brother but immediately backtracked. "No. Look, he went about it the wrong way. I laid into him…laid into him…over it. He's a wreck, Lara."

"No kidding. He needs help."

Nothing tasted good anymore. I was sick to my stomach. I gave up on the salad and was sucking on the straw of an empty cup of iced coffee just to have something to do.

"Not because of that…because of you. He loves you so much, and I know you feel the same way. You can't just stop."

Despite what she said being true, I would not admit to my mutual feelings. I knew it would go directly back to Finn, and he didn't deserve to know that I was not only thinking of him but still ached for and loved him. "I'm sorry. I can't do this." Damn it, I was near tears. I didn't want anyone from work to see me like this.

"Here." Nola handed me one of the cardboard-like napkins. As I turned my head and dabbed my eyes, she continued, "Please give him a chance. Just listen to him. I'm telling you, he's not on drugs," she spoke the last word quieter considering the youthful crowd among us. "He hasn't been for years."

"C'mon, Nola," I crumbled up the napkin and recomposed myself. "I saw him. And when I look back, it was all there. I mean, all of it—the mood swings…being up all night…. Don't tell me you didn't know. That was what you were arguing about at the baseball game, wasn't it?" It clicked in my brain just as it was coming out of my mouth.

"Yes. Well…no. There's an explanation. I swear to you. We were arguing about a choice that he made. It wasn't the right one."

"What? What are you talking about?"

"I can't say. It's Finn's place to tell you. But I will tell you this, things are better now. Believe me when I say that. It's all better. He's better. All he needs now is for you to listen to him. Please, if he calls, can you just listen to him?"

I could see the sincerity in her eyes and hear it in her voice. I believed she was telling me the truth, not only because she was saying it, but because there hadn't been a word about Finn in any type of press for over a week or so. And, yes, despite myself, I was keeping tabs. But then I wondered, still so confused, what was the whole truth?

"If he calls," I replied. "He hasn't lately. And I am not calling him," I added with an adamant tone.

"Can I tell him that?" Her face relaxed.

"Nola," I warned, already unsure that I was doing the right thing. Relenting, "I suppose you would, anyway."

"Not if you truly didn't want me to."

God help me. "I didn't say that." As she reached her hands out to mine across the table, I supplemented, "No promises."

"No promises. No guarantees. I get it. Life is that way. Just listen to him. You don't even have to talk."

***

The acidy feeling in my stomach only grew as I left McDonald's. I figured Matchmaker Nola was probably on the phone with her brother before I even started the Jeep's ignition. God, a good part of me wanted so desperately to hear from him…to talk with him. But another part knew that it wasn't going to be a talk like I was imagining—a talk like we used to have. How could it be? There was so much between us.

I purposefully went to sleep earlier than usual that night, giving myself an excuse for not picking up the phone if he called. But Finn didn't call. I got up the next morning and checked both my cell and my landline. No missed calls or messages. I went to work anticipating being angry when he called me while I was there. But there was still no "Roxanne" belting out of my phone. It would be after dismissal, I thought. But still, no call.

At least the acidy feeling went away by the time he called me the following day. It was Wednesday around dinner time. I debated about leaving it go to voice mail but knew if I did, I would only be playing games. I had to "woman-up" and answer.

"Hello?" I answered generically— something I rarely did with him.

"Lar, it's Finn."

"Oh, hi." I had tried to sound casual, but it came off all wrong.

Finn left out a nervous laugh, for sure knowing that I was nervous too by my comment. "How are you?"

"I'm sad, Finn." Whoa, where did that honesty come from? Let's add some sarcasm. "How are you? Hope *you're* well."

"I was going to call you before, but I didn't think you

wanted me to. I've been thinking of you, and Nola said I should call. But if you want to talk later—"

"No. I told Nola to tell you to call. How's the tour shaping up?" I tried to be kinder thinking back to what his sister had told me. Plus, I could tell that, despite being nervous talking with me—which he never, ever was before—Finn sounded more like himself than he had in maybe a couple months.

"Still on course…busy…just over a week." He had been speaking in a staccato rhythm, but now there was an even more defined pause. "Lara? I'm sorry you're sad. I know I did that to you."

"So, we're actually going to have a real talk?"

"I want to explain some things to you. Can we meet up? I want to see you. I don't want to do this on the phone."

"If you're around." Why did that sound accusatory? I knew he had always bent over backward to see me, which may have, actually, led to the problem in the first place.

"I will be."

"In person?"

His laugh was staggered. "That's what seeing you means."

Of course that's what it means. The idea just made me so nervous. It was like I couldn't even talk.

I tried again. "You know my schedule. I'm free weekends and nights."

"I'm going to be in the city on Friday, but a few days after that I'll be on the road for a while."

"Friday's good." I could see him, and then, if it didn't work out, I knew he would be gone for months on end. "After work? Somewhere around here?"

"Yeah. I'll text you Friday before you leave work."

"Sounds good."

But it didn't sound good at all. In fact, it sounded almost the opposite. It sounded like I was setting myself up to being hurt all over again.

"Okay," he responded.

"Finn," I said, "Don't…." *Let me down, hurt me….*

"What?"

"Never mind." I shouldn't beat him up before I actually listened to him. "Hear from you on Friday."

"Friday," he confirmed.

CHAPTER TWENTY

Amazingly, I slept well the rest of the week. I think having a rational, albeit tense, conversation with Finn helped put things more at ease than they had been in a while. It didn't mean by any measure, though, that I thought Friday would be a dream day and that all would be miraculously right between us. But I had told Nola I would listen, and I would, out of curiosity and out of closure. I wanted to be able to look him in the eyes and know, one way or the other, if it was possible to have resolution on this issue or on our relationship altogether. While I didn't necessarily want the latter to be true, at least it would be closure—something we had never, ever had before.

Always receiving the entire school attendance e-mail, I knew Wyatt wasn't in school on Friday. But there were a greater number of absences in general that day. It was Memorial Day weekend. So, there were probably a lot of long weekend family getaways. Finn might have been going with them had he not been appearing on *Good Morning America* kicking off their summer concert series that morning. I only knew that because I stalked his webpage to see why he was going to be in the New York area.

As the day went on, I slowly started getting more and more apprehensive about meeting Finn. I was only able to eat a banana and a cracker for lunch. Dressed up more than usual for a casual Friday, I had debated back and forth for hours the night before on what to wear. I wanted to look good. No—I wanted to look fabulous so that he could see what he threw away. But I didn't want the situation to be all cheerful. So my ensemble was all black—black skinny jeans and a black top accented by silver ball earrings and a huge circular pendent necklace, neither of which he had bought me. By pure coincidence, my hair appointment had been the day before. So I asked her to add some platinum highlights for extra effect.

Nerves I had anticipated, but the anger I had not. I was getting upset because Finn had clearly told me he would text me before the end of work. It was now way past that and no text or call for that matter. The students had been dismissed over a half hour before and most of the staff had left with well wishes for a relaxing, long weekend. I made copies for the following week but kept my phone nearby. In my rational mind, I knew Finn had a lot going on in the final days before his tour start. Maybe he had lost track of time or maybe he had just figured he would come directly over to the school instead of calling me first. My irrational mind, of course, told me he didn't care, and he was paying me back for bailing on him when he was in need. I thought of looking up the *Good Morning America* website and seeing if I could watch his morning act. But I decided viewing his sexy self performing would sway my judgment, and I needed to stay mad or, at least, neutral. So, not wanting the temptation, I turned the computer off completely.

I had sorted through my numerous copies and was labeling boxes for summer storage when Xenia walked into my room. "Hey, you're still here." I acknowledged my principal's presence. "I thought you would have been gone after a long week."

"I was on my way out." Her voice was very methodic, still, and purposeful. "Lara, I'm guessing you haven't heard."

I finished the last few labels and looked up. "What?"

"You better sit down."

God, those words were never good strung together. I sat on the edge of my desk. But it didn't matter—even a desk couldn't hold me. I nearly collapsed after finally understanding why I hadn't heard from Finn. Xenia explained to me how she saw a breaking news article on her computer just as she was about to leave. There weren't many details, but Finn had been involved in a pedestrian accident. He had been hit. Ambulances were at the scene. His condition was not being released and the location was not being disclosed.

"Okay." I breathed in deeply. "Okay." Breathe again. "Oh, God." And again. "I've got to call his sister."

"All right. Do you have her number, or do you need me to—"

"No, no, I got it." My hands were shaking uncontrollably as I called Nola's cell. Xenia calmly looked to me as I listened to the phone ring and finally go to voice mail. With sporadic breathing, I tried to sound more controlled than I actually was while leaving the message. "It's Lara. What's going on? I know I probably don't have a right to even call. But can you let me know please? I'm worried sick." I pressed end and looked to Xenia. "The news didn't say anything more? Nothing? Not when? Not where?"

"No, Lara, I'm sorry. I don't even know who I could call to find out. Do you want me to drive you home?"

"No. I don't…I don't want to go home. I want to see Finn. God, but I have no idea where he's even at."

Xenia looked at me for a moment. Complete helplessness was strung across her face. She offered the only thing she could. "Well, let me sit with you. Maybe his sis—"

As if on cue, my phone rang. Seeing Nola's phone number light up, I immediately answered. "Nola?"

"No, it's Will." He sounded awful—completely deflated.

I was a jittery mess. "Will, how's Finn? What's going on?"

Instead of answering my question, he instead asked one of his own. "Lara, where are you?"

"I'm still at work." What? How's Finn? "I just—"

Interrupting, "We're at the hospital. Can you come?"

"Finn? How's Finn? What's—"

"Finn is all right. From what I know, they're still running some tests—just precautionary. But emotionally…."

I should have been relieved by that statement. But there was something so foreboding especially how his voice simply, solemnly faded. Did it have something to do with the drugs?

"What? What does that mean? What hospital are you at? In the city?" I looked at Xenia who was scrambling her eyes back and forth as she was processing the information just from my side of the conversation.

"No. Our hospital. General on Fifth Street. Can you come down here?"

"He's here? Yeah. Absolutely. Of course. But Will, what is it? What's going on? If he's—"

"It's Wyatt." His voice broke. "He was with Finn. The car struck him. It's pretty bad."

I made some kind of animalistic screech as the phone started to slide from my face. Xenia's eyes grew wide trying to interpret my movement. She steadied my balance as I lifted the phone back to my ear.

"Oh my God. Oh my God. I didn't know. I—" I wasn't helping matters not being able to put a complete sentence together.

I heard Will's voice re-enter my brain from across the line. "We can't be in two places in the hospital at once, and we need to be with Wyatt. Can you come? Finn's gonna need you."

I was nodding my head in agreement, although Will couldn't see it. "I'm already halfway down the hall, all right? I'll be right there. I'll be," I choked on my words. "right there." I looked at Xenia who waved her hand urging me to go. "Will, Wyatt…he's gonna be fine," I spoke literally now halfway down the hall.

"We're scared, Lara. Just get here. I gotta go."

Oh, man, I was too. Wyatt. Wyatt. His smile was flashing in my brain as I raced up the stairs. "I know your real name." "Pop-pop, good one." "My uncle can sing!" God help me, that little chatterbox just had to be all right. I loved Finn more deeply than I could have ever imagined, and thinking that he had been hurt or worse tore me to the core—shook my very being. But knowing that his nephew, just seven years old, had apparently sustained critical injuries was something simply inconceivable. How could that be? How could the world allow that to happen? He just had to be all right. Nothing else mattered—nothing. I exited the building focused on nothing but getting to Finn and Wyatt.

***

Finding, or more accurately, being able to get to Finn in the hospital was quite the ordeal. The hospital was very protective of the information they were divulging as to his whereabouts. Although it did seem that, mercifully, there weren't any press or other Finn Murphy groupies camped out anywhere. I was assuming this was only the case because people believed, as I had, that Finn was in Manhattan when the accident occurred. It only made sense. It was documented via national television that he was there mid-morning. Why would he be in a small upstate community in the afternoon? Because of me. Because of Wyatt. Damn it! What happened? I had gotten no more information on the less than ten-minute drive to the hospital.

My saving grace to finding Finn was his publicist. Reese spotted me at the counter pleading with hospital personnel to see Finn. She instantly recognized me. Although I barely recognized her because of my crazed state.

"He's all right—just some minor stuff," she said, pulling me aside and sliding her hands down my arms in a comforting way.

"Oh, God. Yeah, I know. I talked with his brother-in-law. I just…I want to see him."

"I know. I'm glad you're here. He practically just forced me to leave. I've never seen him like this. I know you being here will help."

"I'm not sure about that." I paused. "You know, Finn and I…we…we're not exactly together right now." I wasn't sure who knew what. So I played it close to the vest.

"I know, Lara. Just because I haven't put out a press release doesn't mean that I don't know what's going on in our boy's life. It's my job to know. Even if he thinks he doesn't need anyone right now, he does. And Lara, it's you."

Silent tears were escaping my eyes. "Can you take me to him?"

"Yeah." She looked down at her vibrating phone. "Come on. Let's go. But Finn was right about one thing. I do need to leave. I have a lot of work to do, especially trying to make sure that he and his family have privacy."

Walking beside her, Reese started telling me how she had been on the phone with Finn when the accident occurred. That was how she knew about it and how to get to him so quickly since she had been in the city with him earlier. Mid-story and mid-hospital corridor, Reese's phone vibrated again. She frowned and picked it up immediately, starting in on an animated phone conversation. I walked silently beside her with the new knowledge that the accident happened at the local train station. I tried to picture Wyatt and Finn in my mind—happy and talking one minute and in pure terror the next.

Reese erased those conjured up mental pictures when she suddenly stopped and pointed across the lobby-like area. I followed her outreached hand to see Finn. He was talking with someone in scrubs and shaking his head making a "no" statement. Even though I had been reassured by both Will and Reese that Finn was all right, I didn't truly believe it until I saw him in person. My legs got wobbly with pure relief. Reese touched my shoulder and scurried off in the direction we had come, still talking on the phone.

As if knowing that I was suddenly in his presence, Finn turned and looked at me across the way. "Lara?" He seemed surprised.

"Hey."

It was the first time I had seen him in weeks—since that heart-wrenching parking lot episode. That all seemed so pointless now…so childish. I made my way over to this man who, despite his flaws, I loved unconditionally.

I tentatively put my hand up to his cheek noting a cut on his right eyebrow and another just under his left eye. "Are you all right?"

He backed away forcing my hand to fall to my side. "How's Wyatt? Where is he?"

I searched his eyes wanting to understand what state he was in. "I don't know. I came to find you first."

"Oh." He steadied his gaze on me hopefully feeling the compassion that I so wanted him to. Slowly, he turned back to the hospital worker. "I need to see my nephew. I'll sign whatever I need to sign later. Just please tell me where I can find Wyatt."

I could see the empathy in the eyes of the doctor or nurse or aide—whoever he was—as Finn pleaded with him. Sporting long, wavy, hippie-like, salt-and-pepper hair, the man in scrubs told Finn and me which elevator to take and which station to go to. I didn't like how he said the directions in such a melancholy way. I don't think Finn noticed. He was too worked up. But I did.

Finn walked with a slight limp as we made our way to the elevator. I looked down to see that his foot was tightly wrapped in some type of bandage. I imagined it was a badly sprained ankle but later found out it was his Achilles. Other than that, physically, he appeared to be all right. It was emotionally, as Will had cautioned, where he suffered the most.

He was the first to break the silence. "It was awful, Lara. He looked so bad."

"I know." I tried to sound reassuring. But I didn't know. I wasn't there. I couldn't see the horrifying event that Finn was surely replaying in his mind over and over again. Waiting for the elevator doors to open, I reached out my hand for his and, thankfully, he took it.

His grip was tight as if he was holding onto life itself. He looked straight ahead as he spoke. "It was supposed to be our special boys' day. You should have seen him. He was dancing up on stage with me during the breaks in front of all those people. He was having a blast."

I smiled slightly, imagining that active seven-year-old eating up the spotlight. "*G.M.A.?*"

Finn nodded as we stepped into the elevator which, miraculously, was empty. As I pressed the button for the correct floor, not wanting to release my other hand from Finn's, he continued talking. "So, we went for something to eat in the city and rode the train back here. Wy just loves taking the train. I'd rather not put up with the onlookers. But you know that kid. I'd do anything for him. All we had to do when we got back was cross the parking lot, get into the car, and go to Nola's. That's all." And he repeated in frustration, "That's all."

Ah, the pieces were finally starting to come together. "Finn—" I hurt for him.

He continued as if he was not even aware that I was

there. "We had just gotten off. The car came out of nowhere, I swear. It jumped onto the sidewalk. We were on the sidewalk for Christ's sake. I couldn't react fast enough. I couldn't. I tried. It hit Wyatt—hard."

"Finn," I couldn't help it. I was trying to be brave for him, but I was in tears. "It's all right."

"I heard the driver had a stroke. That's what caused him to lose control. I guess he died instantly."

"I…I don't know. I…." The "why" and "how" pieces were now in place for me.

"God, why did we have to take that train?" he questioned in distress. "We should have just driven."

I tried to be the rational one. "You said Wyatt loves them."

"I keep hearing the sound of him hitting. It's the worst sound I've ever heard." Finn whispered in response as we stepped out of the elevator. When I squeezed his hand, not being able to speak myself, he continued, "Wyatt was standing up and trying to move like he was all right, but yet he was screaming and crying absolutely horrifically. Some guy, some guy in a suit, got to him first and put him in his arms. There was blood. He was bleeding." That said blood was still noticeable on the shoulder of Finn's light shirt. "Wyatt reached out for me like he was a baby. I had him in my arms. He wouldn't let go. There were people asking him questions and making sure he stayed awake. 9-1-1 was called. I told them to get on my phone and tell Reese to call Nola. Oh God, Lara, it was all going so fast. He actually calmed down before the ambulance arrived, but his eyes, they were starting to flutter. By the time they had him strapped on that board, he was so still. Oh my God, he was so still."

I was glad that Finn was opening up, but I didn't know if I could handle any more of his first-person account. We had reached the nurses' station before I heard about the, surely, petrifying ambulance ride over. A nurse gave us an update on Wyatt. I didn't understand the medical terminology but realized that what it boiled down to was a waiting game. Wyatt had suffered a traumatic brain injury. A CT scan showed a fractured skull and there was a long medical term that basically meant brain fluid. He was unconscious and not reacting to any stimulus. It was, indeed, critical. Finn kept shaking his head like if he did it long enough, he could shake the horrible words and situation away.

He dropped my hand the moment we got to the threshold of Wyatt's private room. The sight of that little boy lying so uncharacteristically still with monitors and equipment surrounding him was surreal. I looked at Finn whose face seemed to bleach out instantly. I tried to get him to reclaim my hand, but it was to no avail. He was as stationary as Wyatt was and wouldn't take a step farther.

Will was standing near the window while Nola was sitting bedside with her hands in a prayer like position and her eyes fixated on her son. Silently, I crossed the room and gave Will a reassuring hug. I then did the same with Nola as she stood to meet me.

With bloodshot eyes and new tears forming, Nola walked over to her brother and embraced him. "I'm glad you're okay."

Wiping his own tears away, he replied, "How can you say that? If I hadn't taken him—"

Nola interrupted him and pulled away so she could look at him directly. "Don't do that. It wasn't —" She stopped and was able to take his hand where I couldn't and direct him closer to his nephew. "Sit with him. Talk with him. He needs to know you're here."

Finn sat down in the seat that Nola had just vacated. He put his hands on top of Wyatt's tiny right hand, staring at the boy he would do anything for. I went around the other side and touched Wyatt's left hand, pausing to look at him and then catching Finn's eyes before following Will and Nola out of the room. We all silently recognized the fact that he needed alone time with his nephew. It was for

Wyatt. But it was for Finn too.

As Will and Nola walked to the nurses' station, I leaned up against the wall next to Wyatt's room and listened. I wasn't doing it to be obtrusive. I was doing it because I knew how much Finn was hurting, and I wanted to be there for him if he needed me to be.

It took a few moments, but I eventually heard Finn say, with his voice cracking, "Hey, Earp. Hey, buddy. C'mon, we need you to wake up. C'mon, you're never this quiet…from the day you were born." I smiled, despite the dire situation, listening to Finn speak the truth. "I want to hear more of those famous Wyatt stories. It's your big chance to talk, talk, talk. You got our full attention." There was a pause as if Finn believed that just saying that would cause Wyatt to suddenly wake and start talking his normal mile-a-minute chatter. When he didn't, Finn tried again. "Wyatt, c'mon, man." And then it was just heart-wrenching. "Wy, I'm sorry. I'm sorry. I'm so sorry." I wiped my own tears as I heard Finn sniffle out a final, "Wyatt."

Then I heard it. Finn took refuge in the place he knew best—words harmoniously strung together with melody. I recognized the Dixie Chicks song "Godspeed (Sweet Dreams)." It wasn't a particularly popular song, but I knew it. I had first heard it shortly after giving up my baby all those years ago and it had struck a soothing chord in me then. Now I knew, or at least hoped, it was doing the same for Finn.

Crouched on the floor outside Wyatt's room, I started kneading my knuckles into the inner corner of my eyes willing them to give up their relentless tearing onslaught. It seemed to work but, consequently, left my fingers coal black from mascara remnants. I stood, trying to recollect myself, noticing Will and Nola approaching. Nola froze when she heard her brother singing and looked from the doorway to me. I shook my head, helpless.

I was helpless. We all were. I didn't know what to do.

Or even if I should.

As if reading my mind, Nola reached out and clasped both of my hands. "Stay. Please."

I squeezed back, giving Wyatt's mother what strength I had in me. "I need to go splash some water on my face. He…they…don't need to see me like this."

"But they do need to see you."

I half-smiled, gave an extra squeeze, and followed the signs to the public restroom. God, I looked awful —such a contrast to that sleek persona I had prepared to present to Finn when the day had started. A water geyser over my entire head wouldn't be able to reclaim any semblance of normalcy. I dabbed dampened paper towels on my face and reapplied some colored lip balm. Taking an extended moment to breathe in and out, I grabbed the sink edge, said a silent prayer, and started the short walk back to Wyatt's room.

When I returned, Will and Nola were sitting together at Wyatt's side, she leaning into him. They were looking up at Finn who was standing at the foot of the bed, hands shoved in his pockets. He was telling them how Wyatt was signing autographs right alongside him after the *G.M.A.* concert. I was glad Finn was sharing something affirmative with his sister and brother-in-law and not dwelling on the accident itself. Everyone needed positive vibes in that room. I smiled, thinking of Wyatt's boundless energy and how he was a star in his own right. Nola saw me and smiled back causing Finn to turn my direction.

"Lar…."

I was at a crossroads. I so wanted to go up and embrace him and not let go. I wanted to feel the warmth of his chest against my cheek. I wanted to be his security blanket and he mine. A couple of months ago, there wouldn't have been even the slightest hesitation to do just that. But nothing was the same. Nothing.

And I couldn't tell by the way he stopped half-way through my name what he wanted from me. So I put out a generic offer to the entire clan. "How about if I go get everyone some coffee or something to eat?"

"I can't eat," Nola stated.

Standing up, Will agreed to my offer. "Coffee. Coffee would be great. Please." He started pulling out his wallet.

"No, no, I got it. Just coffee?" I asked glad to be doing something.

"Coffee's fine. Three?" Will said looking at Finn.

"Yeah." Finn's voice was soft, serene, contemplative.

"Cream, sugar, what?" I directed my question to Will and Nola.

"Get a sugar substitute for her if they have it and mine with just a little bit of cream," Will answered and then turned to face Finn.

I knew his coffee order, though—strong and black. "I got it." I smiled slightly at Finn's appreciative eyes warming my heart if even just for a moment.

CHAPTER TWENTY-ONE

The cafeteria, of course, seemed to be at the farthest point possible from Wyatt's room. After two elevators and extensive hallways, I finally made my way there. And, of course, I think I hit mid-shift change. So the line of patrons not only included family and friends of patients but scrub-clothed workers. I paid for the java, went to the condiments bar, added the appropriate additives, wrote initials on cups, re-fastened the lids, and started my journey back to Wyatt's room.

The sight I saw when I approached the room is one that I will forever have ingrained in my mind. Nola and Will were just inside the doorway of the room. Nola, barely standing, was crying hysterically in Will's arms. Finn was immediately outside the room. His back was to me as he struck his fist against the wall.

And I knew.

There was only one thing that could onset those extreme emotions. I glanced past Will and Nola to look into the room. There was a doctor with Wyatt but the monitors were silent.

Everything was happening in slow motion. My brain was a foggy mess. I understood the situation but, yet, how could anyone truly comprehend such devastation?

I placed the coffee carrier on the floor against the wall and walked over to Finn. I rubbed his back with my palm in slow, soothing strokes. Acknowledging my touch, he turned around and instantly melted into my arms. I absorbed his weight. I absorbed his pain. I absorbed his grief.

Holding Finn, I mouthed an "I'm sorry" to Will and Nola. I could barely make out the doctor telling them that he was going to give us some time alone. Finn was shaking. I held him tighter and even tighter while watching Nola collapse onto the chair inside the room. She was staring at her son lying so innocently…so still…so gone. I reached up and wiped a tear from my eye. The motion caused Finn to pull away from me. Mere inches away, I met his eyes and slowly nodded my head up and down to give him support and encouragement.

We heard Nola from inside the room, "He's gone. He's gone. How can he be gone?"

Finn turned from me, looking as if he wanted to punch something again. "Oh…God. No. Damn it! No!"

"Finn, I'm—" I reached out for him, but he slowly walked trance-like into Wyatt's room. I collected myself with a huge inhale and followed him.

Will was seated holding onto his wife when Finn and I entered. It was so hard to look at them. I could not imagine a loss any larger. Their beautiful boy was feet away and looked like he was simply sleeping. But he wasn't.

"We…he…oh my God, this can't be real." Nola, eyes swollen with red rims, looked at Finn and me. "He and Kelsea were just getting out their beach stuff yesterday. He told Kels she could have his old floaties. He wouldn't need them. He was a big kid." She scrunched up her nose and squinted her eyes so intensely, but it didn't stop the tears from pouring or the pain from piercing. Finn leaned up against the wall for support just as Nola turned to her husband with a new thought suddenly invading her mind.

"Kelsea…we need to get her. She's been in that place too long. She needs to see one of us. She was so scared when we dropped her off there."

My mind was spinning all over the place. I couldn't focus. I imagined it's what extreme ADHD felt like. Wyatt was gone…gone…dead. He would never again be sitting at that computer or walking down the hall. He would never again be swinging away at the baseball. He would never again tease his little sister. Kelsea…right, where was Kelsea?

I must have asked that last part out loud because Will's voice interrupted my racing mind. "The hospital has a daycare downstairs." Still holding onto his wife, he directed his next statement to her. "Honey, I don't think you're in any shape to pick her up right now. She's not ready. We're not ready."

Will was holding it together. How? I had no idea. But I was sure that it would all fall apart sooner rather than later.

Nola, in contrast, was dazed and bewildered. Trying to rationalize what her husband said, she turned toward her brother. "Finn, will you go get her?"

Finn's answer was immediate and adamant. "No." When we all turned to him astonished, he shook his head stating quite plainly, "I can't be responsible for your children. No. No. No, I can't. No."

I looked from Finn to a distraught Nola and Will. They were three lost souls drowning in a grief more enormous than all the oceans combined. They were suffering from shell shock in a war far greater than one with any physical bullets. I had to be the strong one despite my connection to Wyatt—despite my loss.

I cleared my voice not realizing that it was, indeed, cluttered with emotion too. "I can get her. I can even take her to my place if you need the time. We can have a sleepover," I added trying to bring the slightest spot of sunlight onto the dank situation.

Nola was still staring at Finn as if trying to understand

his response to her request. Finn couldn't keep eye contact, though. I knew his guilt for being with Wyatt when everything went down was eroding his very being. Nola couldn't see it in her grief. She just saw her brother who was always there for her. In her mind, she couldn't understand why he would deny her this…now.

Will tried to register a response from his wife to my proposition. "Honey, that sounds good to me. What do you think?"

"Wha…?" Confused. Lost.

"Lara can take Kelsea home with her. Spend the night, right?" He turned to me.

"Sure. Absolutely. Whatever you need," I quietly answered— the room demanded it.

Nola slowly looked my direction and acknowledged my offer. "Yeah. Yeah. That might be… that might be best. Thanks, Lara."

Relieved that we were getting resolution to one concern, I breathed out. "Oh God, it's no problem. I love that little girl. You know that." There was a time I thought I would end up a part of her family. Watching Finn walk toward the window, I refocused. "I just…what else can I do?"

"You being here. It means the world to us." Nola choked out looking at Finn.

"I'm so, so sorry." What else could I say?

Again, Will found the strength. "We know." He cleared his throat in the first sign that he, as suspected, was vulnerable too. "Uh, so, the daycare is on the bottom floor. I'll go to the desk and call them to let them know it's you picking her up."

Nola perked up suddenly, almost panicky. "Lara, don't tell her anything. Don't tell her, all right? We need to tell her." And then more calmly, more sadly, she added, "Let her have her innocence for one more night."

"Of course. Anything I need to know? No allergies, right? Meds?"

"Nope. She's good," Nola answered and then, remembering suddenly, "Oh, God, her car seat. You'll need her car seat."

The three of us stared at one another not being able to figure out a solution to what would normally be an easy dilemma. Finn was not only not involved in our conversation, he was emotionally checked out, staring blankly out the window. I wanted to help him. Yet I knew it was more important to take care of Will and Nola via Kelsea at the moment.

Will, again the rational one, figured out a resolution. "Just let her drive our car." He stood from his wife's side. "We can switch?" Already getting the key and fob off his key chain, he directed the question to me.

"Oh, um, sure, that's fine," I agreed.

"We're in the emergency lot. Beep it. You'll find it."

"I know where you are—your Cadillac. I'm actually two away from you. You came together?" I asked since, in my mind, Will came from work and Nola from home. Hence, I had believed there to be two separate cars.

"Yeah, I took a half day today. I was home when it happened. We were waiting to all go to the…. Oh, God." Will's voice broke now.

"It's all right," I said immediately and swiftly. Knowing we all couldn't be bumbling messes, I tried hard to keep it under control and handed him my car keys. "Here. Here are the keys to the Jeep." Out of the corner of my eyes, I noticed Finn stringing his hair at the mention of our Jeep.

"Tell her we all love her." Nola spoke with tears rolling down her face.

"I will. I can keep her as long as you need me to. She'll be fine," I tried in a reassuring way but realized there were no guarantees in life that anything will be fine or safe. With that, I took another glance at Finn still so stoic and shut-down. My heart broke. I wanted to take on his pain which, of course, was impossible. "Finn?" When he didn't turn, I offered a more generic goodbye to everyone. "You know

I'm here for all of you if you need anything." I didn't like the distance between the two of us, but I understood that it was an extenuating circumstance, and nothing should be taken as face value. For this, I prayed. And I was not known to be the most spiritual creature on the planet.

***

The first question Kelsea asked when I arrived was where her Uncle Finn was. I suppose the only times she usually saw me, Finn was at my side. So his absence was surely another conundrum in this young girl's already disheveled day.

"He had to be with your mommy and daddy." I tried to put on a smile.

"I want Daddy." She appeared quiet, tired, a little spooked.

"Your daddy dropped you off, huh?"

"Yeah."

She nodded her head while taking my hand as we started out the door. Her tiny hand in mine seemed more childlike than ever. Even that made me want to cry. But I held it together for her and her family.

"Your dad has to be with your mommy and Uncle Finn."

"I want to go."

"You know what, Kels? You and me? We get to have a special princess night together."

Her eyes lit up a tiny bit but, yet, were still wary. "Wyatt too?"

I stumbled on my stride. I couldn't help it. Not being able to look that innocence in the eyes, I said, "No. Just us girls…not…Wyatt."

***

I gained more of Kelsea's trust through food. I made

us whole wheat rotini with ground turkey and marinara sauce for dinner. Kelsea loved the spirals but picked away the meat. Amazingly, she munched away at the broccoli "trees" as long as I provided ranch dressing. Just like her uncle, I couldn't help but think. And she loved the milk. She had a hearty appetite, for which I was glad. I did not.

My phone rang while I was cleaning up after dinner and Kelsea was attempting to play a game on my laptop. I jumped, startled by the phone's sound, and instantly got a pit feeling in my stomach that it was Finn. I should have known better, though. It wasn't his ring. It was, instead, Nola. She was brief, obviously exhausted, and just wanted to check up on her daughter—now her only living child. I gave the phone to Kelsea who handled it like a pro while spilling out the details of our fun girls' adventure. After she said goodnight to her parents, I reclaimed the phone. Will was on the other end this time. He informed me that they would call in the morning to make arrangements for bringing Kelsea home. I reassured him that everything was all right and was going to ask about Finn when I heard Nola crying in the background.

Sniffling himself, Will said, "I gotta go, Lara. Thanks. Thanks again."

After brushing teeth and changing Kelsea into one of my smaller T-shirts—a nightgown for her—we settled on the sofa, sharing my white and blue throw blanket. I downloaded a few children's books on my e-reader and made sure she could see. She zonked out on the sofa next to me somewhere in the midst of the third book. I picked both her and the blanket up, cradling them in my arms. Her soft, wispy hair tickled my cheek as she naturally curved into my shoulder.

"Mommy," she mumbled, and my heart broke, not only for her but for me. She missed her mommy and, with the extreme emotions of the day, I ached for the child that I never gave a chance to call me "Mommy."

I tucked in Wyatt's baby sister on the air mattress

beside my bed. Knowing that Kelsea had graduated to a toddler bed at home, I figured the air mattress was the next best thing in my abode. I didn't want to risk her falling out of my bed or off the sofa, especially since she was in unfamiliar surroundings. And I wasn't ready to go to sleep yet. In fact, I wasn't sure I would be able to sleep at all that night.

No longer did I have the distraction of little Kelsea Jamison to keep my mind circling back to the devastation of the day. Now I was alone with my thoughts and, for the first time in hours, my tears. I allowed myself to openly sob, recalling everything from the moment Xenia entered my room to Finn collapsing in my arms. I tried to muffle my angst with my hands to my face, but it was to no avail. I needed the release. It was the type of messy, ugly, snot running cry that one did when there was no hope left.

Once I recollected myself, I went and checked on Kelsea. Sleeping peacefully, she had her thumb popped innocently in her mouth. She, I thought, would be what would get us all through.

I next turned on my laptop to search for articles about the accident. There were a good number of them now. And, this time, the information was accurate. Of course, the emphasis was on Finn's condition. He was the superstar after all. It was Finn's involvement that made it, for the most part, newsworthy—at least nationally. He was the headliner. Wyatt was the causality. The most updated article, sadly, reported the truth. There it was in black and white—Wyatt William Jamison dead at the tender age of seven.

I put the computer off to the side and curled myself into a fetal position. No sooner had I done that when the phone startled me again. I answered seeing Xenia's name on the caller ID. She had, of course, been monitoring the situation and waited to call, knowing that I would be occupied at some capacity with the Jamison family. I filled her in on what I knew and promised to keep her informed so that she would know what to do for the school community.

Then, in my solemn state, I texted Finn. *I'm here if U need to talk. Anytime…doesn't matter.*

When I didn't get a response back from him, I started to obsess on where he was, what he was doing and, most importantly, how he was doing. I couldn't help but worry about his state of mind. How was he going to be able to survive such devastation? Not only did he love that boy unconditionally, but he was there. He was there when the car hit. He was there in the ambulance. And he was there when the doctor confirmed the most devastating part of all. How? How do you witness that and survive yourself?

Then I thought of something I hadn't thought of in years—the night my father passed away. Although his death was stupid and senseless, it was, nonetheless, eerily similar to Wyatt's. Only it was my Uncle Jimmy being witness to his accident and my mother seeing everything from the moment the medical helicopter landed—she had been one of the nurses on duty that night. I picked up the phone and called my mom to tell her of Wyatt's accident. I listened as she consoled me as only a mother could and, for the first time in all those years, understood what horror she endured watching a life come suddenly, unexpectedly, tragically to an end.

Mercifully, I did manage to fall asleep sometime later that evening. The phone was still only a hand's length away, but it didn't matter. Finn hadn't called or texted.

***

The cheesy eggs and toast were not a hit for Kelsea's morning breakfast. So I conceded and poured her a bowl of cereal with milk. That brought a smile along with the orange slices substituting for teeth.

It was mid-morning when Will and Nola called again. I wondered if they had gotten any sleep. I sincerely doubted it but whole-heartedly hoped for it. They were going to need every ounce of strength to get through the next few days, never mind weeks, months, and years. They, of course, asked about Kelsea who was coloring and gluing outfits onto paper dolls I had cut out for her. They wanted to know if I could keep their daughter until late afternoon/early evening while they dealt with the arrangements… the legalese of a sudden death.

"Of course," I replied. "Of course."

"I mean, Lara, if you have other plans, we can—"

I interrupted Nola. "What plans would I have? Besides, even if I did, they wouldn't matter. Maybe I can see when the new 3D animated movie is playing?"

"Yeah. They both," she caught herself. "Well, they both wanted to see that."

"Popcorn and candy for lunch beats the fruit, veggies, hummus, and pita I have in the fridge." I added humor so that Nola didn't dwell on what she had just said. It would do no good.

"She'd love that." It didn't matter. I heard Nola choking up. "Someone will pick her up and switch back cars. Let's say between four and six?"

"We'll be back by then. And if things change, just let me know."

"Okay."

"Nola?" Was it appropriate to ask? "Is Finn…?"

She sighed at my partial question. "He tore out of the hospital shortly after you left. We were hoping he called you or came to your place." She sounded doubtful yet hopeful at the same time.

"No."

"Okay. Well, we'll deal with it," she said before saying goodbye and leaving me more concerned than ever.

***

The movie worked out perfectly. Kelsea enjoyed it

once she got the hang of 3D objects flying at her. She kept reaching out to try to touch things which got me to laugh for the first time in days. It was exhilarating to hear children laugh and clap during the movie. Yet it was also so sad realizing how precious life went on for so many of them and not for Wyatt. I wanted to scream to the parents, grandparents, care givers, etc. in the audience, "Hug your child. Don't let them go. Be proud of them. Love every moment. It is all so fleeting."

CHAPTER TWENTY-TWO

While I didn't know exactly who would pick Kelsea up, I was expecting Nola or Will or the combination of. In the back of my mind, I hoped that it would be Finn but knew from his reaction to the Kelsea request at the hospital and his non-reaction to my text, that the possibility of him showing up was nil to none. I did not expect his mother.

For obvious reasons, Mrs. Murphy did not look her cheerful, bouncy, put-together self as she stood in my doorway. I hadn't seen or talked with her since Finn and I had broken up and, selfishly, I couldn't help but wonder what she thought of me. I knew she had been one of our biggest advocates from the start of our relationship. But now? Did she blame me for the relationship ending and her son's downfall?

Any doubt was immediately erased as she said, "Oh." Her eyes dipped in sadness as she brought me into an embrace.

I held onto Finn's mother, Wyatt and Kelsea's grandmother, for an extended moment. I didn't realize until she secured me, how much I needed to be held…how much I needed to be comforted. I pulled away, grateful to the woman who was the true matriarch of the clan, and led her into the living room.

"I'm so, so sorry. I don't know what to say. I just can't believe you're here…that this is happening."

"I know." She paused looking at me. "He was just the best—the light and heart of our world. Every time we talked on the phone, he rambled on and on. And he loved that school."

"He's a good kid." I stumbled on the present tense use of the word. "He fit right in. I loved having him in my little club."

"Believe me," she said with the purist of sincerity. "I think that was the favorite part of his week. We all knew it." I was pondering if she purposefully emphasized "we all" in reference to Finn when she spoke again confirming my suspicion. "I want you to know, since Will's parents are with Nola and Will, we decided Zak"—she referenced her husband by his first name—"should go to the city to be with Finn."

"So, Finn… he's all right? He's at the penthouse?" I couldn't help but sound relieved yet desperate for information.

"Yeah. He answered our phone call when our flight got in. He doesn't sound good, but he was willing to have his dad come over while I came here. That's something."

"I'm scared for him," I admitted. "He was there. He saw all of it. He—"

"We're going to make sure he's all right, Lara," she said with as much reassurance, I'm sure, as she could muster under the circumstances. She spoke again more slowly and deliberately while looking directly at me. "You know, you two should be together."

"That's not what's important right now."

"It is and it isn't, huh?"

We both looked at each other for an extended moment. I knew what she was saying—the fragility of life and being with those we love despite the challenges. But, yet, it wasn't Finn's mom that I needed to talk to. It was

Finn. And that wasn't happening right then. Kelsea was what we had to focus on. Kelsea and dear, dear Wyatt.

"Is anything decided?" I continued. "I will do whatever…whatever any of you need. I'm not just saying that."

"I know. We know." She paused. "If Finn doesn't call you, we will. We'll make sure you know what's going on."

Before I could respond, the Flash, better known as Kelsea Jamison, entered the room, diving into Mrs. Murphy's legs. "Nana!"

"Beautiful baby girl." Finn's mother acknowledged her granddaughter with a blend of love and sorrow that were surely going to be a fixture in their family for some time to come.

***

Visitation at the funeral parlor was set from two until eight that Monday— ironically, Memorial Day Monday. A private, intimate service was to immediately follow. There wasn't an obituary cited in any of the local papers. Everything was done via word of mouth, e-mail, or some other electronic medium. Due to Finn's connection, there was enough press surrounding Wyatt's death despite, I am sure, Reese's best intentions. And the family wanted to keep it as personal as possible. So for that reason, and because they simply didn't know how they could bear two, Nola and Will chose just one day of visitation on the holiday itself.

Of course, I didn't know any of this information because of Finn. Mrs. Murphy lived up to her word and called Sunday shortly after noon to give me the details. She told me there truly wasn't anything for me to do. They had more than an abundance of food, and Kelsea was being taken care of between two sets of grandparents, etc.

"Let me know if anything changes. But, otherwise, I will be there tomorrow," I said speaking of the funeral parlor. "Maybe around six or so."

"That's so good of you," was Mrs. Murphy's response.

"Nothing could stop me." I paused. And then, unable to resist, "Will Finn—"

She spoke with a matronly confident tone. "He'll be there."

"Does he know that I will?" I asked so unsure of how our relationship stood.

"We told him all that you were doing and that you would most likely be coming."

"And?" I felt awful pumping Finn's mother for information, but I knew she understood.

"He's not giving any of us much."

"Okay," I lamented.

At least he was speaking with his parents if not me. And even if the circumstances were far worse than years before, they had a grip on him. They knew. They were standing guard. They wouldn't let anything happen. They had to be his rock and his home base because he didn't seem to want me. And could I blame him? Did he know how much I wanted to be there for him? Did he know that since the fear of losing him, since being at his side at the hospital, since Wyatt, that nothing else mattered? Maybe not. But what was even scarier was, if he did, did it just not matter to him anymore?

***

Among so many other vehicles in the parking lot, his sporty, steely blue coupe seemed to beacon out to me. I saw it as I pulled the Jeep into one of the few empty spots. As if the sad situation wasn't awful enough, I was beyond anxious with the anticipation of seeing Finn again. I hadn't eaten all day besides coffee and a granola bar. And they were threatening to come up as I parked my car a row and a few spaces down from Finn's.

And then I just sat in the car and breathed. I was

breathing for control, for strength, for peace. I was breathing for Wyatt, for his parents, for his sister, for Finn. But despite following the inhaling and exhaling techniques that I had seen Finn do so many times, it didn't help. I knew it wouldn't. This was just too intense and sad.

I gathered up my will and got out of the car. It was then that I saw another vehicle that, had I not been concentrating so much on Finn's, I surely would have noticed right away. It was a news van and beside it a few people were gathered in a small circle. Really? Not even now? Not even during the deepest, darkest moments of despair can this family be left alone? A couple heads swirled toward me and, luckily, I recognized one of them as Reese.

Looking at the reporting crew, she held up her hand in a stop motion and then walked over to me. "It's all right," she said. "I got it under control." But both her body and mine were semi-turned to make sure that they weren't filming.

"There's no respect," I admonished.

"It's their job. And, actually, they're being respectful. They're just filming some shots and are going to leave. I gave a generic statement. And I told them to not even consider approaching you."

"Thank you." I did another of those strong exhales. "Thank you so much. Did Finn see them? He'd have a fit."

"He would," she agreed. "But, no. He knew I would take care of it, as well as stopping anyone from the music business from coming too. He said he doesn't want any of it taking away from his family. But I have a feeling he also just doesn't want to deal with it. It's more than he can handle right now."

"I know." I sighed and, God, how I ached.

"Oh, sheez, there's another station," she grumbled, touched my hand, and scurried in that direction.

I went the opposite way, taking a deep breath and entering the funeral parlor. When I stepped inside, the first thing I noticed was the stand with the guest book. I picked up the pen and signed the paper. Along with their names, the few people listed above me had also written their relationship to the family. I stared and stared. What exactly was I?

I had to leave it blank, though— just like I supposed it should be—as one of the aides from work approached. "Lara," he said. "How are you?"

"We're all a little dazed right now, huh?" I commented while putting the pen down and grabbing one of the prayer cards.

"Not used to seeing all of us dressed up."

"Sad that we are," I offered re-examining my black slacks and blue ribbed top that I had purposefully picked out, knowing they were Wyatt's favorite colors.

"I'll see you tomorrow," was his answer as he exited.

Tomorrow? Work? God, how could I deal with that? How could the world just keep turning?

I didn't have much time to ponder as Xenia and Vanessa walked up to me on their way out. "I can't give you a bereavement day tomorrow." Xenia touched my hand. "But, Lara, I know this hits you like it's family. You do what you need to do. If you come in, I'll make sure no one bothers you at all. If you need to go home, you go home."

I gave my immediate boss a hug—something I had never done before. But with the emotional status of the day, it seemed fitting. And I realized it was another way Finn had taught me to let go and open up.

"Thanks, Xenia. I don't know if there would be any reason for me not to be there, though." My eyes did a quick dart of the hallway. I was thinking of Finn. I was looking for Finn. But I was not spotting Finn.

As Xenia exited, Vanessa gave me a hug. "How you doing, girlfriend?"

"I…I don't know," I admitted. "Thanks for calling me, Vanessa. It really helped."

"Have you talked with him since the hospital?"

Vanessa still didn't know what had caused the split between Finn and me. But after calling when she heard the news about the accident, she knew for sure how much I still loved him. I had confessed that much, but I suspected she already knew.

"No," I lamented. "He's here, right?"

"Yeah. But he seems to be making himself scarce."

I nodded my head in acknowledgement. "I better go and…and see." My exhale was strong but so unsure as I said goodbye to my friend and made my way into the main, doublewide room.

There were pockets of people everywhere. Some people I didn't know. But the other sixty-some percent were a weird clash of both halves of my life—my work life and my personal life with Finn's family. Still, like Reese said, I didn't see anyone from Finn's professional life or him for that matter.

Numbly, and ignoring all others, I made my way to the casket and knelt down on the low cushioned pew. I didn't last more than a couple minutes. I couldn't. It was so unbelievably wrong. He was a little boy. He hadn't even been on this earth for a decade. He liked superheroes and drawing and baseball. I saw him in school. I saw him at his house. I could not see him in that casket.

I got up desperate to find something else to hold my attention. Right next to the casket was a massive easel embellished with photographs and mementos—a life so short but filled with such love. There was a photo of a pregnant Nola, Wyatt's christening, him holding a baby Kelsea, recent beach photos, other close-up candids, a baseball card with him as the star, his first-grade picture, the four of them dressed up for a special event, Wyatt with Nana and Pop-Pop, Wyatt with Will's parents, and Wyatt with Uncle Finn. It hurt to look at those smiling memories… especially Finn's. But then I caught sight of something else. Hanging along with some of Wyatt's baseball cards and award certificates was the paper Thanksgiving turkey that we all wrote in during the holiday meal. It was stapled shut so no one could intrude on the details that the family was thankful for. But I knew. I remembered intimately what was written, drawn, and said at that Thanksgiving table. It was all love, and it was all gone.

I started blinking my eyes as rapidly as I could to prevent the tears that were just beneath the surface from appearing. It was then that I noticed Finn out of the corner of my eye. He had just entered the room with Will's parents and Will who was carrying Kelsea. I knew Finn didn't see me as I openly gawked. Adorning a fitted white button down and black tie, he was limping and looked simply tortured. An elderly couple approached their group and Finn attempted a smile, but anyone, short of the blind, could tell it was not genuine. It was then that I think he spotted me, but it was also then that Nola did too.

"We didn't have any photos of you with Wy." She glanced at my hand that was still on the turkey. "And you were such a special part of his life. We wanted to make sure you were represented somehow."

Of course they didn't. I hated getting my photo taken and, on top of that, I was extra cautious about separating my personal life with my work life. Ironically, very much like Finn. Even though I knew why, I regretted it all the same at that moment. For I too, wished I had at least one photograph with that amazing boy. More than that, I wished I had one more day.

"Nola," I managed to squeak out before she brought me into her embrace.

"Thank you for everything these past few days," she said breaking the bond.

"Of course."

I hadn't seen any of them since the hospital, and I was amazed how well she was holding up. Of course, I knew that shock had surely found its home in her soul and that, combined with having to play busy hostess, created an illusion of everything being okay. I talked with her for a few minutes commenting on the photos and letting her relive favorite memories of her son. But there were people gathered around us, waiting in a haphazard line to give the grieving mother their condolences. So, I excused myself, giving her a second quick hug and allowing a distinguished, suit-clad gentleman with goatee to approach her next. As I heard him tell Nola that he was a colleague of Will's, I started to make my way to Finn's parents.

I got sidetracked, however, by a circled gathering of my co-workers. It was sweet seeing the turnout considering Wyatt was only a first grader and some of the teachers there had not had him in class. Wyatt would never make it to second grade let alone fifth. Of course, his first-grade teacher, Gwen, was among the group. She hadn't told her class yet, but she had just found out she was pregnant. New life and death—what a surreal moment. When the conversation started to change to Finn and what I knew, I excused myself. I would have to put up with enough of that at work. I didn't want to do it with Finn just so many feet away. Not that I wanted to put up with it at all.

Luckily, the Murphys and Uncle Eoin were alone as I made my way over to them. As I hugged Mrs. Murphy, dressed in all black with pink accents, I spotted Finn watching me from across the room…now a little closer than he had been before. Shaking his image from my brain, I turned to his mostly silver-haired, broad father who swallowed me into his dark suit via a warm bear hug. They were the type of family I had always wanted, even yearned for, in childhood. They were the family that, just a couple months ago, I had started thinking I might be joining sometime in the future. Did Finn see that when he watched us? Did he see how screwed up everything had become?

"Lara, I didn't see you come in," Mr. Murphy's deep voice resonated behind my back.

"There are a lot of people," I said upon release.

I then found myself in a similar hug with Finn's Uncle Eoin. "Lara, so glad you came."

"Of course. I had to be here for Wyatt and for all of you," I said. "I had to make sure that everyone was all right."

"Thanks," replied the restaurant owner. "I actually have to go meet up with my kids. They took the bus in together, and I have to pick them up before the service."

"Oh, all right," I said and quickly hugged him again.

Mrs. Murphy caught me looking in Finn's direction as Eoin exited. "We told him he's missing out on something good and that he needs you."

It was obvious that Finn knew I was there. Yet he made no effort to approach me. The magnetic force between us was there. There was no denying it. I could feel it. And because I could feel it, I knew he could feel it too. But the opposite sides of the magnets were winning I was afraid, repelling us apart instead of drawing us instinctively together.

"You know I care…so much. But nothing is different. It's not," I said.

"We love you, girl, and he does too," Mr. Murphy offered, seeming suddenly somehow older. His shoulders sank, perhaps in the realization that what I said was true despite what he said being equally as true.

"Just don't give up, please," Mrs. Murphy chimed in. "You don't really know what happened with him—why he was the way he was. I mean, before the accident."

Again with the mystery. "That's what Nola said," I relayed.

"It's true. Don't be stubborn or let him deter you. Talk with him," his mom encouraged.

I looked across the room, again, to where Finn was. His eyes immediately swung in another direction. He had been watching us that whole time. But it was obvious that he didn't want any part of it…of me. He promptly started out of the room.

CHAPTER TWENTY-THREE

The room seemed a little dimmer—the world too. I knew I had a decision to make. It was now or never. I had to speak to Finn, or let it go and be at peace with it.

I found him looking through a photo album in a smaller side room separate from the main area where everyone else was gathered. He was by himself, and he was lost in himself. I watched for a moment, thinking that, despite his worldly travels and fame, he was not much more than a boy himself.

"Hi," I said once he looked up to acknowledge my presence.

"Hi," he echoed, offering, as his mother had warned, not much.

"How are you?" It was a weak question, especially under the circumstances, but so was I.

I wanted to embrace him like we used to…like we were one-being instead of two. But while there was a smidge of progress at the hospital, all that had changed on Wyatt's passing. In that funeral parlor, it felt like we were more apart than ever.

"Thanks for coming." His response was routine, removed, rote. For sure, it was the same mechanical statement he had given hundreds of times that day.

"I'm worried about you."

Finn had been making eye contact with me until that comment. He paused and looked down as if he was trying to gain some type of strength. Slowly, he looked back up, but the vacancy was still in his eyes, which appeared more overcast and ashen than his normal sparkly and steely shade. "You meant a lot to him."

"Finn…." My voice choked out his name.

I wanted to tell him that everything was going to be all right. But the air seemed to be sucked out of the room. There was such an awkward distance between us. I was emotionally paralyzed.

"Make sure to sign the guest book."

If I didn't leave then, I would bawl my eyes out. And I didn't want to do that. I couldn't do that to this poor family whose grief and task before them was so much greater than my heartbreak. I shook my head and turned around determined to leave. When I did, however, I came face-to-face with Nola who had obviously been privy to our conversation.

She looked past me and directly at her brother. "What are you doing? It's Lara. Finn, you need to talk with her. You need to tell her what's going on—now especially."

I slowly turned so that I could see both siblings at the same time. Whatever Nola and Mrs. Murphy were referring to, Finn had been prepared to tell me on Friday—Friday before tragedy had struck. Now, everything had changed.

"She doesn't care. She left me. She left me, just like everyone does." He was talking about me but looking at his sister. God, his pain.

It didn't matter that his anguish was directed at me, I wanted to help him… heal him. "Finn—" I started only to be cut off.

"Lara, walk away. You'd be better off. It's easy. Just put one foot in front of the other." He wasn't zombie-like any more. But the spite in his voice was almost chilling.

I was a fighter, though. I had to be from a very young age. And I couldn't bear to lose. I couldn't just sit back and let things go the way they were going. I spoke honestly, "It wouldn't be easy, and it wouldn't be better. It never has been when I'm away from you."

"Damn it!" he cursed, but it wasn't out of anger necessarily. It was more because he knew that I would challenge him and not let him off the hook that easily. He always did the same with me.

Nola, obviously worn from the past few days, interjected. "Finn, look, I can't deal with worrying about you on top of…on top of…on top of losing my little boy." She struggled on the truth. "I'm telling you, you need to talk with Lara or I will."

It was an ultimatum for sure. I don't know about Nola, but I wasn't expecting the answer that Finn gave. I was used to him being there for his sister, helping her—not walking away. But that was before Friday. And that's exactly what he did.

"Then just do it." Finn's voice sounded utterly defeated. "It doesn't matter. Nothing matters."

Nola looked from me to Finn. "You know what? I will," she said as Finn exited to the adjoining outdoor terrace. Now alone, she said to me, "I can't deal with this any longer."

Recognizing that Nola was most likely at her breaking point after a terribly emotional day, I tried to rectify the situation to the best of my ability. "Nola, please, it's fine. Please be with your family. I'll go."

But she was determined. "You don't know," she said earnestly. "You don't know what storm rages through his head. And you need to know. You're the one that can make the difference. We had gotten him back again, but I'm afraid with all of this—"

I couldn't let her go on. "Nola, I know." I was trying so hard to repress the tears that were threatening due to the extremely high emotional stakes of the day and the past few days. I was determined to be strong as much for her sake as mine. "I get it. I know about the drugs. I'll help if I can...if he'll let me. The program he was in be—"

"It's not drugs. I told you." She was calmer now before striking the proverbial gavel. "Lara, Finn suffers from a form of PTSD."

I think Nola stopped talking. If she didn't, she might as well have. I had heard her, and then I didn't. It wasn't that I didn't believe what she had said. It was just that I needed to process. I needed a moment to let it sink in. PTSD? What? I tried to put the pieces together. I thought about what I knew about the disorder from any psychology courses I had taken and from other sources.

As I thought back to some of Finn's behaviors, particularly in the past few months—the angry outbursts, the sometimes excessive energy, the sadness—Nola's voice started resonating in my ears. She told me that before Finn had been diagnosed, he hadn't been able to control the emotional swings of life. That was when he, yes, turned to drugs all those years ago. It was only once he sought help for his addiction that an insightful doctor asked the right questions, ran the right tests, and took the time to get to the root of the problem.

"It was when he moved to Nashville...his career and...Audrey."

"Yes," she confirmed the story that Finn had told me months before minus the PTSD diagnoses. "That's when things came to a head."

"I...I don't get it. PTSD? I know he wasn't in the armed forces. Something...God Nola, what happened to him? When?" Horrific images ran rapidly through my mind.

"Lara, I really wish Finn would tell you this."

"Was he hurt?" Tears were pooling in my eyes with the mere thought of a younger Finn being abused in any type of manner. I knew that pain too well.

"No. No." She put her hand out to my arm. Here she was, during the worst week of her life, comforting me. "He was left." She paused. "It's post-traumatic stress disorder of abandonment. When he was three years old, our grandmother, mom's mom, left him at the park. From what my parents understand, he was playing on one of the big slides, and she just left. She told him she would be right back and then she left. She just left…never came back. Eventually, I'm sure he grew tired of the swings and monkey bars and whatever, but he couldn't find her. And because it wasn't a popular playground, no one else was there. No one found him until the middle of the night. Thank God it was a random police patrol. But he was too little. He didn't have any ID. He was too scared to say anything. And my parents didn't even know he was missing. He was supposed to be at my grandparents' house for the weekend because I was having my first sleepover party at our house. And my grandfather was out of town. So, no one knew. He was at the station that night and all the next day into the night."

"I don't get it. Why did she leave him?" I was suddenly angry… so furious at that cruel grandmother. "What happened?"

"Well, they eventually tracked her down. She took a bus out of town. It was later discovered that she had a brain tumor. The delusion was the first symptom. She died shortly after. Finn and I actually never saw her again."

"Oh, God, poor Finn."

"Well, he didn't remember any of the whole experience until everything went down with Audrey."

"She left him…without warning." Oh, crap. What a trigger.

"He self-medicated with drugs and then he had a complete breakdown. Thank God, we were able to get him into rehab and therapy. Everything came out. But since then, he has needed a stabilizer."

"Meds."

"And a therapist occasionally."

"But nobody knows, right? He's kept everything in." I knew all about keeping secrets and bottling things up deep inside.

Nola explained that Finn felt similarly to mental illness as, unfortunately, a lot of people did—embarrassed. Plus, with him being such a high-profile figure, he did not want it getting out. Fair or not fair, he would be treated differently by the press, labels, and fans.

"I'm not press!" I couldn't help but blurt it out, feeling hurt. "God, why wouldn't he tell me?"

"I know. I know." She paused ever so slightly. "Here's the thing, though. You couldn't tell, right? I mean when he was taking his meds. No one really could. They worked. We even, you know, kinda forgot—didn't forget exactly but didn't worry about it anymore. There was no need to. But then he starting skipping and then not taking his meds altogether."

"Why?" I asked. "Why did he do that?"

"I think you and Finn need to talk about that, but, essentially, it's what happens with a lot of people in his shoes. He felt good. He felt like everything was good…great. Because of that, he felt like he didn't need the meds. He thought he was fine. He was the happiest he had ever been." She smiled as much as she could, and I knew it was her way of acknowledging that her brother's happiness was because of me.

"But that didn't mean he should go off his meds."

It occurred to me then that his medication was probably what he called his vitamin. When was the last time I had seen him take it? Probably around the same time that his behavior started to become erratic.

"No. It's kinda like a false positive," Nola answered. "Once I confronted him, he said that he wanted to be his real true self, all of him, for you. He wanted to make sure that he didn't need the meds. He just didn't get that the real Finn now meant medication. And once he was off, he couldn't see straight."

His true, real self? God, had I pushed him into making that horrible decision? I had harped about those damn green contacts and how I wanted the real Finn—not a mask. Suddenly, events were flashing back in my mind. Our Valentine's Day rendezvous—he had told me in the shower that I had the "real" him. I thought he was referring to being sans-condom. And the argument we had the night before breaking up. He said he was trying to be the guy I needed and why couldn't he just be himself.

Nola began talking again. "It was you leaving him, ironically, and not giving in, not coming back, that finally got him to wake up. Especially because that is what he can't deal with the most—any type of loss or failure, whether it is personal or his career. Lara, I don't know if you completely understand how devastated…ruined he was when you refused to talk with him."

I did. I felt the same way. I still did.

"He was already messed up because of not taking the meds, but, on top of that…. It wasn't easy to rationalize with him, but he listened. He finally listened. He saw his doctor. He got back on the right dosage. He's been good for a little bit now."

I hesitated, but it needed to be asked. "So, you think he's still taking them even with…." I didn't need to finish. I was standing in a funeral parlor with a mother who lost her child. Enough said.

"Yeah, I think. Our folks are making sure. You have to understand, though, even with medication, extreme highs and lows will still affect him. He can get angry or shut down."

I knew that. I knew with the right medication and dosage, personalities and feelings did not change but problems seemed more manageable. With Wyatt's death and our separation, his emotions, medication or not, were surely imbalanced. I had a better understanding of his indifference toward me over the last couple of days, and it made me more than ever want to help.

"I need to see him," I said plainly.

Nola's answer was to hug me. As I held her, I felt some of the stress lift from her body. Of course, the overpowering grief of losing her son clung to her like nothing else imaginable, but knowing that someone was taking on the task of helping her brother surely alleviated some pressure.

I watched Nola walk back into the main area of the funeral parlor. I took a moment to myself before facing Finn. A lot of information had been thrown at me in the matter of minutes, and I knew the next conversation I had was going to be one of the most important ones of my life.

***

He was alone with his back toward me. His arms, outstretched, were grasping the railing so tightly that I could see the strain of his muscles through the back of his button-down shirt. He was looking at the sky, which seemed to be as confused as we all were. Straight ahead it was celestial blue with a couple of puffy, white clouds. But if you looked to the left, both the sky color and clouds appeared a more ominous gray.

Finn turned to me before I had a chance to even announce my presence. Even though he didn't have his green contacts in, his eyes wore a different mask. Like cold, gray steel, they were void of emotion as he seemed to look right through me.

"Don't," he said shaking his head, knowing what his sister had just revealed. "Don't feel sorry for me."

"Feel sorry for you? I'm actually pretty pissed at you right now." I hadn't known what I was going to say, but that was what came out, and it felt good.

If my response surprised him, he didn't let it show. "Well, join the club. Everyone should be for what I did to Wy—"

"Finn, it was an accident… an accident. A terrible, horrific accident. It wasn't you."

I knew he had been holding onto that. I knew it from talking with him at the hospital and then, consequently, through how he had been shutting down. No one had been able to tell him differently. In time, hopefully, he would be able to see the truth.

I trudged on before he could argue. "And I'm not mad at you for that and neither is your sister. I'm upset that you didn't think you could tell me. I'm upset that you would risk your well-being and, ultimately, risk us by going off your meds. You told me that you wanted me to feel like I could tell you anything. And, yet, you kept *this*? You kept *this* from me? God, I told you my innermost secrets—things only my mother knows. No. Some things my mother doesn't even know." I looked down, embarrassed after all this time, about the encounter with Macon.

With the pause, Finn looked up at me knowing what I was referring to. There was a glimmer of pain in his eyes then. Pain for himself but, also, pain for me. I didn't want to be sidetracked, though.

"I trusted you," I continued. "I felt safe with you and you couldn't do the same with me?" There. That was what needed to be said.

"You wouldn't want me. You—"

I cut him off. "You think a mood disorder would scare me away? Really? Really, Finn? You didn't choose this. Something happened to you. You're not purposefully putting a bottle or—" I stopped myself, not wanting to bring up my own baggage. "And I love you."

"I don't want you to love me," he said instantly and vehemently. "I don't want anyone to love me." The last sentence portrayed a dent in his stoic stance. His voice quivered, just slightly, but it gave him away nonetheless.

I eased up looking for my opening to reach him. "Let me help you. Hold onto me."

As I took a step forward, he took one back. And just

like that, his shield was back up. I wasn't the only one with walls.

"No. Lara, go. Go ahead and leave. I don't need this." He paused and then spoke slowly so that I was sure to hear it. "I don't need you." My unwillingness to move or react to his comment, unfortunately, made him say something even crueler, although in a softer voice. "I can have anyone I want, you know."

I admit it, that stung. I tried not to show any physical reaction, but I wasn't made of stone. I wasn't the ice princess I had been accused of being in the past. I blinked physically but not mentally. Emotionally, I was hurt, but, intellectually, I knew Finn was composing his words carefully to hurt me on purpose. It was his defense mechanism. I knew him too well. I knew him deep down. I knew how he felt about me and about himself. He didn't want me to see him broken because of the accident and not perfect due to his disorder. I refused to let him push me away, though.

"You could," I admitted plainly and solidly. "And if that is what you wanted, it would break my heart."

Upset that I wouldn't just give in, he cried more than yelled, "Damn it, Lara," and turned around not wanting to expose his feelings.

"Finn, did you ever think that I might need you? I loved that little boy too, you know. I loved him for all his enthusiasm, his wonderment, his compassion, his determination, and because he was a part of you. And to think that I lost him, and I lost you too? I need you to love me. Finn?" I stepped so that I was in his line of vision affording him no other choice than to acknowledge me. "Or is that it? Do you not love me anymore?"

His eyes were watery and bloodshot, but they were on me. "Like that would ever be possible."

"Oh, God." It was my turn to break. I knew deep down his feelings for me, but hearing those words definitely helped. I watched as Finn bowed his head, accepting that I was there for him no matter what. "Please, let me in."

As he had at the hospital, Finn let himself go and folded into my arms. We melted into one another, absorbing each other's sorrow and love. There was no other place for either one of us. Only together could we travel the unknown roads still ahead.

Read the next part of Finn and Lara's journey in Book Two: *Almost Heaven*

SNEAK PEEK AT *ALMOST HEAVEN*

CHAPTER ONE

It was weird thinking that we were leaving him there. Sure, the beach was picturesque and serene with its rippling water and stretching coastline. It was a place where any young boy would love to spend hours on end running, swimming, and making creative structures along the bank. But knowing that the sandy shore was, in part, his final home instead of a bedroom full of books, stuffed animals, and model airplanes, still seemed so wrong. And hearing his sweet, three-year-old sister ask when he was coming back broke our hearts. No matter how much we tried to keep a positive spin on the evening by eating Wyatt's favorite mint chocolate chip ice cream and splashing in the water, the fact that we were scattering some of his seven-year-old ashes could not be eclipsed.

It had been one day less than a week since the accident and, consequently, Wyatt's passing. It was only three days since the funeral parlor. Three days since I found out the real truth about Finn's erratic behavior. Three days since I had been able to understand. Three days since I had held Finn's hand as we listened to the preacher say a few words of supposed closure.

Finn offered to drive me home from his nephew's beach memorial. His parents, who were staying with his only sibling, Nola, had driven me there which, I am sure, was an obvious set-up to have Finn make the return offer. He didn't need the push, though, which made me feel a little more secure about our questionable relationship status. That drive would be the first time we would truly be alone together since the gut-wrenching day, over a month before, when I had told him I didn't want to see him anymore. I hadn't understood back then. He hadn't told me why he had acted the way he had. But after the tragedy, I had learned that Finn suffered from a form of PTSD and had went off his meds. Now, back on, I hoped we were too.

Coming June 2018

Want to read about how Lara and Finn first met? *ALL MY MEMORIES* is a special prequel, told from Finn's point of view, that details their days in college. The novella is a featured in the anthology *CAN'T BUY ME LOVE.*

SNEAK PEEK AT *ALL MY MEMORIES*

Can't Buy Me Love

https://www.amazon.com/dp/B076BSXNGK

Seven romantic tales of love where royalty, celebrities, and passion meet. A case of mistaken identity, protecting the one you love, or proving you aren't all about the money...these tales will entice and thrill.

All My Memories by Grea Warner
The possibility of reconnecting with an unrequited love leads country music star Finn Murphy on a journey of memories in this special prequel to the Country Roads series.

EXCERPT:
"Ugh—the light. Why is it so bright?" I squinted my eyes and threw my forearm across them.

I felt like I was in a vacuum. There was a low buzzing sound in my ears. No, it was more like my head.

When I finally adjusted to my surroundings, I realized I was in my bed. The sheets were tousled and thrown. The pillows laid haphazardly on the floor. I could hear some of my fraternity brothers talking in the nearby lounge. I could tell it was probably closer to mid-day than morning by the slightest ray of light that beamed a little too brightly through the crack in the window's drapes. My stomach swished a little. And then I remembered. I remembered the night before.

"Oh, geez. Oh, God. Lara," I mumbled to myself.

What had I been thinking?

Also Including the following stories:
A Royal Pain by Abigail Drake
Getting shot in the bottom saving a visiting royal turns out to be the best thing to happen to, impoverished socialite, Chloe Burkhart in a long time, especially when the prince's very handsome, very sexy bodyguard, Nicolai, comes to her aid.

Caught by Him by Tammy Mannersly
Blockbuster movie actor, Brody Nash doesn't quite know what to make of the gorgeous woman precariously perched on his neighbor's gate, but as they start to get to know each other better, he begins to wonder if she might just be the *one* for him.

Romancing the Princess by Bridie Hall

A commoner, Sebastian, and Princess Alixandra are set to get married until he begins to wonder if fitting in with royalty is worth sacrificing his principles. Love rules all. Or does it?

Me and Tillie by Lisa Hahn

1950s musical film star Oren Cooper returns to Broadway to find new inspiration. Unexpectedly, that inspiration comes in the form of Tillie Parker—his childhood friend's little sister and an up-and-coming ingénue.

Defending Demma by Melissa Kay Clarke

When faced with an unsavory past, can Demma St. John, rising new starlet, trust ex-Marine Ryker "Digger" McMillan with her secrets and her heart?

His Royal Typeface by Stephanie Keyes

When all is lost, love can be found. Will Prince Asher Tarrington's unique font design be enough to salvage a royal family and set the tone for true love?

ABOUT THE AUTHOR

There really wasn't any other path. Grea Warner knew from a young age that she wanted to write. She was born to write. First it was in diaries with little metal keys and in written tales that she slipped to friends in study hall. School newspapers, a college television drama, and internships in the soap opera world were next. After producing and writing a local show, she decided to delve into the world of the novelist. When her fingers aren't tapping out her latest book filled with angst and romance, Grea can be found hiking the trails or jamming to her favorite country artists on the radio.

Facebook: https://www.facebook.com/grea.warner.7
Twitter:@grea_warner

CPSIA information can be obtained
at www.ICGtesting.com
Printed in the USA
BVHW030159120219
540055BV00001B/30/P